Lucy Sweet was born in 1972 in Hull, but hasn't let that stop her. She got her first writing job at nineteen and is a regular contributor to a wide range of publications as a journalist and cartoonist, including *Punch*, the *Independent on Sunday*, the *Express* and the *Sunday Times*. She lives in Glasgow with her husband, where she currently juggles multiple careers as a girl-about-town columnist, magazine editor and struggling musician. *Coming Apart at the Seams* is her second novel. Her first, *Have Love Will Travel*, is also published by Black Swan.

Also by Lucy Sweet

HAVE LOVE WILL TRAVEL

and published by Black Swan

COMING APART AT THE SEAMS

Lucy Sweet

BLACK SWAN

COMING APART AT THE SEAMS
A BLACK SWAN BOOK : 0552773026
9780552773027

First publication in Great Britain

PRINTING HISTORY
Black Swan edition published 2006

1 3 5 7 9 10 8 6 4 2

Set in 11/14pt Melior by
Kestrel Data, Exeter, Devon.

Black Swan Books are published by Transworld Publishers,
61–63 Uxbridge Road, London W5 5SA,
a division of The Random House Group Ltd,
in Australia by Random House Australia (Pty) Ltd,
20 Alfred Street, Milsons Point, Sydney, NSW 2061, Australia,
in New Zealand by Random House New Zealand Ltd,
18 Poland Road, Glenfield, Auckland 10, New Zealand
and in South Africa by Random House (Pty) Ltd,
Isle of Houghton, Corner of Boundary Road & Carse O'Gowrie,
Houghton 2198, South Africa.

Printed and bound in Great Britain by
Cox & Wyman Ltd, Reading, Berkshire.

Papers used by Transworld Publishers are natural, recyclable products made from wood grown in sustainable forests. The manufacturing processes conform to the environmental regulations of the country of origin.

To my crazy artist parents

Thanks to Gail Haslam at Transworld and Susan Smith at MBA for their invaluable input and advice, Andrew Symington for being a human thesaurus, all my fabulous local and international lady friends for inspiration and encouragement, and Ian Murray for everything else. Also, thank you to Pinkie McClure and John Wills, Stella Kane, Cora Kipling, Joe Veltre, and the musicians, artists and characters of Glasgow. Any similarities to persons living or dead are entirely coincidental. Honestly.

Step One – The Pattern Is your Guide

> If you are holding your scissors aloft ready to cut your fabric, take a breath and step back. Remember, a pattern is a map and should be thoroughly consulted before you begin your dressmaking journey. Disregard it and you will surely be lost, but follow it correctly and your pattern should direct you successfully to your final destination – sartorial perfection!
>
> *Paris Fashions the Easy Way* (1932)

Snip snip snip. I balance the book on the sink, open at a picture of a glamorous film actress from the 1920s, and try to cut my fringe into a similar straight black line. I bet this faded star spent her afternoons riding around in cabs in Jazz Age New York and drinking cocktails at the Ritz with exotic gentlemen. As for me, I will be working in Kirkness Fashions, the least fashionable place on God's earth, watching my octogenarian boss adjust the tubular bandage on her gammy knee. I don't usually indulge in lunch-hour home hairdressing, but I figure if I change my hair, some old-fashioned pizzazz will attach itself to me somehow, in the same way that static clings to beige polyester, and the rest of the day will be transformed into a wonderland of glamour and adventure. It's a long shot, but you never know.

The cuttings fall satisfyingly into the sink, and there I am – not exactly Hollywood material, but sufficiently transformed to make today a bit different from the rest. And soon it won't just be my hair that'll be different. Casting around the bathroom looking for the wastebasket, I realize it's disappeared – instead there's just a ring of talc and used tissues and squashed toothpaste tubes. (My dad's probably got it on his head, trying to summon up the spirit of Matisse's Moroccan period.) Even if you were a tramp living under a railway arch, you'd have to agree that this place is a mess. Nothing is where it's supposed to be. If you're looking for an apple, the last place it'll be is in the fruit bowl, because that's full of paper-clips, keys and cat toys. Instead, try the shoe cupboard or, better still, the U-bend. Even very important things lose their way with miraculous efficiency. The other day I found unpaid bills from 1995 in the piano seat. One of them was a final notice from the electricity board threatening to cut us off, and on the back of it my dad had scribbled a diagram for a 55-foot-high sculpture called *Windscape*, which he reckoned would act as 'a monument to the power of the alternative energy resource, which will challenge visual expectations of the landscape and raise issues about man's interference within it, in both an industrial and a creative capacity'. It's a pole. With a propeller on it.

I've just got time to grab something to eat before my lunch-hour ends and I have to go back to work. Mrs Morrison will be working her way through her soup at Vanelli's, so I've got about fifteen minutes to wolf down something and get back to the shop to take the 'Back at 2 p.m.' sign off the door. (It's a very slick operation, as you can see.) Coming out of the bathroom, past the mannequin with no arms, I can hear my mother Charlotte holding court downstairs. I do a quick calculation: by this time she'll be approximately 45 per cent red wine. She's having a liquid lunch with 'Morticia', aka Carol, the witchy woman from two houses away who makes jewellery out of random things she finds on the beach – shells, plastic toys, rusty razors. They're planning an exhibition together. Mum shows her ceramics twice a year, once in a tiny local gallery owned by her friend Sheila Warren, and then at the bistro/coffee shop in Stainton. If she's lucky, she gets a write-up in the local paper with a cheesy picture of her holding up a plate and some kind of witty caption like: 'LOCAL ARTIST GOES POTTY'. You wouldn't know it to listen to them, though. The way they're talking about it you'd think they were organizing a retrospective at the Tate Modern, not two weeks in the display cabinet at the Wobbly Wheel café. For a second, I make idle circles with my foot, collecting a ball of cat hair from the carpet, eavesdropping.

'Ceramics are notoriously difficult to light,' Charlotte

is saying, her voice full of loud, booming, posh authority. 'So much so, they often don't bother to light them at all.'

'Oh, I know,' squeaks Morticia. 'People don't put enough effort into showing them. With painting, it's different, the blank wall is there to be filled. But displaying ceramics and jewellery is a very exact art. It's so easy for them to get lost.'

'Ooh, I know,' I say to the dummy. It beams at me with a showroom smile, but its eyes are glazed and I can tell that it's not on my side. I used to dress this thing when I was young, wrapping it in anything I could find. At one point, it had a bubble-wrap dress and a hat made out of banana skins and its nose was covered in green felt tip. No wonder it doesn't like me much. I always thought it'd end up in one of my dad's sculptures, decapitated and melted to a bit of driftwood, and called something like *Figurehead Number 5*, but no, there it is, watching over me like a hawk.

'Stop staring at me,' I whisper. Trembling from the impact of hammer blows coming out of my dad's studio at the far end of the hall, it starts to wobble in reply, as if possessed by the devil. With a terrible slam, the mannequin pitches forward, disturbing a stack of dusty wicker kitchen stools, and looms heavily towards me, grazing my shoulder and leaving a trail of plaster all over my smartest black sweater, before crashing messily to the floor. I yelp and rub at the stain but it appears to have mashed itself permanently into the wool.

'Shit!' I try to push the dummy back into place but

it's lying on the tatty carpet, face down. It's dead. I give up and slip into my own room and lock the door with the sliding bolt, take off the sweater and change into another one, green cashmere – a Kirkness Fashions discounted special, 30 per cent off for members of staff (although I suspect the only other member of staff just swipes what she wants off the shelves). In here, everything is tidy. My sewing machine lies ready on the table near the window, but all my colour-coded reels of cotton are packed away and fabrics are kept rolled and folded in the corner. Next to it my black leather chair, liberated from a car boot sale, is spotlessly shiny and uncluttered, with no yellowing newspapers or dog slaver or cat sick on it. Downstairs, it's a different story – like one of those washing-powder adverts featuring every possible stain known to man. The sofa is a big, sagging, hairy, jam-covered monster, the tables are held together with Sellotape, and everything you pick up has something dubious smeared all over it. This is my safe haven – my jam-free zone. Even the sea looks neat out of my bedroom window, a grey flat line undisturbed by breakers or trawlers.

I lick my finger and smooth down my hair. Oh well, onwards and upwards. Just keep smiling and stick to your guns. Remember the Spirit of the Blitz, as Mrs Morrison says when a particularly depressing delivery of massive support bras comes on a Monday morning.

Compulsively, just to check it's still there, I take out the box file marked 'Plan A', which I keep under my bed. In here there are numbers for letting agents, tourist information and public transport leaflets, and the passbook for my building society account, which reads '£4,117.82', scraped together from days and days of toil at Kirkness Fashions and nights and nights of staying at home. I pick up one of the transport authority leaflets and trace the subway line with my finger, over and over. It's a circle – well, more a flattened oval – studded with unfamiliar, clipped names like St Enoch, Cessnock and Ibrox. They call the tube line 'the Clockwork Orange'. Such a neat idea: tangerine trains, ticking along underground, one after the other. The city is a simple, reassuring grid, not like round here, where everything is wonky and illogical and at the mercy of rock formations and tides. Buildings slapped on top and to the side of each other, doors in places there shouldn't be doors, seashells pasted into the plaster like an infant school art project. It's time to move on. I glance up at a postcard of my heroine, Edith Head. Edith is the real deal, a Hollywood costume designer who dressed all the greats – Audrey Hepburn, Grace Kelly, Bette Davis, all those women with true style. I want to be like her. I'll bet there was never any plaster dust on *her* jumper. In my photo she's leaning over a fashion sketch, wearing a crisp tailored suit, showing off a severe pageboy haircut and strange shaded glasses, like Second World War aviator's goggles. She wasn't much of a looker, but she was technical and stylish and brilliant and I wish I could be as good as her. Unfortunately, nobody I've ever met knows who she is. When I once told my friend Mona that I wanted to be like Edith, she looked at the postcard with narrowed eyes and said: 'Ewww! He's a funny-looking bloke.'

Hmm.

But even Edith had to start somewhere, and so do I. From the box I take out the letter with the logo for MetroTech College at the top, an optimistic graphic with searchlights radiating from it, stretching into a bright future.

Dear Ms Kaminsky,

RE: HND Fashion Design

We are delighted to inform you that your letter of acceptance has been processed and we would like to welcome you to MetroTech College. To enrol, students must attend an induction event in the main hall at 10 a.m. on Tuesday 22 August. Please see enclosed details for bursary and student loan information. Thank you for choosing MetroTech.

Yours sincerely,

Maureen Ballantyne, Admissions Secretary

I did apply for London but it wasn't to be. MetroTech was what you might call a last resort: when I went to my interview, they seemed to be amazed at my portfolio, and it wasn't even that good. The original one, the really great portfolio, which was the result of years of work and might have secured me a place at Central St Martins (the most prestigious fashion school in the land, no less, where I'd always dreamed of going), died a terrible death, which I still can't bear to think about. It left me stranded here for another year, and it was too late then to try to get a place anywhere else. But this time I've got it all worked out. I have approximately two weeks to look for a place to live. I'm going over to Glasgow twice next week (undercover, dark glasses optional) to check out what's on offer, and I will officially announce my departure on the 20th in time for my college induction day on the 22nd. I will move into my new flat later on in the week and begin the course on Monday 28th August. I've written it all down.

This time, my parents can't spoil it. They really can't. I haven't even told them about it yet. Just to be on the safe side.

'Evie!' my dad barks outside the door.

I tense up and slam the box file under the bed. I can hear him breathing through the door, a wheezing, foreboding sound like an intensive-care patient on a ventilator. He's always wound up about something. According to him, we Kaminskys work like dogs and do everything with passion. His family have endured great hardships that no other human beings could possibly understand. Usually, by his fourth whisky, his grandmother, who probably never left her home town, ends up travelling from Kazakhstan to St Petersburg on the back of a three-legged yak. Sometimes I wonder whether I'm the milkman's daughter.

'Evgeniya!' he shouts again, using my full, awful, horrible Russian name, which he does when he wants to get a rise out of me. In Russian, it means 'well bred'; here, it sounds like a gynaecological ailment.

'Don't call me that!'

'You said to me that you would save your hair cuttings, and then I see you have flushed them down the sink. What am I gonnae do?'

I take a deep breath. 'Sorry, Dad. I didn't know you needed them. It was only a wee bit anyway. I'll save some next time.'

'You say this again and again. My sculpture needs to have female hair otherwise it will not be a real expression of femininity, will it? Can I come in? Let me in!' He starts rattling at the door handle.

'I'm busy!' I yell. 'Use some of Mum's. There's tons of it all over the bathroom floor.'

'Your mother has hair like a horse!' he rumbles. I hear him stop to put the dummy back, then he stomps off down the hall, knocking over something else on the way.

When he's safely back in his studio, banging, I look once more at the letter – holding it delicately, like the golden ticket it is. I really have to get out of here.

'Oh hello, Evie. Have you cut your fringe? You look like a lesbian!' says Charlotte delightedly. She and Morticia are now well on their way through their first bottle, and the buckled ashtray (Mum's handiwork) is full of Silk Cut ends. (Amazing how we're supposed to be dirt poor, but somehow she can afford endless packs of cigarettes and limitless trips to the Majestic Wine Warehouse.) Charlotte is wearing some kind of pale blue linen smock, accessorized with a jagged, rusty metal necklace that seems like a recipe for tetanus. She rakes her hand through her famous horse hair, or at least she tries to. I peer closely at it. There could be all kinds of stuff lurking in that scary grey cloud – leaves, twigs, crumbs, Christmas ornaments, families of squirrels.

'She looks like one of those freewheeling surrealist women, doesn't she, Carol?' she says. 'You know, the ones that hung around with Man Ray and Picasso and all that mob and got their boobies out all over the place. Very Twenties.'

Carol, showing blackened red-wine teeth, smiles ghoulishly in agreement. I smile weakly back and head for the cooker. The top of it is covered in an explosion of brown stuff that has congealed into greasy rubber, and it's groaning with dirty dishes, which I feel compelled to clear out of the way, even though I haven't really got time. There's no point in raising the housework issue – I just get on with it. Whenever I say anything about the mess, Charlotte just shrugs and says: 'Life's too short to stuff a mushroom.' I've told her where she can stuff her bloody mushrooms more times than I care to remember.

'Don't do that now, darling,' she trills. 'Want some wine?'

'No thanks. I have to go to work.'

'God, if I worked in that shop I'd have to be pissed to get through the day!' she bellows. Then, in a quieter voice, to Carol: 'It's like something out of *Are You Being Served?* Well, it would be, if nothing ever happened and all the characters were dead.'

'I'm only over here, y'know – I can hear you.'

'Oh Evie, you're so serious all the time,' she whines. 'Chill out.'

My chest tightens. I fill the kettle, manoeuvring it over the other pile of festering dishes in the sink, and bang it on the Aga.

'Hey, Carol was saying that there's a job going at Sheila's gallery,' Charlotte chirrups. 'Only part time, but it would make a change, wouldn't it? You're too young to be hanging about with old women all day.'

I think of Sheila Warren's gallery, a cosy converted farmhouse selling innocuous art, more eventful than Kirkness Fashions, but only just. It would probably make a change from Mrs Morrison's ramblings about powdered egg. But no.

I start trying to scrub the blackened deposits off the kettle with a scouring pad and suddenly feel steely. They have no idea about my secret plan. It's mine, something shiny and original that I can keep just for me. They can't take the gleam off it with their sticky fingers. A glossy image of me fleeing the village in a convertible sports car happily springs to mind and quickly pops.

'I don't think so,' I breeze, giving up on the kettle and trying to find a mug that hasn't got something unexplained lurking at the bottom of it. 'I'm really busy at the shop.' I think of my typical day at Kirkness Fashions, catatonically folding neck scarves and enormous pants. There's no way they're going to buy that excuse.

'If you're that busy, why does it close for lunch?' Carol inevitably pipes up, beady as a crow.

'It's Ramadan,' I lie.

There's a small, unconvinced silence, ended abruptly by a very loud and sustained banging from upstairs, during which something slips off a shelf and crashes to the ground. Nobody sees fit to comment on it or even bother to find out what fell on the floor.

'Don't be a smart arse, dear. You know, Carol, you can't make Evie do anything she doesn't want to do,' Charlotte says, making a joint. 'She's very independent. And practical. Very good with her hands. We'd be lost without her.'

I briefly wonder how they *will* cope without me. Soon there's not going to be anyone around to remember to pay the paper boy and fumigate the toilet and clean the burnt grease from the inside of the oven. If nobody does it, are they going to be found years later in layers of crust and gunk, like the people of Pompeii? I make a mental note to buy oven cleaner before I go. Behind me, as if I'm not here, Charlotte is now wittering on about how creative I am, a whiz with the sewing machine, destined for great things.

'All she needs to do really is let her creative side flourish,' she says, 'and soon enough her work will be marvellous.'

'Is there anything to eat?' I ask, overtly cheerful and very loudly, trying to railroad her off the topic of creativity before she starts comparing me to free-wheeling lesbian surrealists again.

'There's some crisps and nuts in the larder,' she shouts, waving her arms towards the back door. 'Open a big bag. And grab us another bottle of red, will you, darling? What's Anton doing up there?'

I ignore her and go to the 'larder' – less a food cupboard, more a hole in the wall, a nightmare lurking within. This room, more than any other, sums up the true state of decay and disorganization in the house. Crates of empties and unopened wine boxes are stacked waist high like a deranged game of Tetris, and apart from the crisps and nuts and a pack of pretzels, I can't see any real food.

'He's always banging about,' she tells Carol. 'He's been in a shitty mood ever since the Arts Council turned down his other proposal to turn a boat wreck on Creggan beach into a sculpture of a whale. I kept telling him it was a great idea but who goes to Creggan? There's not even a ferry – he'd need to charter a helicopter to get to the bloody thing. He's impossible. I can't communicate with him when he's like this – he just locks himself away and stews in his own juices. I really hope something good happens for him soon. He hasn't touched me for weeks. And then there's the wind thing . . .'

I squash myself further into the cupboard so as not to hear about the state of my parents' sex life or their gastric health. Something smells funny in here, a powdery green smell, like mouldy oranges, but I can't see any oranges. I can now see a tin of baked beans that expired three months ago, though, and a cucumber in the process of turning into slime. I grab an old carrier bag and sling them both in there for the bin. Do other people live like this? The only vaguely edible thing in here is a tin of Pal. I'm suddenly so hungry that the picture of meaty chunks in gravy on the label looks quite appetizing. Can humans eat dog food?

'So what are you up to tonight, Evie?' shouts Carol. 'Are you going to stick around for the party?'

'What?' I murmur, hypnotized by dog meat.

'The party! Tonight!'

Oh no. I stop and look at the pretzel packet in front of me. Sure enough, it has 'PARTY MIX' emblazoned on it in jaunty red letters. I completely forgot. 'Er, I don't think so.'

'Aw, why not?' asks Charlotte, pouncing on the bottle as I emerge from the larder. She can move fast when she wants to. 'It'll be great . . .' she dribbles, 'Svetlana is coming, and Gaynor and Barry, and Malcolm. And according to Jean, Victor McDougall said he'd be dropping in. Victor McDougall – The Painter! It'll be a blast!'

'Mmm.'

My parents' parties are legendary, and not in a good way. They generally involve a bunch of self-important artists drinking too much and smoking foul cigars and talking about themselves and then trying to hump each other's legs. At about half past ten, Charlotte will start dancing 'meaningfully' to Led Zeppelin like she's suffering from agonizing irritable bowel syndrome and someone will throw up in a plant pot. Still, when the booze starts flowing things can get pretty funny. The time my mum decided to celebrate the Solstice with a Wicker Man style bonfire, and tried to get everyone to run around in the altogether, almost made the national news. I hid in my room, but the fleeting sight of my dad's hairy arse will haunt me for the rest of my life.

'Mona invited me round,' I say, which isn't true, but I'm going anyway.

'Well bring her!' Charlotte shrieks. 'She loves a party, that one – you can't wrestle her drink off her, can you? Ooh, and tell her to bring her dad. He's gorgeous. Carpenter. Big arms.' Charlotte flexes her upper arm and mimes a 'Phwworgh' sound to Carol, who gives a cooing, gurgling giggle like a pigeon trapped in a mangle.

My head feels too heavy for my body and it's nothing to do with the turpentine fumes that are finding their way down the stairs. I put down the pan I was about to wash, wipe my hands twice on a dish rag before realizing it's dirtier than anything else in the kitchen, and pick up my red coat, which has somehow fallen into the dog's basket.

'See you later. I'm going to work,' I tell them.

'Loosen up, Evie, I'm only joking!' Charlotte chuckles.

As I shut the door, Dad bashes the final nail into whatever he's making, and a large chunk of masonry falls off the porch roof, narrowly missing my head and plopping into a terracotta plant pot full of old trainers and a vacuum cleaner attachment.

It's an omen, I tell myself. It's a sign that I'll be much safer in Glasgow. If I stay here I'll either die in a sculpture-related accident or, even worse, end up wearing rubbish jewellery made out of rusty old tap washers. I head purposefully into the village. But although my departure date is imminent and my fringe is pure Fifties Hollywood, the slow afternoon at Kirkness Fashions stretches out endlessly, like the elastic on a size-24 girdle.

Step Two – Cutting Remarks

Some dresses just won't fit, no matter how much you tug and tweak. A bad fit is a bad friend: frumpy, awkward and uncooperative. But it takes two to make a friendship work. Simply make sure your cutting out is accurate at the beginning, and your creation will never turn against you.

I walk down the steep, uneven hill to the harbour, where Saturday is in full swing, hoping that five o'clock will miraculously creep up on me unnoticed. Perhaps there'll be an afternoon rush at the shop – there's a first time for everything. The National Lottery sign outside the Spar rocks in the wind, permanently thronged by a bunch of bored kids who can't afford the bus fare to St Andrews or Edinburgh. Slow, meandering groups of gawkers, day-trippers and window-shoppers steel themselves against the stiff sea breeze, with 'is this it?' plastered all over their faces. Yes, I always want to tell them, this is it. Kirkness.

There's the High Street, then a couple of mostly residential back roads, a church and the community centre, and the small, usually closed Maritime Museum featuring the odd salvaged shipwreck and interactive exhibit about fish. Visitors usually find a café or go to the chippy, then quickly get back in their cars and go off to somewhere more exciting. Maybe they'll buy a postcard from Strathie's, or a box of Kirkness rock, but it's not somewhere that sticks in your mind – just one of many seaside villages up the coast, with wee shops boasting 'Best Fish and Chips in the East' or 'World Famous Italian Ice Cream'.

As I get to Kirkness Fashions, the 'Back at 2 p.m.' sign is off the door, and I can see the well-padded figure of Mrs Morrison bustling behind the counter. I take a deep breath and hover outside. The script is well worn. 'Ding!' (That's the bell that rings as you open the door.) 'Hello, Mrs Morrison. Did you have a nice lunch?' 'That place is going downhill. [Insert complaint about service, or quality and temperature of soup.] I shan't be going back.' 'Not to worry. I'll put the kettle on.' 'Aye, you do that. Then we'll get to work.'

Half crazed from hunger, I decide to stave off the boredom with a grand sweeping entrance in the style of Holly Golightly in *Breakfast at Tiffany's*.

'Why, hello, Mrs Morrison!' I chirp, wide eyed. 'Did you have a nice lunch?' (And by the way, that slightly stained blouse you're wearing is positively darling!)

'Aye, no bad,' she sniffs. 'Tea?'

'Tea would be just wonderful!'

She eyes me with suspicion, as if I've been mind-probed by aliens during my lunch-break, and retreats into the back. I drop the act and assume my usual position behind the wide wooden counter, a relic from the 1930s, glassy from decades of polishing. Behind here, though, is a mess of cardboard and balls of wool, bags of shopping and well-thumbed *Puzzler* books. She won't let me touch anything or tidy it up, claiming to have a 'system'. As far as I can tell, her main system seems to involve sticking stray American-tan tights and outsized knickers into a big cardboard box, flinging it on the floor and writing 'Have A Rummage, Only 50p!!' on it. Everything in here is old, cracked, overlit, falling apart, with the yellow cellophane over the window giving the room a jaundiced, sallow look. I wipe at a stain and fold the cloth up into a neat square while listening to the clock, which is as old as Mrs Morrison herself, with spikes of gold radiating from it and dots instead of numbers. The place reminds me of a documentary I once saw about the wreck of the *Titanic*, where silver dinner services still languish inside, gathering barnacles – everything spookily untouched by progress. In Kirkness Fashions, it's still about 1937. It's one of the reasons I liked it at first, but now I feel suffocated, like a refugee from the future, stranded here for ever because there's not enough plutonium for my time machine.

'The soup isn't what it used to be. Full of bits. It's that new Vanelli boy – he wouldnae know a minestrone from a black-and-white minstrel.' Mrs Morrison laughs at her joke and comes back in with two mugs in her shaky hands. The 'new' owner of Vanelli's has worked there all my life, but to Mrs Morrison, he's still about twelve. 'Ah'm just off to the Ladies,' she wheezes, handing me the cup. 'Hold the fort, will ye?'

'Will do, Mrs M.'

I'll be giving my notice in next week. I hope she doesn't have a turn, like when they threatened to discontinue salad cream a few years ago. Still, it's not as if there's much to do round here now. And rather than helping the occasional big-armed old lady into a tent-like disaster, I could be doing what I love. I could be making clothes. Not ordinary clothes, but beautiful ones, like the great couturiers and costumiers used to make, created with care and attention and skill. Clothes that make the women that wear them feel magic, with luxurious fabrics and fitted waists and seamless curves. Soothed by the woozy fumes of the paraffin heater, I drift off into a trance. I'm in a neat and tidy studio, wearing glasses on a string, gliding silver scissors through an acre of silk, a seamstress, in great demand, working in Paris, with a couple of assistants to help me out. In between lightning flashes of inspiration, I go downstairs to the patisserie and drink tiny black coffees and do broad, confident sketches just like Edith's. In some distant yet-to-be-published issue of *Vogue*, I'm a real hit – Nicole Kidman is a huge fan, apparently. 'Her dresses just make everyone feel so special,' she swoons.

'Ding!' The sharpness of the bell makes me jump.

Oh no. Please no. It's Boreen.

'Hello, Evie dear. Only me,' she says, in a monotonous voice, beginning her slow shuffle across the carpet. Doreen/Boreen is the bane of our lives, a retired domestic science teacher who hangs about all day being miserable and stealing our biscuits.

'Hello.' I smile, breaking out my *Tiffany's* routine. 'Isn't the weather terrible? It just gives me the screaming reds.'

'Whit?'

'They're worse than the blues . . .' I say, not being able to remember the exact line.

'You're as bonkers as your ma and dad,' she says, shaking her head.

I tense up. 'They're not bonkers, they're . . . creative,' I reply, feeling surprisingly defensive. (I can say what I like about them but she can't.) 'Anyway, Bor— I mean Doreen. Would you like a biscuit?'

'Och no. I haven't had a movement since Tuesday.' She shoots me a resentful vinegary look, the bags under her eyes giving her the appearance of an aged turtle poking its head out of its shell. Her thinning hair stands up in wisps, stiffened peaks of egg white on top of her misshapen head. I wish Mrs Morrison would come out of the Ladies, but she's probably suffering from a similar problem. Either that or she's doing the crossword on the toilet again.

'It's all right for you, eh?' Boreen wheezes, plonking herself down on a threadbare chair. 'At least you're regular.' At that moment, she tips back, showing me an acre of off-white gusset encased in lumpy American-tan mesh with ladders along the thighs.

'Yes,' I say, through gritted teeth, nails digging into the counter. 'Well, that's a blessing, I suppose.'

Ahead of me is the small village of Culdrossie, nestling in an armpit of land further up the coast. It's even sleepier than here, if that's possible. Mona is, as is usual for a Saturday evening, sitting in the bus shelter, bathed in the sweaty light from the chip shop. She's got a quarter bottle of Buckfast on the go and is talking to Teresa Donegan, or 'corned beef legs' as she's otherwise known. Teresa is a big, perpetually angry and obnoxious girl, who wears a zip-up tracksuit top and a liberal amount of ugly gold jewellery advertising the fact that she's called Teresa. I sometimes wonder whether it's a style choice or whether it really is in case she forgets. She's hard, from the housing scheme on the outskirts of the village, so everyone's scared of her, but for some reason, I can't bring myself to care. Next to Teresa, Mona looks tiny and impish, engulfed in a black hooded top, with a couple of spikes of pink hair lolling over her eyes.

'Hi,' I say.

Teresa grunts, lighting a cigarette and pointedly ignoring me.

'All right, Evie!' Mona takes a careless swig from the bottle, patting the bench next to her. 'What you up to?'

'Nothing much,' I say, perching on the seat. 'What you doing?'

'Nothin'. Teresa says she might be able to get hold of some eckies for tonight – maybe go to the woods? Her pal Tommy and some guys from Kingsferry are going too.'

'Hmm. I dunno . . .' I say, trying to sound non-committal.

I am definitely, categorically, not going in a million years. But the only social options round here are hanging around the harbour eating chips, going to the Anchor Hotel (which I used to work in and know like the back of my hand) or driving to the woods to take drugs with a bunch of guys with a one-way ticket to the remand centre. I don't want to do any of it. Maybe there are other people who don't want to do these things too, but I've yet to bump into them. I turn away and pull a long-suffering face, as if addressing an invisible person, one who wouldn't be seen dead in a bus shelter on a Saturday night. Staring out at the familiar street, with its cobblestones and twists and turns, I get a sudden but very deep yearning to visit an art house cinema.

'What's up? Is that no posh enough for ye?' Teresa harrumphs, sensing dissatisfaction. She hoists herself up onto her spongy white feet, encased in the latest back-of-a-lorry Nikes. 'No enough . . . champagne for ye, eh?' she adds, unconvincingly, trying to think of some suitably posh scenario she might have seen on TV. Then she seems to find her thread.

'I ken your type. Arty-farty twats. Think you're fucking it. What you still doin' round here anyway? I thought you were away in London wi' all they trendies. Or did Mammy and Daddy put a stop to it?' She reaches into her pocket and menacingly flicks her Bic lighter into life with her fat thumb, holding it up to her face.

I try to open my mouth, but nothing comes out. The night before I was due to take a train to London for the interview, my portfolio somehow managed to get embroiled in what I can only describe as 'an incident'. Needless to say, my parents were implicated, as was the cat and a candle and a bottle of white spirit, which my dad probably uses to gargle with in between bouts of frenzied banging. It was the kind of thing that seems to happen only in silent films and my house. I put my portfolio on the kitchen table for five minutes, and when I came back Charlotte was attacking the flames with a fire extinguisher and Dad was running after the cat with a rolled-up newspaper. Nobody had a very satisfactory explanation for this farcical event. Although I'm certain it was an accident, I can't help thinking that it was somehow, subconsciously, deliberate. 'We're so sorry, darling,' Mum crooned. 'But there's no way we could have afforded to send you to London anyway. The course fees are astronomical, the rents are even worse, and even with funding we'd be really stretched. I know it's heartbreaking, but maybe it's for the best.'

Dad was even worse at disguising his relief. 'Oh well, fate has spoken. You wouldn't have liked it. Fashion school is full of wankers,' he said.

That night, my dreams went up in smoke along with the portfolio.

I glare at Teresa and she looks back at me

triumphantly. Amazingly, she must have been listening when I told Mona all the awful details.

'They didn't burn it on purpose,' I finally say, my mouth curling down at the corners. 'It was an accident.'

Teresa lets out a hoot. 'Maybe see ya later, Mona,' she says, knowing she's hit a nerve and proud of it. 'If you come dinnae bring her, right?'

I watch as she thunders across to the pub and slings the door open like a thirsty sailor.

Mona, as usual, offers nothing.

'What? Do you want to go?' I fire back.

'No, but it's nice to have the option,' she says with a sigh. 'What else are we gonna do? Sit here all night?'

'Whatever.' I feel lousy. There's a silence, and my ears fill with the constant, queasy glugging of the water against the harbour. Mona shoves me the bottle of Buckfast, but I decline.

'Get over yourself,' she says.

I stare at her, and she stares at me. Reluctantly, I wipe the top of the bottle and take a swig of the sticky wine. It goes down like cough linctus, lighting a fire in my belly, and we sit there, saying nothing, huddled in the concrete cave of the municipal bus shelter. There's the usual smell of wee and chips, the graffiti (Tam '84, Leanne luvs Donald IDST, Fife Boyracerz!!! to fast to furius [sic]) and the feeling that tonight, like every Saturday night, I'm trapped.

'There's a party at mine,' I volunteer in a small voice.

'Really?' Mona gasps, jumping up. 'Why didn't you say?'

'I didn't think you'd be that interested. It'll be full of old people.'

'So what? There'll be booze, right? And your ma and da are a right laugh. They're all crazy! Come back to mine and we'll get ready.'

'Let me just get some chips first,' I mumble, but Mona is already halfway up the road, singing to herself like she's won the lottery.

Mona and I have known each other since we were small, about five years old or so. She used to sit next to me in school. Back then, her hair wasn't pink, it was the colour of sun-bleached corn, and she was really quiet, to the point that her mum took her to a special doctor in Edinburgh to find out whether she was all there. When I was eleven I read a book called the *Midwich Cuckoos* and the children in it reminded me of her: blond, blank eyed, possessed by some invisible sinister power. Except Mona was never sinister, she was just an agreeably empty space, like the first white page in a new notebook. I'd tell her things, about the names of birds and animals, who said what about this or that, and make up my own myths – that my father was a disgraced Russian count and I was actually a princess, and that one day I would go back to the motherland and ride horses and take my rightful place on the throne of Moscowrovia. I talked a lot of nonsense. Even when the stories got more and more far-fetched, she would never react to anything, and after a while it got pretty frustrating. Sometimes I would say nasty things to her or hit her and give her a dead arm, which I now regret, of course, but she wouldn't even fight back. It was like it never happened. One day I told her to wait for me at Strathie's newsagent's on High Street after school and I deliberately went home without meeting her. The next day, she appeared at my side as usual, and nothing was said about it. Racked with guilt, I bought her sweets every day for about two weeks, which she gracefully accepted. It was only when we were about fifteen that she admitted she'd forgotten to turn up to Strathie's herself, but telling me that would have interrupted the flow of free cola cubes she'd got used to stuffing her face with.

Now, Mona has found a voice, a very loud one. She's perched on top of the washing machine in my parents' kitchen, talking to my mother about what a freak I am, and trying to shotgun a can of lager with a broken ballpoint pen.

'She'sh always been so uptight, Mrs Kaminsky,' she slurs. 'She ushed to tell me to tuck in my blouse at school . . . I mean, we were seven or schumthin'! It's mad!'

My mother, rather than supporting her daughter, is sticking her oar in too, waving a stumpy roll-up and sloshing red wine around in her glass.

'Yes, dear, I remember when Evie was a wee girl – primary three, maybe – she would lay out all her clothes for the next day on her bed, and when I asked her about it, she said, "Mummy, I like to know where everything is in the morning, and that way I won't be late for school." God knows where she gets it from – I'd be late for my own funeral!' My mum lets out a wheezing sea lion's honk and Mona spills a river of lager down her front, consumed with the giggles.

I sigh heavily. The kitchen is a bombsite. Fag ends and sticky plastic glasses everywhere, crisp packets and dips and cans and bottles. I know that I'll be cleaning it up. The house is crawling with the area's most prolific local artisans. There's Linda Appleby, who paints watercolours of flowers and fruit and is, rumour has it, addicted to painkillers. She's talking to Malcolm Chance, a teacher and part-time painter who thinks he's a total genius because his tedious landscapes are sold in a teeny wee gallery in Perth. Then there's Barry and Gaynor Melville. Gaynor works in a home furnishings shop in St Andrews and does weedy drawings of plants in her spare time, while Barry, a blustering retired carpet salesman, fancies himself as a regular Picasso, boring everyone rigid with his pervy theories about the female form. In the shadowy corner near the grandfather clock is my dad, Anton Kaminsky, a dark scribble, wearing the same bobbled jumper he always wears, discussing something very intense with the woman who works in the Spar. Everyone is drunk out of their minds.

I bite my lip and try to imagine the room filled with people I've learned about from library books and afternoon films on BBC2. People with a bit of dignity and poise. I think of Jean Seberg in *A Bout de Souffle*, buying a newspaper and skipping down the Parisian streets. I think of Marlene Dietrich in *The Blue Angel*, her whippet-thin legs draped around a chair. I think of

Dorothy Parker, wrapped in fur, sipping a Martini and saying something fabulously witty, but then she morphs into my mother, talking about how ceramics are notoriously difficult to light. I pour myself a cup of red wine from a Stowells of Chelsea box and edge closer to the wall. Who would have thought you could feel so out of place in your own house? The blank-faced phrenology head on the shelf looks more at ease here than me. I busy myself by absent-mindedly making an origami boat out of a receipt.

'Hello there,' a man says. 'Nice boat. Very sculptural.' He sidles up to me like jam oozing out of a doughnut, wearing a wide-brimmed black hat that announces his position as a very important and iconic figure. I don't need to ask his name – this is Victor McDougall, The Painter. Everyone is in awe of him. He has a chirruping flock of middle-aged women around him at all times because he is monumentally rich. He's here as a guest of Svetlana, some gallery owner my dad knows, who is very high up in commercial art. Victor's bow-lipped women are used on mugs and postcards and glossy prints and we're all supposed to be delighted that he's lowered himself to our level for this evening. I agree with my dad, who thinks Victor's work is highly derivative. What's more, close up, he smells of taramasalata.

'Victor. Pleased to meet you,' he says, breathing all over me. 'I'm sure my reputation precedes me.'

I try to think of some scathing and fabulously witty retort, but the only thing that springs to mind is 'back off, fishy breath'.

'No, I'm not crazy about parties,' he says, as if I've asked him a question. 'Standing around, talking about the weather. I'd rather be working. But it's the eternal conundrum, isn't it? One must observe so that one can create. There must be a period of looking, a period of contemplation, a gestation period.'

I sip my wine and smile blandly. Go and gestate somewhere else.

'Usually I get tired of parties because you see the same old faces, but when I saw you, I thought, What a fascinating creature. Your disconsolate, almost insolent energy, this bobbed hair and A-line skirt reminiscent of a French schoolgirl, a mixture of cool, self-contained composure and dark, tempestuous ferocity.'

I look at him with dark tempestuous ferocity, but he doesn't notice. He's too busy looking at my chest.

'You know, I'd very much like to . . . paint you,' he leers.

Here we go. He edges even closer and I can feel his arm near my boob. This kind of thing happens all the time at my parents' parties – I should have invested in a baseball bat years ago. Under his hat his eyes are blindly beady, like a randy ferret. He must be about seventy – what does he think he's doing, cracking on to twenty-year-olds?

'Of course, Victor, the hardest observations are the ones we must make about ourselves,' I declare loftily, the red wine and lack of food making me feel quite bold. 'One must step back and be self-critical, and ask oneself, "What am I talking about? Am I making a total arse of myself?"' I try to catch his eye, hoping he'll get the message, but he's too busy thinking of his next killer line. I glance away across the room and see that someone has ordered an Indian take-away and is in the process of spreading oily lids and vivid globs of orange sauce all over the table. That's going to stain. Rothko is peering upwards hopefully, slavering and drooling on the floor tiles.

'Very true, very true,' Victor says. 'You're Evie, right?'

'Hmm.'

'Sexy name,' he slithers.

Suddenly, gloriously, there is a horrendous thud from near the sink.

'Mona!' my mother shrieks. Mona has fallen off the washing machine, dragging four full cans of Stella and a packet of Bold Ultra with her.

'I'm sorry, Victor, I've got to go. Nice to meet you.'

With more speed than is entirely necessary, I dash to pick up Mona, who is laughing in great, breathless gulps. All around her is a festive sprinkling of washing powder. It's all very funny now, if only this wasn't such a familiar performance. Soon her eyes'll start to water, she'll go pale – and there's no way I'm going to let her puke in the house. Again.

'Come on – come into the garden . . .' I say, hauling her up underneath the armpits.

'Nuuh, leave me alone. I wanna stay here!' she protests.

'Shh, I'm taking you outside,' I tell her, dragging her limp, five-foot-nothing frame towards the door. She weighs a ton, but everyone else is too engaged in their intense conversations to bother helping me.

'Youso BOSSY! Chill out, Evie, GOD . . .' Mona moans, but doesn't resist. When I've got her into the garden, I sit her down on a flat rock near the path. It's a warm night, with a salty breeze coming off the sea.

'Are you OK? Do you want some water?' I ask, looking down at the top of her head, a tender mesh of pinky blond hair and white scalp. The harsh flamingo shade looks inappropriate somehow, like seeing a baby with its ears pierced. We're quiet for a while, and I'm starting to think I might bring a chair and a blanket out here and look at the stars, when a demonic growling sound comes out of Mona's throat; a noise far bigger than she is. Then she opens her mouth and barfs all over my shoes. As I yelp and jump out of the way, puke pitter-patters all over the flagstones and in between the clumps of grass and slides onto the path in a damp stream.

'Thanks.'

'Uuuh,' Mona whimpers, and does it again.

I go inside and wipe the vomit off with a piece of damp kitchen towel. In the few moments I was away, the party has moved up a gear – Charlotte is doing the IBS shuffle to Pink Floyd; Dad, charm personified, is entertaining Sheila Warren and Gaynor Melville at the newly stained kitchen table; and Victor McDougall is now lolling on the threadbare sofa, flanked by Svetlana, in a terrifyingly low-cut electric-blue evening gown, along with a woman who appears to be wearing a skunk on her head. Victor sends me another ferrety look from under his hat that could either be flirtatious or scornful, but I can't be bothered to figure it out. I'm more concerned with the state of the house. It really looks like someone has put a wrecking ball through it. The kitchen hums of chicken jalfrezi, grass and patchouli joss sticks, and the dog is eating all the leftover curry out of a foil carton on the floor.

'No, Rothko!' I say, grabbing it off him. He licks his chops and looks hurt, then sneezes twice. We're all going to pay for that in the morning. I realize I have a thumping headache and feel about fifty years old. Remember, Evie, this is the last push, it'll soon be V-Day. I experiment with a smile but my mouth refuses to co-operate.

'Hi, Evie,' says Malcolm Chance, suavely. 'Don't have an ashtray anywhere round here, do you?'

I hand him the drool-covered curry carton. 'Here you go.'

Through the glass panel in the back door, I keep one eye on Mona, who is in an advanced state of elasticity, her feet splayed at right angles and her chin hovering above the ground. A strand of hair trails in her puke. God knows what she's been eating. I quickly kick my ruined shoes off and go to the porch to find some alternatives, but all I can see is a monstrous pair of hairy Ugg boots belonging to my mother.

'Your friend doesn't look too chipper,' Malcolm Chance observes wryly, scratching his grey stubbly chin with a bony finger as I wrestle to put on the ridiculous boots. 'I remember when I was your age – I could drink ten pints and still drive home.'

'Er, right.'

'Not advisable these days, of course. But at least we

were free. We had great music and a real sense of possibility, y'know. Nineteen sixty-nine and all that. I was really living then.'

'Yes, Malcolm.' I grimace, while simultaneously submerging my feet into a pair of dead yaks.

'Nowadays, youth is wasted on the young. The kids I teach haven't got a clue how to have a good time. I mean, check out Charlotte over there – she really knows how to let her hair down.'

Oh God. I look over at my mum, who is making sensuous arm movements and running her fingers over her body in a, quite frankly, distressing manner. I think of other mothers in Kirkness, the normal parents of schoolfriends, who always paid up for school trips and baked rock cakes for summer fairs. I never asked her to bake any cakes. She'd have probably put hash in them.

'Could you find me a clean glass?' I enquire in my sweetest voice, hoping to distract him from any more philosophizing about the swinging Sixties. Maybe he's right, though. I try to remember the last time I had a really good time, but all I can think of is the bus shelter and the slick condensation running down the window of the chip shop.

Malcolm, on his quest to find a glass, bumbles about and very helpfully knocks over a lamp.

'Never mind, I'll get it,' I say, padding in an unwieldy fashion towards the sink and grabbing the nearest plastic cup. The water is full of bits (some ongoing plumbing problem nobody can get round to fixing) but Mona won't notice.

'You should have a drink, Evie,' Malcolm slurs. 'You need to loosen up a bit.'

Aaaaargh!!

'You can stay in the spare room if you can get in it,' I tell Mona when I'm outside, straightening her up and examining her for signs of brain malfunction. Her head lolls back and her eyes open up a crack, happily glazed.

'Thanks,' she says. 'I don't know what I'd do without you.'

I grab her arm and ease her off the rock. When she leans in on me too heavily, I feel a short stab of irritation. I wish she wouldn't get so hammered. Every time we do this little dance – she passes out and I haul her around – but tonight it's even more undignified than usual. At the moment, she's doing a good impression of a ventriloquist's dummy with no hand up its backside, and I'm waddling around like the Abominable Snowman. It's really not a very classy state of affairs.

'Help me out here,' I tell her, shoving her through the door and into the barely used narrow hallway at the side of the kitchen. She stumbles and her hand fails to grip the banister. It seems wiser to get her upstairs via the servants' staircase, a secret remnant of when this tumbledown house was grand, and not stuffed to bursting with damp, mouldy crud. The old wallpaper is covered in dusty-coloured leaves and cabbage roses, a quiet ecosystem that seems to exist quite happily by itself, hidden away from the light and noise in the rest of the house. When I was small I would sit here by myself in the gloom and stare at the wallpaper, until my eyes started to play tricks on me and the roses turned into sinister puffed-up faces and I had to run away.

'Allow me,' says a booming voice. Victor McDougall is standing in the doorway like a cut-price Humphrey Bogart. He looks remarkably pleased with himself, as if he's expecting a round of applause.

'It's OK, I can manage . . .' I tell him, but he's in full alpha male mode, and scoops Mona up in one movement, grazing her head on the wall. She lets out a strangulated cry, but he ignores her, thundering up the stairs with no idea where he's going.

'Turn right,' I call to him.

'It's dark!' he yelps.

There's a clatter as he dislodges something large and metallic sounding.

'Wait there.'

I follow him up. The only thing I can see are the white skull and crossbones on the soles of Mona's shoes, the shoes I once drove her to Edinburgh to get.

'Let me get past – there's a light at the end of the hall.'

Victor does his best not to move out of the way, and I have to practically molest him to get by, with Mona as a human contraceptive. I'm so fed up with all this silliness that I consider leaving them both there, stumbling about in the pitch black, while I go to bed and bolt my door, but I find the light switch instead. The scene is instantly and unattractively illuminated: a fat Fifties gangster holding a dead punk girl. At their feet, the mannequin lies like a bloated corpse – all it needs is a line of chalk drawn round it and this could be a case for the NYPD.

'Er, it's probably better to put her in here,' I say, getting my key out of my skirt pocket and opening the door. Stumbling over the threshold, panting like a pig, Victor makes a big deal about putting Mona on the bed in the recovery position.

'Thanks, Victor,' I say, in an artificial, upbeat voice. 'You've been very helpful. I'll take it from here.'

Overexerted, he takes a hanky out of his breast pocket, lifts his hat, and wipes his brow, which is such a ridiculously old-fashioned gesture it makes me want to snort with laughter. Under his hat, he's going bald – black strands of hair stick to his head like strips of liquorice. He looks around at my room and, without even asking, decides to sit in my leather chair.

'Let me get my breath back, Evie,' he smirks, his eyes lingering yet again over my boobs.

Mona rolls over onto her back, and begins to snore musically.

'I see you're a woman of taste,' he says. 'Interesting collection of glassware. I collect Murano myself.'

Oh really, Victor, well in that case, we must have sex immediately. I stand around rolling my eyes, with my hands stuffed in my pockets, hoping to make him feel awkward enough to leave.

'So if she's in here, where are you going to sleep tonight?' he asks fruitily, showing suspiciously neat, probably false teeth.

'I'll think of something,' I snap, and start to quickly

untie Mona's shoelaces. Maybe the smell of her feet will cool his ardour.

'You know, I'm very interested in you. Your black hair and pale skin is so perfect, and what's amazing is that you don't even know it. You're so young, so guileless – so angry with the world. A child, yet fully formed, overflowing with womanly ripeness.'

What makes him think that I'd be interested in him?

Anyway, if he wants ripeness, I'll give him ripe. I unveil Mona's socks, pink and white grubby things with holes in the heel, and a yeasty pong briefly fills the air.

'Well that's nice, Victor, but I really think we should have this conversation some other time. Perhaps when I'm ten years older. Now, if you don't mind I need to put Mona to bed and I think she'd appreciate some privacy.'

It takes a moment for my rejection to sink in. Suddenly he leaps to his feet, startling me and almost knocking off his hat on the sloping ceiling.

'Evie,' he breathes, fishily, 'I don't think you quite understand who I am. I'm Victor McDougall.'

I stare at him. He's trying to be masterful, but the threatening tone and damp sheen of sweat on his cheeks make him seem thoroughly sinister.

'That means,' he says, advancing closer in a creepy fashion, 'that I always, always get what I want.'

With that, he grabs either side of me and pulls me towards him like a rag doll, in the same way silent movie heroes manhandle their leading ladies. This guy is so cheesy, it's unbelievable. I feel like laughing hysterically – surely he can't be serious? But oh, God, he is, all 5 foot 4 of him.

'Get off me,' I growl, stamping on his foot. He doesn't move, and his ferrety eyes have gone all gooey. Yuk, he's about to kiss me. On the bed, Mona is snoring like a steam train. I dimly recall my self-defence training at school – if you're going to kick a man in the family jewels, do it with your foot pointing upwards for maximum damage. And preferably don't do it with a pair of Muppets on your feet. But I can't get far enough away from him to get a good swing at them, and if I brought my knee up now he'd go stumbling backwards into my bookcase and knock the whole thing flying.

'Evie, Evie, Evie,' Victor dribbles. 'Come to bed with me and you won't regret it. I'll paint you and make you a star. I'll take you away from all this. We'll go to Paris. I'll show you things you never even knew existed.'

Despite the desperate situation, I quickly wonder what it would be like to be Victor's Parisian lady friend, the face that launched a million mugs and mouse mats, staying in the Ritz and charging Chanel to his platinum credit card. Perhaps he would buy me my studio near the patisserie. Then reality comes crashing in as his lips, two glistening slug trails, loom towards me alarmingly. With my mouth clamped shut, I turn away, scrunch up my eyes and let out an involuntary high-pitched squeal.

'What the HELL is going on here?'

I open them and see my dad in the doorway, the very picture of a marauding peasant. His curly hair is matted, his vast chin like a prime cut of ham, everything covered in jet-black bristles and resonating with hot-blooded anger.

'You bastard! Get your dirty hands off my daughter!'

I start to say something reasonable and calming to diffuse the situation, but falter, and in that moment, just as Dad balls his shovel hand into a fist and Victor McDougall's grip turns to jelly, I instead start to utter a wee prayer that nothing gets broken and that my room can return to its original state, untainted by horny painters and bilious friends and drunken violence. Then I hear the moment of contact, the cartoon smacking noise of knuckle against jaw, and I know what's going to happen. It's like a domino rally I once saw on TV when I was small – a spectacular and inevitable matter of gravity. I watch helplessly as Victor barrels backwards, snapping the chrome stem of my leather chair, his shoulder colliding with my shelf of glass in silly, pantomime slow motion. Everything slides off in a deranged tea party of clinks and clunks and each object self-destructs, thudding heavily to the floor, shattering in mesmerizing bursts of red and green against the end of the bookcase. The sound is deafening, the sound of the world ending. From somewhere behind me I can hear a scream and I'm caught up in the panic, hardly able to breathe.

Afterwards there is a stomach-churning silence. Then a delicate, comically refined tinkle of glass, like a disturbed chandelier.

'Oh God,' says Mona, woken from her coma.

'Oh,' says my dad, staring at the damage he's done.

His hands hover in the air, thick and beefy and blistered, but wavering, as if they're made of paper.

'Anton!' says my mother, who has appeared in the doorway along with several other stricken houseguests.

'I think someone should get him some ice,' somebody says after a while, as Victor nurses his jaw and whimpers. Nobody moves. They're all just standing around with their mouths open, wooden Cluedo characters confronted with a body in the drawing room. The floor is a mosaic of glittering, lethal shards. I mentally add it to the horrors downstairs and I feel like I'm being strangled. I think my parents have finally made a mess I'm not sure I can clean up.

'I can't live here any more,' I announce, the words tumbling out of mouth. My voice sounds like it belongs to a person on the verge of a nervous breakdown. 'I'm moving out first thing tomorrow morning. To Glasgow. I have a place on the HND Fashion Design course at MetroTech College.'

It doesn't sound as thrilling as I'd hoped. In fact, I may as well have announced I'm doing a City and Guilds in boiler maintenance. Still, so what? My knees stop buckling and I say it again.

'That's right. HND Fashion Design. I enrol on my course on the twenty-second of August, and from now on, I will no longer be living in this ridiculous place.'

There's a weird swishing silence. All I can hear is the blood pounding in my ears. I turn to see my mother standing in the doorway, looking at me uncomprehendingly.

'I can't believe it,' she says, genuinely stunned.

'That's Victor McDougall. The Painter. What have you done to him?'

The first thing I see when I wake up is the chair, listing unnaturally to the right. How much of a big fat lump do you have to be to snap a piece of metal? I don't want to face the carnage. I was too exhausted to clean it up last night and nobody offered to help. The mess seemed like a good motivator – evidence of the unreasonable nonsense I have to put up with, day in, day out. Now I just wish it was gone.

Victor McDougall decided not to press charges and left with Svetlana, under a considerable cloud. Mona, who was starting to turn green again, was taken home by Gaynor Melville in her 4 x 4, and probably puked in the glove compartment. Then the party continued, fuelled by that brief, thrilling flash of testosterone and the ensuing gossip. The music was turned off at 6.37 a.m. I know because it was me who turned it off. Everyone had left and 'Wish You Were Here' was blaring out on repeat, with Dad slumped asleep in an armchair, a cut on his knuckle and a mug of whisky cradled in his other hand.

I roll over and look at the ceiling with all its familiar dents and buckles, the damp patch in the shape of Australia in the left-hand corner, the old glow-in-the-dark stars I used to marvel at when I was little, permanently welded to the plaster. The sun comes out unexpectedly and the ceiling is immediately fragmented by sparkling red, blue and green dots of light, glinting off the remains of my glass collection. I stare at it for a while and the kaleidoscopic colours swim before my eyes. The effect is quite beautiful, really. But then I get a suffocating feeling that I'm underwater and clawing my way towards the light – this is the glimmering, panic-stricken, euphoric moment you're supposed to get before you drown.

I prop myself up on my elbows, freaking out, gasping for breath.

Damn you, Victor McDougall.

Perhaps I should just slip out, unnoticed. But then I would have to leave a note, which is even more overblown and stupid, like I'm committing suicide or something. It'd be more ridiculous nonsense we just don't need.

I sit up and decide that lying here feeling sorry for myself isn't the solution. Outside, it's chosen to be a bright, insidiously cheerful seaside day, all buckets and spades and fleeting clouds, whipping wind-breakers, fish teas, and happy families. I put on some shoes and take a suitcase from the top of the wardrobe, but even doing that seems too drastic. I think for a minute, absently chewing my thumbnail. Maybe slipping out unnoticed might not be a bad thing after all – they probably won't regain consciousness until about two o'clock anyway, and it'll take them a few hours to realize I'm not in my room – more if they think I'm in a huff with them. By that time, I would be able to phone them from a hotel. 'I'm in Glasgow,' I'd say, my voice hard with resolve. 'I told you about it last night – remember?' (Of course, they'd have been too pissed and shocked to remember, an oversight I would triumphantly use against them.) Afterwards, I would lie on the springy bed and drink in the austere, refined hotel silence like Scarlett Johansson in *Lost in Translation*, and get on with beginning the rest of my life. Maybe it'll be glamorous as well as character building. But the idea seems so foreign and out of reach I can't believe it'll ever happen, never mind as soon as tonight.

Anyway, best to get on with things. I pick out what to wear today, a black shift dress with white stitching that I copied from a book about the Sixties – it seemed cool then, but now it feels funereal. Then I systematically pack the rest of my clothes into layers. The books will have to be packed into boxes and labelled, such a time-consuming process that it might be better if I come back for them at a later date. The only thing sturdy enough to survive the glass massacre was a chunky bright orange ashtray, which I wrap in a copy of *Architecture Now* magazine and bury deep within my clothes. I close the lid easily and the swish of the zipper is encouragingly final, like the sound of a hard pencil drawing a line under all this ridiculous business.

But I can't leave without cleaning up this glass. What if Rothko or Hepworth come in and cut their paws on it? Then there's the matter of Mrs Morrison, who I'll be leaving in the lurch at Kirkness Fashions. With nobody around to fold the enormous pants or fend off Boreen, things could quickly get out of hand.

Nervously, I go to the bathroom, shivering as I hop across the landing, which seems to have acquired a brand-new set of junk overnight in the shape of a dirty water-filter jug, a saddle and an old silver artificial Christmas tree. The dummy is back where it was.

I rattle the door handle. That's strange. There's someone in there. From inside I can hear the sound of coughing, followed by a thin trickle of water. It can't be my dad, because he's still passed out on the chair downstairs. And although she sometimes takes the dog out, I'm pretty sure Charlotte won't see the light of day till September. It's definitely a man. Perhaps it's a stray who fell asleep under a pile of coats and was forgotten, now getting ready to stumble up the road. But I could have sworn that my dad was the only person down there first thing this morning. It's not Victor McDougall returning to the scene of the crime, is it?

I backtrack into my bedroom as the toilet flushes, and just as I reach the door, the lock is opened and someone comes out. He's tall, wiry, wearing a pair of faded pinstripe boxer shorts. It's Malcolm Chance! 1969 and all that. His grey, porous wig stands on end, and from here I can see he has two repulsive wire-wool tufts of hair on each shoulder. Then he goes into the bedroom. *My parents' bedroom.* Through the diminishing gap in the closing door, I can just make out a shape under the mountainous duvet.

Oh my God.

Please, no.

I lean weakly on the doorframe, feeling like a piece of overcooked spaghetti. *Your father hasn't touched me for weeks,* Mum said, when I was in the cupboard. *Charlotte really knows how to let her hair down,* said

Malcolm, tipping his ash into the empty curry carton, acting the smart arse. They're not. They can't be.

I don't seem to have any bones any more. My parents don't have affairs. Do they? The mannequin on the landing stares impenetrably at me. What has it seen?

I think back to all the other parties there have been in this house over the years. When I was about twelve, was Dad snogging Gaynor Melville in the garden or were they just talking? I remember Mum and Malcolm slow dancing in the living room once, and she tripped over a wine bottle and fell backwards on the sofa. He landed on top of her and there was a lot of giggling. Was that the start of it? It didn't seem serious at the time, but maybe I missed something, maybe some spark passed between them when I wasn't looking, a squeeze of the knee or a wink. And now here he is, keeping the bed warm while my dad is downstairs. It's so cheeky! It's so humiliating. I feel like going in there with a bucket of water and breaking it up. But does my dad know? Is it one of those 1969 things? Their idea of a good time? Are they all in it together – a bunch of arty swingers, swapping fluids like other people swap gardening tips?

I don't want to go into the bathroom and smell whatever manly odours Malcolm Chance has left in there. Instead I put on my clothes as quickly as possible, gather the rest of my things in a duffel bag, including the box file with all my Glasgow stuff in it, and lock my room from the outside. I try not to look at the door to my parents' bedroom, which stays shut, as simultaneously anonymous and obvious as the entrance to a back-street brothel.

Instead I lose myself in the straightforward business of planning. According to my timetable, the one and only bus to Glasgow on Sunday leaves at quarter to twelve. When I get there, I'll call Mrs Morrison and tell her that I will be terminating my employment as of today. It's really not like me to let people down like this, but I just can't face staying here to work a two-week notice. It's not as if she needs me, not really. In fact, I've long suspected that my role in the shop is to listen while Mrs Morrison tells me how she had to draw a line up her leg during the war because you couldn't get stockings. Anyway, she barely remembers my name half the time, and when she does she calls me 'Edna'. I tell myself it's all going to be OK. My teeth are chattering.

Downstairs, the living room stinks of stale smoke and my dad is still slumbering in the chair. The table is a muddle of cups, plates, flattened foil pouches from wine boxes, mugs and plastic glasses with soggy filter tips at the bottom like dead slugs. There's a terrible, stifling smell of stale curry and musky incense cones. A blizzard of washing powder is sprinkled across the kitchen tiles, along with broken pretzels, half-chewed cubes of scarlet-coated tandoori chicken, sticky red wine stains, beer spillages, and a crazy paving of muddy paw- and footprints. Hepworth comes tinkling in, propelled by a purring motor, full of hungry adoration. I know without looking that we've run out of cat food.

I drag my suitcase and bag through the filth and try not to wake my dad, who, despite his hulking frame, looks like a vulnerable little boy with his hair sticking out and the crocheted throw from the sofa pulled over him. Poor Dad. What if I woke him up and told him about Malcolm? Would it do any good? Or would everything just get broken again?

No – it's better he doesn't know. I go over to him anyway, and pull the blanket further towards his chin to keep him warm.

'Bye, Dad,' I whisper. He stirs, briefly, and puts his hand over mine. 'Take care and I'll see you soon.'

He grunts and goes back to snoring. I take one last look at the mess, an unsolvable tangle of party debris and extramarital lunacy that I can't possibly begin to sort out, and leave the chaos behind.

Outside, it's practically idyllic, with bushes and trees waving greenly in the breeze. I shouldn't even be leaving, but my legs are taking me to the bus stop regardless, even though I'm consumed with a horrible feeling that as soon as I go, my family will slide catastrophically away from me and fall to pieces like my shelf of glass, undone by a nudge from Victor McDougall's elbow. On the seafront, populated by carefree day-trippers, the seaside scene starts to seem like a freakish parody. The oversized fibreglass ice cream outside Vanelli's is disturbingly out of proportion, the sky is an artificial dyed blue, like food colouring in a Slush Puppy. People's smiles are the medicated grins of the insane, and the canopy over the closed fishmonger's is an unnecessarily cheerful Toytown yellow.

I set my bag down on the cobbles. The smart thing to do is to keep my nerve and leave. I was going anyway, even though, ideally, I wanted to get a place to live first. Still, what does it matter? I couldn't stand another day in there, and that's that. I steel myself against the wind, willing away the uncertainty. In fact, it's not long before I convince myself that leaving today, at this very moment, without warning, is absolutely the right thing to do. It's only when I'm actually on the bus and I see my mum, coming back from the Co-op with Rothko trailing behind her, that I realize my mistake.

Step Three – Try and Try Again

You wouldn't buy an outfit off the peg without first checking that it fits, would you? The same goes for your own project. Once tacked loosely together, your outfit may look marvellous on your dressmaker's mannequin, but do try it on for size first, otherwise you'll be the dummy!

'Ma! Ma! Look! A bus!'

'Shut up, Ashley! I'm tryin' tae have a fag!'

Buchanan Street bus station is swarming with people, all seemingly in the same state as everyone at the party last night. There's a football match on, and a knife-edge of tension in the town – I don't want to look anyone in the eye. I go straight to the exit, ignoring the *Big Issue* seller and the homeless guy who has a limp ribbon of trouser where his left leg should be, and spill out into the street, carried by a scary wave of foul-mouthed teenage girls from the Teresa Donegan school of fashion, dripping with nameplate gold and kitted out in cheap, sugary pink. When I snuck out of the house and came here to present my portfolio to Duncan Howitson, the course leader, on a slate-grey Monday in July, the atmosphere was calm and businesslike, and I arrived feeling purposeful and grown-up. Now the office workers are replaced with shoppers and children and football fans, it's a madhouse. Everyone seems to be agitated, almost running along. Even the clock – a piece of mediocre public art, which would probably have my dad beating his chest in despair – is fleeing, sitting atop two mammoth metal legs that are breaking out into a sprint.

I briefly wonder whether I should just turn round and go home. It's not like I left a note or anything. I could say I went for a walk. (With a full suitcase.) But there's no time to form any other thoughts as I'm propelled into the crowd, and I'm painfully aware of my stupid short black dress and matching black bob. I look like I'm trying too hard. I may as well have a sign on my back that says 'Mug Me'. Everything is just so big, much bigger than it seemed when I came here before. The massive multiplex cinema raises its confident fist to the sky, and the concert hall seems uniformly vast, filling my field of vision with great broad slabs of sandstone. At the mouth of the bus station is a hotel, but it's too posh and overwhelming for me even to contemplate entering. There are so many people: negative and positive energies crashing together, newborn babies and weather-beaten pockmarked lunatics; students with staggered, unsymmetrical haircuts stumbling through hangovers;

neat beige old ladies from the same mould as Mrs Morrison. I keep having to sidestep folk coming the other way, a hick from the sticks lost in the city traffic. Buskers and Chinese girls selling annoying, bleeping, squeaking toys crowd the pavement – everyone is *shouting*. 'It's just a city,' I keep saying to myself, but my bearings are gone and now, somehow, between the bus station and the city centre, I've managed to get lost on a wide road with nothing much on it apart from blocks of flats in the distance. I stumble onward, realize I'm in the shopping centre car park, and end up in John Lewis, in the carpet department. I've only walked about a third of a mile and I'm hyper-ventilating.

Evie.

Calm down. You're in a carpet department, not Chechnya.

I stare at the black-and-white diagonals on a rug, hanging by invisible thread from the ceiling, a magic carpet ready to transport me anywhere.

Chill out. Loosen up.

I wonder if, by now, Charlotte has realized that I've gone. I wonder whether Dad and Malcolm Chance and the mystery lady in my parents' bed are all having scrambled eggs, cooked by my mother in a rare fit of culinary competence. 'Where's Evie?' someone might ask. 'Probably in her room,' Charlotte would breeze, piling up the sink with more dishes. 'God knows what she does in there all day. Probably reading about minimalist German architecture and kicking herself for not putting her socks in alphabetical order.'

OK, I can do this. I've been here before and seen the same sights and it didn't bother me then. I've been to Edinburgh and navigated multi-storey car parking and visited the shops on Saturdays with Mona. I don't know why I'm so rattled all of a sudden – it's not like I'm from the Outer Hebrides. I rouse myself and head for the exit, eventually finding a taxi rank outside the concert hall. I take a deep breath. 'Travelstyle Hotel, please,' I say in a woolly voice. He doesn't hear me so I have to say it again, and I sound like such a total tourist. My face is burning red.

It takes me ages to lug my bags through the door, and he makes no move to help me. In fact, I get the paranoid impression that he's enjoying watching me sweat in the rear-view mirror while he sits there slowly folding his copy of the Sunday paper. Then, he speeds off before I even get a chance to slam the door, throwing me back into my seat. The cab reeks of chemical vanilla air freshener. Even putting on my seat belt is one achievement too far – he keeps pulling out and braking, swinging wildly round corners, and before I've managed to get the buckle in the slot, we're pulling up into the hotel, a tall box overlooking the M8, hardly a stone's throw from the centre of town, but separate and featureless, existing in its own bland touristy vacuum. It's more Alan Partridge than *Lost in Translation*. Instead of splendid isolation, there's a family carvery and a bar called Smokey Joe's, and it's a concrete underpass away from a lapdancing club. I try to stride purposefully into the lobby, as if I'm being trailed by a bellboy carrying hatboxes and trunks, but it's no use. At the reception there's a queue of lairy blokes, each wearing a charming T-shirt with a pair of breasts printed on the front. One turns round to reveal the slogan 'ANDY'S GETTING MARRIED – WHAT A TIT!'

Scarlett Johansson, eat your heart out.

'A-guggh-aaaa-jugggg-aaaaa-aaaarrrrr!!' My mother's laugh is a complex and not very attractive sound – like a lorry trying to do a three-point turn in a vat of porridge.

'Evie, are you having some kind of nervous breakdown? I wouldn't sleep with Malcolm. He has appalling hairy shoulders! That was Linda Appleby – she's been having a terrible time recently, what with her divorce from that wretched car salesman. Malcolm was comforting her, and you know how these things go after a few drinks . . . I slept in the spare room.'

Oh. Now I'm here, everything feels like a silly overreaction, and a hotel, any hotel, is a stupid place to be. Especially one that has microscopic soaps in the bathroom and a large, very dubious stain on the carpet. I look at my reflection in the dressing-table unit, framed by the tray of complimentary tea and shortbread and a Corby trouser press. The room is dismal and sterile – in the mirror is a belligerent kid having a ludicrous tantrum.

'If I'd known you were going I'd have given you some money,' my mother tells me, evenly.

'I did say something. I told you last night.' Charlotte ignores me.

'But, darling, you can't live in a hotel for the rest of your life. You're not Howard Hughes.'

'I'll be fine. I'm going to get a flat.'

'Yes, well, that's nice, dear,' she says.

'I've left home,' I say, balling my fist. 'I'm a student now.'

'Yes, I know. It wouldn't have hurt to tell us before you ran off, though, would it?'

I sigh and unclench my palm, which is white and flabby, like a jellyfish. I did try to tell them.

'I have savings,' I say, mildly. 'I'll be OK.'

'Yes, well, you're very practical.'

I don't like this one bit. My mother is being weird and reasonable, as if she's reading her replies from a script. Is she stoned? Did she score some skunk off someone at the party? Maybe it's some kind of trick to get me to come home and clean up the kitchen.

There's a crackle and a thud and my dad comes on the line.

'Hello, Evie,' he says pleasantly. Now I know something's up. 'I am very sorry about the glass. I will pay for all replacements. How are you?'

'I'm fine,' I say, unnerved. 'What's going on?'

Charlotte comes back on the line.

'We're very sorry about the incident,' she says. 'Victor McDougall is *persona non grata*, shall we say. He won't be coming back, that's for sure.'

'Well, good. He smells of taramasalata.'

'Taramasalata? Well, anyway, we're crossing him off the Christmas card list. And if he thinks he's going to get an invite to my show at the Wobbly Wheel, then he can think again. Still, I'm sorry you had to leave like that. I mean, the postman told me he'd seen letters from MetroTech College, and I knew when you sneaked out in July with that portfolio that you were going for an interview, but I didn't want to ask in case you didn't get it. Anyway, I knew our clever girl would be OK. Congratulations, darling! Anton is going to put some money in your bank account and if there's anything we can do, give us a shout. You know where we are.'

They knew! Damn. I was so careful. But I should have known you can't fart in Kirkness without someone posting it on the village messageboard.

'I'll be fine,' I say quickly, feeling anything but. 'I'll phone you in a couple of days. Say bye to Dad.'

I hang up and lie there for a while, listening to the hum of the air conditioning, or heater or whatever it is. The reasonable, considerate, sympathetic voice of my mother hangs in my ears. Since when did she turn into Kofi Annan? I feel like everything is completely upside down. Now they're the sensible ones, and I'm the one who wears cheesecloth kaftans and wipes my bogies on the curtains.

Mrs Morrison wasn't very pleased when I called her. I suppose I didn't realize I had such a vital role in the empire of Kirkness Fashions. I told her that personal circumstances had required me to move away quickly, and instead of saying, 'Och, never mind, it'll all come out in the wash,' like she usually does when anything goes wrong, she just went very quiet and told me she wasn't sure she could manage without me, but that worse things happen at sea, and she would pay any remaining wages to my mum next week. It all left me with a sinking heart and a weird, metallic taste in my mouth. The thought of her on her own behind that vast wooden counter – getting electric shocks from all those static-charged artificial fibres – doesn't bear thinking about.

Maybe I'll feel better if I reaffirm my plans. I take out the box file and the itinerary (bullet points in pink, yellow and green fluorescent ink), but it doesn't give me the optimistic buzz it usually does. I study the locations, bus routes and places of interest but they just sound flat and uninspiring: 'The Kelvingrove art gallery shouldn't be missed . . .' according to my city guide, 'and the Willow Tearooms are a must for fans of Charles Rennie Mackintosh's simple elegance.' Whatever.

There's nothing else to do but wait until tomorrow. In my wee capsule high above the motorway, time passes, elastic and unchecked. There's no dust to pick up with my finger, no dishes to stack away, and the sanitary, fake hotel quiet I've been praying for is starting to freak me out. I get the remote and flick through the channels. Finally, I stop flicking and settle on a nature programme. A baby chimpanzee leaves its mother for a life of swinging in the trees, unaided. He makes it look easy.

'Oooooooooh . . . arrrrgh!!!'

A girl with long green socks and wild, curly black hair rides past on her bike, through a red light, causing a screech of brakes. Instead of wobbling and falling off, though, she speeds onwards, hoiking herself upwards off the bicycle seat and careering around the corner. Although it's a reckless violation of the Highway Code, I can't help feeling a twinge of admiration.

I walk down the street with purposeful strides. Here you are, Evie. I like it here, I tell myself, over and over again, I like it. That's why I chose it. I like the way the tenements look lined up, stretching all the way down the road like a splayed deck of cards. I like the shops and cafés, the cars and the movement, the sense of urgency and structure. If I was at home, I would be in the shop, drinking Mellow Bird's out of Mrs Morrison's mug with the squirrel on it, and rain would be battering the window, sealing us in our dusty, forgotten wee corner. Instead, I'm here, in the thick of the modern world. I'm alive. I'm my own person. It should be exciting. It is. I think.

The thing is, though, my house hunt isn't going very well. I'm trying to be optimistic, but I've already seen two condemned dungeons calling themselves basement studio flats, with faulty gas heaters and fleas, and I've got a horrible feeling there are more where they came from. This creepy woman called Mrs Kyriakou tried to sell me a hole in the ground that looked as if it had been used as a safe house for the Manson family – squished fag ends on the floor, blood-red spray paint on the walls. 'Only £350 a month!' she said delightedly, showing me the kitchen, where a lone bottle of ancient milk was curdling on the sticky counter. 'Perfect for a person on their own,' she said, but she didn't add: 'who has no sense of smell.'

My next port of call is Copeland Street. The advert in the newsagent's window was pink with WOW! written on it, festooned with lightning bolts and stars. 'Big bright flat to share with girl student', it said. In reality, though, it's less 'wow' and more 'Ugh'! Number 17 has a peeling red door with a pane of dirty frosted glass in it. There are a million buzzers beside it, clogged with peeling Sellotape. So many names: Hassan, Green, McDonald, Wilson, Sweeney, Kapoor, some people called Oliver and Markus, Cooper, Piggott, Svensson. How could so many people live in one house? I press the buzzer, as instructed by the girl on the phone, which just says 'ALICE' in a childish scrawl. The doorstep is littered with free leaflets advertising gleaming double glazing and uPVC doors, sorely needed by the look of it. The entire house looks like it's rotting, held together with putty and dirt.

'Hello?' says a breathless voice. Have I interrupted something?

'Hi, I'm here to see the flat. I'm Evie Kaminsky.'

'Hellooooo! Top floor.'

A buzz and a click and I'm in the hallway, which was probably once grand, but isn't any more. The floorboards are bare and dusty. A huge pile of mail sits by the door, more leaflets and copies of local papers – I get an urge to tidy up but decide to leave them as they are. 'Housing Crisis Looms', says the headline on the *Glasgow Advertiser*. (I hope it's not trying to tell me something.) Smoothing my hair and my skirt, and feeling more like a benefit fraud investigator than a potential flatmate, I navigate the echoing, empty stairs, past festering rubbish bags and bikes. Looking up to the top, I see a pale face looking down at me, framed by a mess of curly black hair. Through the banister rails I can see she's wearing green socks.

'Hellooooo!' she trills again, the echo making her greeting sound eerie. Behind the face, angular rock music pumps out of the doorway.

'I've just seen you!' she says, as if we're old friends. 'You were walking up Byres Road. I thought, I like her style.'

'I saw you too . . . you were going through a red light,' I reply, before realizing it sounds a bit snooty. Not that Alice seems to mind.

'Oh I know! I haven't even passed my Cycling Proficiency!' she cheerfully bellows. 'Come in!'

I follow her in. She is wearing a flowery shirt and a black knitted tank top, which is full of holes and looks ready to unravel.

'The room's a bit of a mess, I'm afraid . . .' she's saying, shouting over the loud music, which is like a million squeaky bedsprings. 'My old flatmate moved in with her boyfriend and left all her crap here. I've been meaning to do something about it, but you can see what it's like.' She gives a goofy smile and waves her arm around, pointing out the madness everywhere. I smile back, but with slightly more desperation.

Walking through the hallway is pure sensory overload – there's not a single space unadorned. The walls are a tangle of fairy lights, posters for bands, postcards, photo-booth shots of Alice and friends unknown, and a large, possibly stolen, old shop sign that says 'MORE UPSTAIRS'. The floor is even more muddled, a crust of matches, tickets, receipts, discarded clothes and a puncture repair kit that seems to have been methodically spread around for maximum messy effect. My mother would love it.

'I've got a terrible hangover,' she shouts over the music. 'I'm not very organized.' She can say that again. This all seems horribly familiar. I poke my head into the living room as we pass the door. It's big and bright, just like the advert said, or would be if there weren't heavy velvet curtains blocking the window. I notice there's a threadbare chaise longue with chipped gold leaf, some beanbags, and what seems to be the remains of an art project on the rug, thronged by empty mugs and ashtrays and wine bottles. Then I realize there's a figure lying slumped against one of the beanbags, mummified in a duvet.

'Once it's cleared out though, it's a lovely room,' she's saying, heartily pushing her way through the door, causing things behind it to clatter joyously to the floor. She doesn't seem to realize that there's a dead body in the living room. 'Gets a lot of light,' she's saying. 'Not that Gina ever needed light – she never got up before five o'clock, the lazy cow. Do you think I should hire a skip? I thought if I did I wouldn't have to drag all her stuff downstairs – I could just throw it out of the window. How much do you reckon it would be to hire a skip?'

'Well, I don't know, I've never hired one.'

'Me neither,' she murmurs, as if she's somehow failed in an important aspect of life.

This might sound mean, but as far as I can see, this place is already a skip. The room is tiny, emitting the rich aroma of foosty old books and vinegary trainers. On the wall, there is the most inept mural I've ever seen, a pale psychedelic mushroomy nightmare painted in what could be Dulux matchpots with 'UTOPIA' written underneath in rubbish melting letters. I try to keep my face cheerful, but it's obviously not working.

'I know what you're thinking,' Alice says, brightly. 'It's nasty, isn't it?'

'Yes.' I smile, relieved that she didn't paint it herself.

'Too much acid . . .' She whirls her finger at the side of her head to denote a screw loose.

'Mmmm,' I reply, knowingly. I don't elaborate, but I know all too well what too much acid looks like. Mona once got hold of some and tried to fly off the end of the harbour, shouting, 'Um Bongo, Um Bongo, they drink it in the Congo.'

'You should paint it out, probably,' she says, fiddling with a snake of black hair. 'You can paint it any colour you want – the landlord won't mind. My room's glittery green. I thought it would be mysterious and glamorous, but it just looks like a drag queen's eyeshadow.' Alice laughs, a musical tinkle. 'So are you a student?'

'Er . . . yes,' I say again, unpleasantly aware that I've now got something sticky attached to the underside of my shoe. 'I'm going to be doing fashion design.'

'Really? That's great. I'm at the Art School. So do you make your own clothes?' she asks, seeming really,

really interested. 'I love that skirt you've got on – it looks like a nineteen forties Dior.'

'Yes,' I stutter, yet again, staring down at it. I've never heard anyone casually slot the words '1940s Dior' into a conversation before, not without sounding like a moron, anyway. 'It's a copy, from a vintage pattern. I just altered the length . . . put some detail on it.'

'You made it? Wow! That's amazing! I wish I could do stuff like that. I'm doing visual communication. Drawing, pissing around on computers creating "concepts".' She rolls her eyes.

I smile, unsure of what to say. Luckily, Alice has already steamrollered ahead.

'Anyway, about the room – if you took it . . . I'm pretty easy going here – you can do as you please and have friends round whenever. Parties and stuff, whatever, I'm not bothered.'

I look at her mouth as she says 'parties' and my heart sinks.

'OK,' I say, but I already know this isn't going to work. Alice seems very friendly, but her flat is a crazed junk shop. Throw in some drugs and art students and I may as well have stayed at home.

'Er, let's see . . . council tax is included, but not bills . . . but they're not much if you split them. I don't have a phone – I just use my mobile, but if you want we can get a landline. Blah blah blah – it's all very boring. I'll just show you the bathroom and the kitchen so you know what you might be letting yourself in for.'

She does, skilfully skipping over a pile of old newspapers that are lying uselessly by the door jamb. As we pass the living-room door the mummified figure stirs under its duvet, like something about to emerge from a swamp.

'Bathroom,' Alice says, waving at a long narrow room with an ancient cistern at the end of it (I dread to think what evil lurks under the seat). Improbably there's a small stuffed animal nailed to the wall, another of Alice's rather bizarre interior design ideas. Is it a stoat? Is it a marmot? Either way it's a hygiene abomination.

'Kitchen,' she says, gesturing towards the opposite room. 'And that completes the tour. You can see my bedroom too if you're interested. But it's not that fascinating.'

'No, that's OK.' I'm still busy registering the kitchen, where months' worth of dishes lie stacked up, issuing forth complex and vile smells, which Alice herself has obviously noticed.

'Yeah, sorry about that – somehow I never get round to doing the dishes . . .' says Alice, screwing up her nose. 'I'll do them before you move in, though, don't worry. If you do move in.'

'Well, it's nice,' I say carefully, 'very nice. I've got a couple to see, so—'

'Sure, no bother,' she chirps. Her expression is one of glowing, open friendliness. When she smiles, her whole face lights up, and I find myself instantly smiling back. Then I realize she isn't looking at me any more. 'Hey, Mickey! What time do you call this?'

I turn round, the sticky thing on my shoe squelching

'This is Mickey. He's a friend of mine.'

The Swamp Thing has emerged.

'Uhhh,' says the boy wrapped in the duvet. His brown hair sticks up at all angles, he's practically got a beard, his eyes are half closed, he isn't wearing a shirt. His shoulders are broad and solid, like those stylized propaganda posters of athletic Russian shot putters. I quickly look away.

'It's OK – he doesn't come with the house,' Alice notes, sticking her hands in her jeans pockets and smiling with mock disapproval. 'He's been kicked out of his flat so he's just staying for a couple of days. Mickey, this is Evie.'

'Hi,' he says, in a sandpapery voice, squinting in my general direction, then clatters into the bathroom. A thought pops into my head quite out of the blue. *I wish I was the stuffed marmot.*

'So, you'll think about it?'

'What? Oh yes.' Shocked with myself, I quickly regain my composure, remember my fake-Dior-clad poise, and smile briskly. 'Thanks, Alice. I've got a couple more to see, so . . .'

Alice looks evenly and agreeably at me, but there's something else behind it, as if she knows more than she's letting on. I double check I don't trip over any bicycle repair kits, glad for the cool air in the hallway, and say my goodbyes. I would never live there in a million years. Not only is it untidy, but it's unsanitary too. And there's still something on my foot. When I get to the litter-strewn steps outside, I check under my shoe. It's a used condom.

I cross Alice off the list.

* * *

I turn back down to where the shops are, feeling restless. I wish Alice hadn't been so nice. On the one hand, she would probably be an interesting flatmate, but I just couldn't stand to live like that. My mum says I'm uptight, but it's not that, not really. I just have this vision of how I want my life to be, and it's clean and ordered, just like Edith's. I like storage, and books in alphabetical order, and toilets that don't give you cholera when go within three feet of them. Is that so wrong? I remember when I was about twelve, I turned to Charlotte, who was probably in some kind of artistic fog at the time, and said that I thought the world would be a better place if it wasn't so disorganized and dirty. She looked at me with horror and asked me whether I'd ever thought of joining the Conservative Party. But what I meant was, if people looked after things, they'd be happier. There would be fewer obstacles and life would be simple, streamlined and certain. That's what I want things to be. But there doesn't seem to be much chance of that today, not with a contraceptive stuck to my foot. Anyway, it's getting late – five o'clock, and the sky is turning a doom-laden, waterlogged grey. Before I call it a day, though, I decide to trail back to the newsagent's to join the permanent huddle of people by the window. This flat-hunting oasis, this magical pane of glass papered with possibilities, already seems the most familiar place in town, a place to go when all other options are exhausted. Even so, I think I might have exhausted them. But as my dad would no doubt remind me, if Great-Great-Aunt Natalya could whip through the May Day harvest with a baby on her back and another one on the way, then I can get myself a place to live. But Aunt Natalya knew nothing of the state of student housing in the West of Scotland. She wouldn't have lasted five minutes. I look again at the flutter of different coloured cards that are all beginning to blur together – dodgy requests for 'artist's models', people wanting drummers for their mythical bands, gleaming expensive flats with all mod cons and 'NO STUDENTS' written across them with relish, and sink into a state of apathy.

Just as I'm about to turn away, though, by a dead wasp on the windowsill I spot a modest white record card I hadn't noticed before, like the ones we use in Kirkness Fashions to keep up to date with the orders. Instead of old lady scribblings, the writing is painstakingly perfect. 'Unfurnished, newly decorated room in neat, tidy flat, would suit clean, quiet non-smoking student, £260 a month. No pets, no loud music, no timewasters. Call Lorna . . .'

It's quite expensive but the words 'TIDY' and 'NEAT' are like life rafts. I look shiftily around at the group of flat hunters, but none of them has spotted it. I type the digits into my phone, feeling furtive. As I struggle to get the number right, I tell myself that I'm prepared for a 'no'. I mean, to get a room today, on the first day, would be a triumph, and you have to be philosophical about these things, but no loud music . . . tidy . . . no condoms on the floor and stuffed rodents and semi-naked deviants – that would be bliss. My hands are shaking. This is either too good to be true or one of Mrs Kyriakou's dirty tricks . . .

'Hello?' says a wary voice.

'Hello, is that Lorna?' I chirp, sounding like a loony. 'I just wondered if the room was still available.' Trying to keep the excitement out of my voice and be pleasant and quiet and soft spoken is difficult over the rumble of rush-hour traffic. 'I'm a quiet, tidy, non-smoking student,' I say, sounding like a screeching harridan standing in the middle of the motorway.

'Yes,' she says, then says something else I can't hear. Jamming my finger in my ear I dip into the newsagent's and stand near the magazines. Glossy women stare back at me, women who probably have somewhere to live.

'Sorry, can you repeat that?' I ask.

'I'm doing viewings tonight,' she says. Her voice is polite but clipped and businesslike. 'If you could come by at seven o'clock, the address is one-left, sixty-eight Dryden Terrace. What's your name?'

'My name is Evie Kaminsky.'

There's a strange pause.

'Right,' she says, drawing out the 'i' as if she doesn't quite believe me. 'So that's one-left, sixty-eight Dryden Terrace. Can I have your mobile number in case there's a problem?'

OK. Now this is more like it. When I phoned Alice, she couldn't even remember her own address.

'Of course. It's 07724 729471.'

'07724 729471,' she repeats, with call-centre efficiency. 'Thanks very much. See you at seven.'

'See you then.'

I type the address into the reminders file of my phone. Now we're getting somewhere. I feel like I've just been offered an interview for a perfect job, or been given a clean bill of health after months of anxiety. I start walking, happily and randomly, and it's not long before I'm outside the university, looking at the wrought-iron gate and stone archways, thinking that in two weeks' time I'll be in the squat concrete building in town, shuffling to my induction day, registering and getting my student card, taking the first steps into a bright new future. The students are still on holiday, but there are plenty of people around. There's so much to be done before my life can officially start, so much to learn. I take a tin of lip balm from my bag and absent-mindedly smear it on my lips, watching gaggles of people about my age laughing and joking and wandering around. What do you have to do to learn the things that they know? What to wear, where to eat, how to get from A to B? At the moment, I can't imagine ever finding out these things.

Still, there's no point in moping about it. Perhaps my parents have done me a favour, giving me two weeks to become the most clued-up student ever. While they're fumbling around with maps, I'll be traversing the city by clockwork orange tube and discovering the cool places to be. In fact, I may as well start now: there's nothing much to do before seven but walking and waiting. 'St Luke's Church,' I whisper to myself, determined to memorize the landmarks and street names and shops and bars, and to pass the time productively. 'You must go – it's like only the best

Episcopalian place of worship in town. What's that? Oh yes, I know GIBSON STREET,' I would say to my imaginary new friends. 'It's just near OTAGO STREET. Would you like to go for coffee at ROCKET FUEL? For a haircut at the hilariously named "HAVING IT OFF"? Or perhaps you would prefer to loiter awhile at THE BANK OF PAKISTAN?'

After several streets' worth of this, my brain can't take any more. Then I realize I'm standing outside a strange café, with overstuffed chairs and mismatched lamps, selling funny teas. I hover around outside for a while, wondering whether I might go in. It looks quite interesting, in a vaguely hairy, scary way. Then I remember I'm not here to sit on the floor with a bunch of hippies, sipping Vietnamese Ping Pong tea out of an egg cup. That's not me. I'm here to get away from all that. So I go back to the generic, clean confines of Rocket Fuel instead and figure out what I'm going to say to Lorna. Smoothing my fringe into a neat, perfect line in the gleaming mirror in the bathroom, it's not long before I've convinced myself that we could be soul mates.

'I'd need a deposit of £260, plus a month's rent up front,' says Lorna, holding an A4 pad and a biro. We – that is, me, a large peroxided lad in a rather unpleasantly aromatic T-shirt and a mean-looking girl with a spray-on tan and a top that screams 'Flirtalicious Babe' – are perched on her sofa. When she said she wanted somebody tidy, she wasn't kidding. The living room is completely spotless, like a grown-up's house. I gaze in awe at the uncluttered coffee table, the defluffed skirting, the calm and serene air of a place well kept. Even the ornaments – simple white vases, glass bowls with baked curls of pot pourri in them, table lamps with heavy bases – look as if they've just come out of a warehouse.

'Just a few questions and then I'll show you the room. Does anyone have any medical problems or long-term illnesses I should know about?' Lorna seems very efficient. She has lustrous magazine hair, slick and long, full of amino acids and hydro-ceramides. She has already told us that she is doing a course in management, and that it's very hard work, so she needs her sleep. I imagine she's going to be very successful, with her well-groomed appearance and confident air. She has a shirt on that I can't help but stare at. It's cheap and not very well made, but it's as starched and crisp as if she was due to meet the Queen. In fact, she could probably go in for an ironing contest, if such a thing existed. It also matches her teeth, which are large and brilliant white.

Anyway, once it's ascertained that none of us is going to bring leprosy into the house, she asks if we have any objection to a noise curfew.

'It's very important that I get someone who understands the value of peace and quiet,' she says, looking in my direction, as if she knows that's what I'm looking for too. 'I'm not saying you can't have friends round, but I would ask any prospective tenant to respect the privacy of the other tenant and keep the noise levels to a minimum. I will also not tolerate drugs, late-night gatherings, or people who I consider to be unsuitable as house guests.'

Flirtalicious Babe shifts in her seat and yawns. She's out of the running already, I bet – the kind of person who leaves cotton buds and orange-stained cleansing pads clogging up the sink and goes off on shrieking nights out in white stretch limos. As for Smelly T-shirt, he's probably not had a bath for a month. Uncharitable thoughts come to me thick and fast, and my mind is closing like a trap – all that matters is she chooses me. I just want to tell her that this is a formality. I like rules and structure and peace and quiet. I'm her flatmate – me.

'As you probably saw on the ad, I'm looking for someone neat and tidy. By that I mean someone who will clean and pick up after themselves, and someone who will keep all communal areas clean . . .' Smelly T-shirt looks at his shoes and sighs, making a raspberry noise with his lips. Lorna flinches but continues, without losing her cool. 'Nothing too strenuous, but you know, it's really important to me to live in a clean house. Just a decent standard of cleanliness is all I really ask.'

Oh, I understand so well. It's like looking into a mirror. I wonder if Lorna grew up in a dog-hair-clogged midden like me. I wonder if she woke up every morning to be greeted by a shop dummy and a bathroom stacked with damp books and talc-covered dreamcatchers and chipped tiles. I really get where she's coming from. Having high standards is not a crime.

'Now, would you like to see the room?'

There's a general murmur of agreement and we all shuffle off to the back of the flat, where we are presented with a plushly carpeted square room, recently painted white. It's perfect – a clean slate.

'There are two power points and a lovely aspect to the back of the house. If you want to go in and look around, I'd appreciate it if you'd remove your shoes.'

Nobody moves. I'm relieved that Smelly T-shirt doesn't attempt to take off his trainers. In fact, neither of them seem that enthusiastic. As for me, I can imagine my stuff in here as clear as day – my savings could stretch to a new bed, I could put my remaining glass ashtray on the built-in shelves in the alcove . . . It's all I can do not to slip off my shoes and dance around on the shag pile.

'So with this in mind, do you have any questions?' Lorna enquires.

There's an awkward silence.

'I have a question,' says Flirty, in a thick, grating Glaswegian accent. 'Is it all right to breathe in here or do you need a letter from your ma?'

Lorna's face darkens. Her eyes, made up with a subtle shade of shadow, grow murky.

'I beg your pardon?'

'Nothin',' she sulks. 'I've got to go. I'll let myself out.'

With that, she stalks down the hallway, and after wrestling with the catch on the door, slams it behind her. Me, Lorna and Smelly stare at each other, unsure of how to arrange our faces. 'Letter from your ma . . .' It's quite funny really. But Lorna isn't laughing.

'So rude,' she growls, clutching her A4 notebook to

her chest. She looks hurt. I instantly feel guilty for finding Flirty's outburst vaguely amusing and want to tell her that it's OK, that she's found her flatmate anyway, and I'm ready to move in straight away, paying my deposit and rent in cash, if necessary. But Lorna has pulled herself together before I can open my mouth, and with a toss of her shiny highlighted hair, regains control of the situation.

'Right, well, one down!' she laughs uncertainly, elaborately crossing out Flirty's details on her pad. 'Does anyone else have any objections?'

There's an uncomfortable pause. Perhaps it's her management training, but she's pretty scary. And I've honestly never seen anyone so immaculately groomed. She seems to have been scrubbed from head to toe with Pledge and her French-manicured nails are as hard and shiny as diamonds. In my house, nails aren't a priority – they're usually black and falling off, after hitting your fingers with a hammer or dropping a kiln on your toe.

'I'm genuinely interested,' I squeak, really wanting the room, which at the moment seems like it might be the only place in Glasgow that doesn't come with its own rat infestation. Smelly, who looks terrified, shoots me a look and clears his throat. He has needlepoints of ingrowing hair all down his neck, and a faint crust of toothpaste or flour around his mouth, neither of which I imagine are at the top of Lorna's wish list.

'I've got a couple more to see . . .' he murmurs.

Yes! It's in the bag.

'OK, that's fine,' Lorna says. 'Well, Michael, it was nice to meet you and good luck with your search.'

Michael shuffles out, saying his goodbyes, leaving me standing on the verge of the new carpet.

When he's away, I'm half expecting Lorna to collapse with relief, put the kettle on and ask me when I can move in, but she leaves the door hanging open and doesn't drop her smiling, efficient persona.

'So, Evie, just so we're clear – if you are genuinely interested, I'll need you to sign a contract that is a written affirmation that you will abide by the rules of the house.'

'Sure, no problem.'

'And I'll phone you just as soon as I've decided, OK? Thanks very much for coming,' she says, a light hand on my back ushering me out. 'Really lovely to meet you.'

'I'm very quiet and tidy,' I say, but I'm talking to the door.

A whole day has passed and Lorna hasn't phoned. I woke myself up this morning, half dreaming, images of Victor McDougall playing like an old film reel in my head – the silent-movie villain in his pantomime hat, the explosion of glass, my angry dad rushing in with a hatchet. Then I was walking through a cartoon Gotham City, on my own, all dark angles and shadows and a weird, threatening humming noise, and Alice rode past on her bike wearing green socks, cackling like the wicked witch in *The Wizard of Oz* and saying, 'It's OK – he doesn't come with the house.'

When I came to it was pitch black and it felt as if the duvet was strangling me and I was in a coffin, and then

I realized that I was in a hotel and the low humming was coming from the air conditioner/heater, but I couldn't remember why I was in a hotel, or where, and I couldn't breathe, and I had to leap out of bed and go to the bathroom and look at myself in the mirror to check I was really all there, and when I did, I looked terrible and pale and terrified, and it took me what seemed like five minutes to remember what I was doing and where and who I was.

Now I'm walking around, trying to get my bearings, trying to look like I'm not holding a map, even though I am, and wrestling with an umbrella at the same time. I've got a plan to see some Places of Interest, but my heart isn't in it. I wish Lorna would phone and put me out of my misery. She seemed so on the ball that I have no reason to doubt her, but I can't help feeling uneasy. Why wouldn't she want me? Is it my problem? Do I have 'daughter of weirdos' written across my forehead? Is it engrained in me like the letters in a stick of rock? Perhaps she's being just extra cautious.

I think I'm going to have to start working on Plan B. There's no way I can stay in that extortionate hotel for much longer. Every night I can hear my savings trickling away down the plughole of my hotel bath, and there's only so many miserable economy meals of complimentary shortbread, Cup-a-Soup and crisps a person can have before they crack up and start ordering furtive midnight snacks from the carvery. I've spent £300 since I got here, mostly on overpriced roast beef baguettes with a horseradish sauce that tastes like grout. I suppose I could get a bed and breakfast or somewhere cheaper while I look for flats. Or move in with that Alice person. Or get a job at the lapdancing club near the hotel. Or, even worse, go home. Talk about rocks and hard places. I can't even begin to imagine what new lows my parents have sunk to since I've been away. Walking around naked, leaving half-eaten bowls of cornflakes on the stairs, forgetting to feed the dog. Who am I kidding? Dad probably lit a roll-up halfway through spray painting a sculpture and burnt the entire place down.

I check my mobile is on for the fifteenth time and trudge up an enormous windy hill to the Art School, which, according to my city guide, is 'a masterpiece of Mackintoshiana'. From the outside though, it just looks grey, unloved and shut. So I head further down the hill and find a fabric shop instead. The hot smell of sewing-machine pedals and the spectrum of different coloured threads soon relaxes me. Without hesitating, I go even further into my savings and buy a few metres of blood-red duchess satin to cheer me up, with the idea of making a dress once my course starts. I can't wait for everything to start. I just want to get on with things, but my sewing machine is still in my old room, and I've got nothing much else to do but drift around aimlessly, ticking off Places of Interest. I went on one of those tourist buses and almost got hypothermia, and I've been to art galleries and museums, but all I found was Rennie Mackintosh as far as the eye could see. Surely there must be something more to Glasgow than tea-rooms full of straight-backed chairs. Where do the glamorous people go? Where's the action? Phone me,

Lorna. Phone me phone me phone me. It's so blindingly obvious that I'm the perfect candidate. It's a no-brainer.

After the haberdashery shop, I'm on the main drag. It's not frightening at all, not like it was on the first day. I must have been suffering from culture shock. There are only chain stores and charity workers in their annoyingly cheery coloured aprons ambushing you to sign up for Greenpeace or Oxfam. It doesn't even seem that big any more. I wonder what I'll feel like when I go back to Kirkness to visit, once the transition has been made and I'm actually a cosmopolitan grown-up who has Left Home. How tiny it might seem! The town will be the size of a postage stamp and the Anchor Hotel will be quaint and clueless, and I will squish Teresa Donegan with my sophisticated Oscar Wilde-style wit. Mona, a pink-haired country lass, will ask me awe-struck questions about the big city and wonder why I don't want to come to the bus shelter to drink Buckfast from the bottle. Meanwhile, my parents will have lost their emotional hold over me and be transformed into two provincial, naïve local artists – pottering about on their potter's wheels and tinkering with shop dummies, as harmless as Rolf Harris.

Maybe.

I head down a street looking for a café and see Luigi's, a place not unlike Vanelli's, with lots of plastic onions hanging up on the wall.

Perhaps a bit of work is just what I need to get rid of this feeling of doom and uncertainty. I order a cappuccino from a lank-haired waitress, then take my sketchbook and start drawing some designs to give me a head start for college. But it's not very easy to concentrate over the hiss of the milk steamer, and come to think of it, Luigi's isn't very clean. I get a stab of anxiety, and feel compelled to wipe the sticky tablecloth with a napkin and rearrange the ashtray, salt, pepper and tin of condiments into a more pleasing arrangement. I'm organizing the mustard and ketchup sachets, and notice that someone near the window is staring at me, quite unashamedly. There's a touch of the Victor McDougalls about the way he's looking at me, but he's about fifty years younger than Victor, fair skinned to the point of near-death, with a glossy mane of blue-black hair cut into something resembling Rod Stewart's Highland terrier.

I ignore him and go back to my sketchbook. Obviously his mother never told him it's rude to stare. Not that Charlotte ever told me that either.

OK, I'm going to make a dress. I've always wanted to make a really classic dress, something so perfectly tailored that it makes anyone look good. The kind of gown Audrey Hepburn or Grace Kelly might have worn to a premiere or a dance, simply constructed, almost seamless. I want it to be so wonderful that it could work magic, like Dorothy's red slippers or Joseph's technicolour dreamcoat.

He's still staring at me.

Look at something else, weirdo.

I untuck a piece of hair from behind my ear and hide behind it. I bet Edith Head didn't have to suffer this kind of distraction. OK, so she looked like a goat, but

I'm a serious person, I'm not some bit of fluff to be molested by the eyes of some stranger under a bunch of plastic onions.

I get on with sketching ideas for necklines, but by the time my cappuccino arrives, this person has made me totally self-conscious, and I take one sip and it goes all over my nose. I cover it up successfully, I think, but when I glance over again, he's laughing at me. Who does he think he is? Sitting there with his daft hair and his far-too-small leather blouson jacket like he owns the place. And he's got bumfluff. I make a face at him and furiously turn back to my sketchbook. So anyway, the dress. The dress, the dress, the dress. Shall I go for a simple shift pattern, or more nipped in at the waist, or shall I—

'Excuse me?'

Like a crow descending from the skies to rest on a fence post, he swoops into the chair opposite me. I look up, reluctantly. He's grinning down at me, full of confidence. His face, which probably never sees the light of day, is bloodless, and would be beautiful if it wasn't for his goofy expression and the faint hint of a monobrow. But I don't care what he looks like – I'm busy.

I slam my notebook shut.

'Sorry to disturb you,' he says, in a surprisingly high, squeaky voice. 'Mind if I join you?'

'Actually, I'm quite busy,' I begin, but he's already sitting down. I'll bet he's some kind of musician, or someone who thinks he is. He's got an air about him like he's had too many late nights, and he seems very sure of himself for some reason.

'You've got some . . .' he murmurs, pointing at the remainder of the foam on my nose. He makes a lazy, half-hearted reach to wipe it off, but I flinch and back away and he smirks again. I'm dimly aware that this move was in a film I saw. He settles back in his chair, his foot tapping relentlessly on the floor to an inaudible beat.

'I thought, I bet she's an art student,' he says, pointing at my book.

'I'm not.'

'What are you then?'

'I'm a fashion student.'

'Fashion? A dedicated follower, I'll bet. What's your name?'

'Evie.'

'Evie? That's cool. You're a pretty cool cat, y'know. I've been watching you. The cat that got the cream. On her nose.'

Oh God, you're so funny with your wordplay and super-cool banter.

'Yes, I know you've been watching me. Is there anything I can help you with?' I snap.

'Meeeow. Easy, tiger. You should lay off the coffee – it makes you catty.'

I can see that he's not going to take a hint. Time for one of my supercharged evil stares, willing him to go away with the sheer force of my feminine fury. But he just smiles.

'OK, I'm sorry, I'm just messing with you,' he says, dropping some of the overblown swagger and sipping his drink. 'My name's Johnny. And you're Evie.

Sounds like a double act. Tell me – do you believe in fate?'

Oh GOD.

'No, Johnny, I don't.' I sigh. I don't even believe his name is Johnny. He blows up his fringe and lights a cigarette – a cartoon rock star. Is someone secretly filming me for a hilarious reality TV show? I want the waitress to come back, but she's probably too busy moulting into the bolognese sauce.

'Well, I do. I believe that you're here for a reason. And I'm here, right here, now, for a reason. It's like, we were always going to come here together, today, and meet, for a reason.'

'Er . . . what?' I enquire, suppressing a smile at his eloquent speech.

He's leaning in now, pointy elbows invading my half of the table, breathing smoke all over me. I sit back in my chair and crane my neck to find a member of staff.

'I don't know, do I? Do you?' he says.

'No.'

'Where you from?' he frowns.

'Kirkness.'

'Kirkness,' he ponders, like he's sucking a gob-stopper.

There's a silence. Perhaps he's trying to figure out the exact latitude and longitude of Kirkness, biting his big dumb bottom lip.

'We're the same, you and me,' he says, without a trace of irony.

I stifle a laugh.

'I don't think we are, somehow.' I smile, and put

£2 on the table for the coffee. I suddenly feel quite cheerful about this amazingly lame encounter. At least it's been marginally more thrilling than standing outside in the rain looking at Rennie Mackintosh's mackintosh.

'I reckon there's more to you than you let on, Little Miss Prim,' he continues, as I pick up my bag and sling it over my shoulder. 'Look at you, rearranging the salt pots, messing with your fringe . . . Who do you think you're kidding?'

I look at him and he looks at me. I don't know what the look is supposed to mean, but Johnny seems to think he's made a significant enough point to hold my gaze for about ten seconds. It certainly gives me enough time to notice that he should wash his hair more often.

'Here,' he says, taking a crumpled, inky flyer from his pocket. 'That's my band – come and see us. Get over it, doll. You're a firecracker. You're a libertine. Takes one to know one.'

I take it off him casually, peeking at the flyer before crumpling it into my own pocket. His band is called Bottle Rocket, and they're playing soon at a place called the Temperance Hotel – which sounds like one of those dives where your shoes stick to the floor and you can catch MRSA.

'I am not like you,' I tell him, certain of that at least. 'Bye, Johnny.'

'Bye,' he says. And as he does so, he pulls a digital camera from his pocket and there's a whip crack of white light.

'Hey!' I protest, and he cackles at his own prank. I'm just about to demand he deletes it, but my phone starts vibrating in my jacket pocket. The screen says 'Lorna'. It's the call. Oh, thank God. Please, please let it be good news.

'Hello,' I say, in my best well-brought-up phone voice.

'She's a libertine!' shouts Johnny, and I have to practically run out of the door to get him out of earshot.

Step Four – An Instrument of Pleasure

The sewing machine is to the dressmaker as the piano is to the pianist – without it, you cannot create. Lavish it with care and attention, making sure your needle is shiny and sharp, and the mechanism is well oiled. Keep your sewing machine in tip-top condition, and you will make sweet music together for a lifetime. Neglect it, and you will be conducting a symphony of errors.

It turns out that Lorna is from Dundee. One day she dreams about having her own property portfolio, and I wouldn't be surprised if she gets it. She has a crisp way of speaking, smells of summer meadows, and I'm her new flatmate as of today. I'm so excited. I have arrived! No more Travelstyle Hotel, no more bitchy women on reception with their hair scraped back off their faces like Spanish dolls, no more lonely nights staring at the walls and nibbling complimentary shortbread. I love this flat. Not a crazed asthmatic artist or overflowing ashtray in sight. On second viewing, it's even cleaner than I remembered – like a furniture showroom. She even has double glazing. Civilization at last.

'Of course, you can do what you like in your own room, but as I said at the interview, I do need to chill out in the evening, so I'd prefer it if loud music and other types of noise were kept at a minimum. When my dad bought the flat I don't think he checked the walls, and they're paper thin, they really are.' She bashes the wall with the side of her surprisingly powerful fist, rattling her River Island bangles as she goes. I nod, sagely, making a sympathetic face.

'Would you like a cup of tea?' she asks cheerfully. 'I have ordinary, Earl Grey, decaf, apple and mango and blackcurrant. Unless you'd prefer coffee, but I only have instant.'

'Tea's fine. Just ordinary. With milk.'

My choice seems to meet with her approval and we go into the kitchen, a fabulously appointed place with all the modern fixtures and fittings you might see on an advert.

'So how long have you lived here?' I ask, surveying her fridge magnets. One says 'To Our Special Little Girl', with a poem about how children are flowers that bloom in the heart.

'Oh about a year. I'm just going into my second year of management and finance, so my parents bought this place as an investment,' she says, passing by me and opening the fridge to reveal an icy white landscape of branded products, with labels facing front. I can't help but be impressed. Our fridge at home is so spectacularly bogging it should have police tape round the door with 'Do Not Cross' written on it.

'It was £140,000,' she says casually, opening a fresh carton of milk. 'The market being what it was at the time, I think it was quite a fair price, and we've improved it no end, so we should make a profit.'

'Hmm.'

'I really enjoyed fixing it up, you know, doing all that *House Doctor* stuff. Keep the decor neutral, make sure it's got a wide appeal for when you're selling it on . . . but I like that kind of clean look anyway. I can't imagine why people want to fill their houses with all sorts of rubbish. I love all those TV makeover shows, don't you?'

'Oh, yeah, they're great,' I say. The times I've dreamed of completely renovating Kaminsky Towers are too numerous to count. 'I love the ones when people don't have a clue what they're doing.'

'I know!' says Lorna, excitedly. 'Really, though, I think I'd be better at it than some people you see doing it, wasting money and getting into debt with their big ideas,' she continues, placing a used teabag into a white bowl by the sink. 'They're so silly, aren't they? They just barge in there – they haven't got a clue!'

'Yeah, knocking down walls, putting toilets in the living room . . .'

When Lorna hands me the milk-chocolate-coloured tea, I feel we're starting to bond. She's my first friend in Glasgow, I realize with a sudden dizzying clarity, and this mansion really will be my home. There's something both fascinating and reassuring about her gleaming confidence and spotless work surfaces. How does she do it?

'So if you want to move in at the weekend, that would suit me best,' she says, putting the milk back. I notice she's got V8 juice in there, a six-pack of Diet Cokes, a bag of salad, and a whole pile of Be Good To Yourself ready meals. 'Do you have furniture?'

'Pardon? Oh, not yet.'

Ah yes, furniture. I know I'm going to have to involve at least one parent in my moving-in day, and at this very moment it doesn't bear thinking about. The idea of Charlotte and Anton marauding through this beautiful, dust-free environment, trailing shreds of Golden Virginia, fills me with horror. What if they pee on the rug?

'I'm going to get my stuff on Saturday,' I tell her, hoping I sound like I know what I'm doing.

'Oh, about weekends,' chirps Lorna precisely, as we trail back into the living room. 'My boyfriend Charlie comes down from Gleneagles, usually every Friday night, so we kind of have a bit of downtime then. We really appreciate our privacy.'

'Oh that's fine. Sure.' A disturbing mental image of Lorna and Charlie romping on the sofa with a bottle of baby oil pops into my mind. But Lorna would never tolerate such messiness, I'm sure.

'He's a golf caddy up there and I really, really miss him during the week,' she adds, her voice changing into a little girl's squeak. 'Look – isn't he gorgeous?' She shows me a photo of her and Charlie, standing to attention in someone's parents' lounge, dressed in formal evening wear. He looks fairly unremarkable to me, an identikit Prince William type with eyes that are too close together, but I manage to produce an exclamation of delight. After all, Lorna is my saviour, and without her, I'd be living in a lice-ridden hovel with only carbon monoxide poisoning to look forward to.

'Oh yes. Very nice.'

'Do you have a boyfriend, Evie?' she enquires.

'Oh no.' I smile.

There's a small gap in the conversation, and the way she's discreetly turned her attention to an invisible blemish on the carpet gives me the impression she might think I'm a lesbian.

'I've had a few boyfriends,' I say, careful not to go into too much detail. I very much doubt that Lorna would be impressed with the male specimens Kirkness has to offer. Let's see – there was Paul McGrath who tried to stick his hand down my bra at the end-of-term ceilidh, Martin Lambert who stalked me for three weeks until I agreed to go on a miserable date with him (which culminated in him trying to stick his hand down my bra) and a disastrous night with a sullen goth friend of Mona's called Kyle, who stayed well away from my bra because he was more interested in pants. Men's pants. 'The right one hasn't come along yet,' I tell her.

'I met Charlie when I was sixteen,' she reminisces. 'He was working as a silver service waiter at the National Builders Association conference, one of my dad's things. He was very attentive, if you know what I mean!' She giggles. 'We were going out for a couple of years, and then, on my eighteenth birthday, he took me to this fantastic hotel in Skye and proposed. Now I know we were young, but it just seemed right. You know when things just seem right?'

I nod, not really knowing.

She thrusts a frosty, glittering rock into my field of vision that would probably cost the average caddy a year's wages.

'It's eighteen-carat white gold with a two-and-a-half-carat princess-cut diamond,' she says, gazing at it fondly. 'We're getting married in 2008 when I finish my course. Do you like weddings?'

'Yeah, they're OK.' I smile. Actually, the only wedding I've ever been to was a raucous reception at the Kirkness community centre that Mona and I gate-crashed. We didn't even know who anyone was.

'I've been planning it for ever,' she tells me. 'Charlie says I'm the organizing type so he's left it to me. I want everything to be perfect. That's the way it should be on a girl's big day, right?'

'Right,' I say, still blinking from the after-image of the diamond.

'Anyway, we love each other very much,' she adds, as if to put an end to that subject, and places the photo back on the shelf. 'So, Evie, tell me about yourself,' she says, fixing me with a penetrating look. 'I'm always fascinated by what makes people tick. What kind of things are you into?'

I pause for a second, aware that I should try to sound as normal as possible. No mention of my previous life as dogsbody to two mental people whose idea of fun is welding a dustbin lid to a broken mandolin and calling it *Music Is Shit #12*.

'Well, I like dressmaking, which I'll be studying at college,' I say carefully. 'And I love collecting Sixties stuff. I'm very into design in general, too, like furniture design and architecture. Reading – I like reading . . .' I sound like a Miss World contestant. I love children, small animals, scuba diving . . .

'Are you one of those arty types?' she asks, with an edge of trepidation.

'Well, not as such,' I say quickly. 'I'm interested in the technical side of things. I like things that are structured and organized, you know, not chaotic. I try to apply that rule to my life, to keep it uncluttered and uncomplicated, but it's not always easy. But that's why I love your flat, it's so clean. I suppose I'm quite into minimalism.'

Oh God, you sound like a right tool. How is she going to reply to that? 'Oh yeah, I like minimalism too, it's brilliant.' Duh. Poor Lorna is obviously completely lost. Did I also mention that I'm very quiet and tidy?

'Really, I'm just into making things. I want to be a seamstress. A fashion designer,' I say, trying to claw back some self-respect.

'Wow,' says Lorna, obviously relieved that I've said something remotely understandable. 'I love fashion! What designers do you like?'

I think of my postcard of Edith, her helmet of black hair sitting on top of her head like well-groomed road kill. Better to start with people she's actually heard of.

'I prefer vintage designers. Mary Quant, Givenchy, Chanel – stuff like that.'

'Oh right,' she says, tweezing a bit of fluff from the carpet with her nails. I notice she has freckles, which she covers up with flawless foundation.

'I'm really into Versace, do you like them? Have you ever been to TK Maxx? I got a great pair of Miss Sixty jeans in there for £19.99. You should check it out. Tons of stuff. They might even sell Chanel there too – there's a perfume counter. Oh God, we have to go shopping. I expect that Kirkness hasn't even got a post office.'

'Well, it's not very big. I used to work at this place called Kirkness Fashions. We sold big old ladies' girdles and enormous bras.'

'Really?' says Lorna, seeming horrified. 'That sounds awful! Well, we'll go to Princes Square – it's got a Ted Baker and a French Connection and even a Whistles. The shops in Glasgow are great.'

I nod, and sip the last of my tea.

'So, let's say Saturday, then.' She stands up, revealing long legs, straight and skinny all the way up to her tiny eight-year-old's bum, encased in sprayed-on jeans. She's so self-possessed, with not a hair out of place, and I find myself briefly wishing I had thinner thighs. 'I'll draw up the contract, give you a key, and then you can move your stuff in. OK?'

'OK,' I say, standing up too.

'Shake on it?'

As I shake her hand, it feels cool and confident and smooth compared to my porky, sweaty palm. For the second time in a week, I'm shown out of the door, but this time, I'm coming back. With my mum. I'm really not sure how that's going to go down.

'It's very clean and tidy, isn't it?' says Charlotte, amusement playing on her lips. She's driving (badly) into the rush-hour traffic, unable to stay in lane.

'Mum, watch that lorry!'

'Gas-guzzling bastards,' she growls, nudging and jerking ahead like she's driving a dodgem. 'Still, you always were tidier than me.'

'There are tramps that are tidier than you,' I say, sinking into my seat, which is covered in crumbs. I can barely move my feet for crumpled old road atlases and empty cartons of antifreeze. On the dashboard, Charlotte has Blu-tacked a carved wooden Celtic angel that is supposed to bring luck. It could have brought a Dustbuster while it was at it.

'Don't you think it'll be a bit restrictive, though?'

'What do you mean?'

'Well, she's awfully precise. I'm sure I saw her counting the teabags. And when I came in to drop off your sewing machine she was lurking in your room.'

'Look where you're going!'

Charlotte's Bronze Age bracelets clank like dustbin lids as she veers her way into the wrong lane and then out again. After five minutes in the house, I had to hustle her out, as Lorna appeared to be allergic to her. Whether it was Charlotte who caused the gale of sneezing and streaming eyes or stray hairs from Rothko and Hepworth, it was impossible to tell, but poor Lorna had to take an antihistamine and muttered an excuse about having to go out. I was mortified.

I thought that maybe some distance between me and Charlotte would have changed things, but everything is still the same. Instead of meeting on equal terms as two adults, we're back to the old routine – I'm looking after her, picking bits of fluff off her cardigan, trying to stop her from ploughing into the central reservation.

'It's the A889 to Braehead – there. Left!'

'It's about time you did something original though, darling. You've been cooped up in your stuffy room for far too long. It's time you had an adventure. You know,' she says, as if she's about to impart some amazing wisdom, 'if you let it, the world will open up to you like a giant and beautiful flower.'

She's too busy reaching for a packet of biscuits in the glove compartment to see my horrified expression. How a grown woman can seriously believe all that mystical nonsense is beyond me. Mid crunch, she brakes suddenly and nearly crashes into the back of a silver Lexus. The person behind us honks angrily. My nerves are in tatters – checking out of hotels, emotional upheaval, new and confusing situations. I turn over the list of things to buy. Charlotte thinks we can get a bed in the back of the car but she's hardly renowned for her spatial awareness.

'Just try not to kill me before I can start the best years of my life,' I snap. 'And watch the road.'

'Oh stop telling me off. You sound like an old woman.'

After what seems like hours, we're at the big blue box

of Ikea. She parks miles away, so we have to walk past rows and rows of cars and cheerful fluttering flags for about ten minutes, stopping every other minute so that Charlotte can adjust the slapping brown strap of her sandal, which is rubbing against her toe ring and causing her to utter some deeply unhippyish swear-words. Whenever I go to retail parks with my parents I go into a deep emotional slump and today is no exception. We haven't even got to the self-service warehouse and had an argument about Pløgbløg shelves and Slaggi wine glasses yet, and already I feel like crawling into the ball pool and hiding.

'Right then,' Charlotte says loudly, when we're in the bed section. 'Will you want a double or a single? I suppose it depends on whether you get lucky, doesn't it?'

'I beg your—'

I want to slope under one of the beds. A man passing by gives me a funny look. I'm going to die of embarrassment. My chest feels crushed. I stare determinedly at some mattress samples that look like I'm feeling – raw springs poking out, stuffing on display. Soltan Blugsplud – basic; Soltan Nogbo – medium; Soltan Droggart – luxury. 'A good mattress is a friend for life.'

'I think you should get a double,' she muses. 'You never know.'

'Shut up,' I hiss.

'Well, it's up to you, of course.'

'This one is fine,' I say, pointing at a single Nogbo. 'Now let's go to the warehouse.'

'Evie, you're just as moody as your father,' she snaps. 'You're the one who asked me to come. I could murder a cup of tea. Shall we go to the café? I have to say all that Swedish food intrigues me . . .' I start walking purposefully. 'Smorgasbord,' she says, rolling the word over on her tongue in an obscene manner. 'Grrrravadlax.'

It's like taking Rainman out for the day. Ignoring Charlotte's requests for a café stop, I plough on, picking up sheets and pillowcases. I try to keep things as simple as possible. Occasionally Mum tells me not to be so boring and waves something ludicrous and pointless in my face – an apple slicer, strawberry-flavoured candles, primary-coloured rubber clocks that project the time on the roof of the building across the road. Finally we get to the checkout. Ahead of us is a girl with wild black curly hair, wearing a peculiar skirt with small drawings of sushi on it, paired rather alarmingly with a pair of yellow leggings and some green platform shoes. Next to her is a tall, good-looking guy with three days' worth of stubble, toying with a washing-up brush.

'Oh, I love your shoes,' I realize Charlotte is saying, slinging things indiscriminately onto the conveyor belt. 'They're gorgeous! Are they vintage?'

Alice beams at my crazy mother and they start discussing footwear. Charlotte shows Alice a really disgusting blister on her toe, which looks like something from *Dr Who*, and I turn away, standing in what I hope is a cool, casual manner, with my eyes fixed on a box of very small pencils. Maybe if I stay quiet they won't notice I'm here. 'Please Take One', the box of pencils says, so I do. Maybe I could use it to gouge my eyes out.

'Evie,' my mum trills, 'this is Alice.' Alice smiles hello, while Mickey, who's with her, gives a cool, vaguely amused stare and digs his hands into his jeans pockets.

Rapidly dissolving, I try a nonchalant smile but it's more like a cornered chihuahua baring its teeth. My entire body is twanging with shame. As well as the fact that that boy seems to cause alarming physical agitation whenever he appears within a five-metre radius of me, there is also the matter of a little white lie that I told Alice. I told her I'd found somewhere cheaper. But if she found out I lived on Dryden Terrace, she would know that was a load of rubbish – it's one of the best streets in the West End, and a flat there would cost much more than Alice's. I hope Charlotte keeps her mouth shut.

'She's moving into her new flat today, on Dryden Terrace,' says Charlotte (oh God in heaven). 'Evie has gone and got herself a room with Eva Braun. You know, Hitler's girlfriend. She's very strict. *Achtung!* Ha ha! Do you live in Glasgow?'

'Yeah. Evie looked at the flat actually,' says Alice, in a confident, breezy voice, craning her neck round my mum's frizzy wig to meet my eye. She looks curious rather than put out. I look at my shoes.

'Dryden Terrace is really nice,' she says to me kindly.

'Yes,' I reply, attempting phase two of my chihuahua smile. She's probably thinking what a stuck-up cow I am, but Alice doesn't seem bothered at all by the obvious knock-back, or by my new-age loon of a mother.

'Really? You've already met?' says Charlotte, regarding me with arched eyebrows. 'Well, that is a coincidence.'

Much as I'd love to keep this awkward conversation going, thankfully Alice is called away by Mickey, who is loading up at the other side of the till, and I'm saved from further scrutiny. Charlotte, of course, is oblivious, looking all pleased with herself.

'And they say Glasgow isn't friendly,' she mutters, nudging me with a dry elbow. 'Why didn't you move in with her? She looks like fun. And that boy is gorgeous!'

'Shut up, Mum. Let's just concentrate on getting this stuff home. It says here we've got to pick the bed up from over there,' I mumble, trying to appear independent and efficient but looking at the wrong side of the trembling printout in my hand. Out of the corner of my eye I can see Alice and Mickey exchange glances. I bet she hates me. I bet he thinks I'm a wee weirdo. All I want to do is get back to my new abode and start sorting out my stuff – Mum can go back to Annoying-on-Sea and I can start again, really start this time, no more nasty surprises – just concentrate on college and Lorna and my smart, shiny home and get settled, get into a routine, make my life my own.

'See you,' says Alice, when they're loaded up and ready to go.

'Bye, dear!' my mother yells. Hovering around our purchases, I catch Mickey's eye and my face goes red.

'Look, Evie! These mugs are called "FARTE"!' Charlotte whoops, and once again I pray for invisibility.

The bed fitted into the car, but not the trestle table Charlotte encouraged me to get for sewing – that stuck out of the boot in a highly illegal fashion all the way home. On the way back our already strained relationship deteriorated further (she called me 'emotionally constipated', I called her something worse), and it didn't help that we couldn't even find the celebrated Dryden Terrace, now known to the world and his wife as the most fabulous address in Glasgow.

'I can't believe you signed this,' Charlotte is saying, waving Lorna's contract in the air. '"Clause 24: Waste – kitchen bins must be emptied once every two days and no accumulation of waste must be allowed to build up in both personal and communal living spaces, including newspapers, magazines or bottles." Surely there's no way this could possibly be a legal document.'

I'm eternally grateful that Lorna is out. Although, I can't decide whether Lorna's absence is a good or bad thing, conscious that I've blown everything on the first day with my allergy-inducing mother. I wish she'd just go home and let me get on with things. Having her lurking about the place taking the piss out of a simple contract is hardly going to help my future prospects.

'A few ground rules are fine,' I say, in the midst of assembling my new Nogbo bed. 'At least then we know where we are. Insert screw A into slot Y,' I say to myself.

'Well, things have certainly changed since my day,'

she mutters, casting the contract aside and popping some bubble wrap. 'Everything is so efficient now, isn't it? Everyone thinks they know what they want and they're not afraid to go out and get it. Of course, the reality is that they don't know what they want at all. I wouldn't last five minutes in the modern world; even how you figure those things out is a mystery.'

'It's not so hard,' I tell her, tightening the Allen key.

No, it really isn't hard, it's a joy – the first step to independence. With a bit of planning and common sense, life should be as straightforward as inserting screw A into slot Y. Easy. If you concentrate on the task at hand and don't get distracted, if you are accurate and focused, then everything will turn out well. It's like dressmaking: if you follow the guidelines properly, there shouldn't be anything wrong with the end result. I feel more in control than I have done for ages. I can feel everything about to click into place.

'Oh, look at you – all grown up and independent,' Charlotte witters. 'I wish I was your age again, with everything in front of you. It's so exciting. I went and got married the minute I left my parents' house. I sometimes wish I'd waited and had an adventure first – maybe got a groovy flat with a girlfriend. Had some more sex.'

'Mum!'

'Of course, your father came into my life and I fell in love straight away – it was me and him against the world and nothing would get in our way. Even so, I've often wondered what it would be like if I was to do it all again, if I was in your position. I'd be fabulously creative, I'd have a vast array of exciting lovers, I'd be someone's muse – I'd live like every day was my last. It's true, youth really is wasted on the young.'

I look up at her silhouetted against the window, wistfully thinking of rose-tinted days gone by – all those ancient faded Polaroids stuffed in shoeboxes in the wardrobe are blazing Technicolor in her memory – Cambridge Folk Festival 1975, Glastonbury 1978, people in kaftans waving their arms about in the days before hair straighteners and decent conditioner – to her they only seem like yesterday. Is she having a mid-life crisis?

'Well, Mum, I'm not you,' I say somewhat piously. 'I'm not interested in going wild and sleeping with loads of men. I just want a quiet life.'

'Ah, my sensible daughter,' she says with a touch of sarcasm, twisting the bubble wrap. 'Such a rebel.'

I briefly feel like inserting screw A somewhere the sun don't shine, but I'll need it for slot Y. In fact I have everything I need – my sewing machine, my box file, my new bed – all the ingredients for this new chapter in my life. I don't have to do anything I don't want to do now. It's a delicious feeling – to be totally in charge. By the end of the week, my frustrating cluttered past will seem like a distant memory.

'Help me with this, will you?' I ask Charlotte, who is now slouching on the windowsill bending the spine of one of my books. She comes over and we move the bed into the centre of the room, headboard expertly attached, a springy, white field of virgin mattress. I get a twinge of pride for building it, and of something else – relief, like dropping off at a charity shop bin bags full of things you've been meaning to get rid of for ages.

'Lovely,' says Charlotte, flipping off her sandals and throwing herself on it.

'Mum, get off, please. You'll make it dirty.'

'Ooh, Evie, look, there's a cobweb up there near the light. Better not let Eva Braun see it.'

'Get off the bed! And stop calling her that. Lorna's nice, OK?'

'All right, simmer down, I was only joking,' she says, leaping off the bed with surprising agility. 'And I'm sure Lorna is very nice when she's not having a violent sneezing fit and being rather rude.'

'She is,' I sulk.

'And it's a great flat, isn't it? Lovely street. She must be loaded.'

'Hmm. Her dad bought it for her. He's a builder, I think.'

'Friends in high places already, eh?' she says.

I start to tidy up the plastic wrappers and bubble wrap, careful to pick all the tiny screws and staples out of the beautiful carpet. While I'm doing that, Charlotte takes a break from winding me up, produces her big brown leather purse, the one I always expect to see moths flying out of, and puts £20 on the bed.

'Get yourselves a couple of bottles of good red wine – get to know each other better. I always find a decent Merlot helps to clear any blockages.'

I look at the grubby money. 'Thanks.'

'Right, well, I better go,' she says, fiddling with her

bracelets. 'You take care, my little grown-up. And come and see us soon. I miss you. And so does your dad.'

She gives me a jangling hug, and I smell her signature scent of jasmine and dust particles and the ancient, ingrained mildew of the house. After spending the last three hours wishing she'd go home, I suddenly don't want her to leave me in this stranger's flat, with its gleaming paintwork and blank walls.

'Ooh, I almost forgot – I brought you this.' She reaches into her bag with the faded Toulouse Lautrec print on the front and produces what looks like an old dishrag.

'I found it in the cupboard when I was getting your stuff together,' she says.

'Ugh . . . what is it?'

I take it from her and slowly realize what I'm holding. It's Soggy the rabbit, so called because I used to suck its ears when I was five. Now Soggy is looking distinctly unwell, as if he's had an altercation with a steamroller, in fact – a flat, grubby piece of stuffing with an eye missing and paws like pancakes. I shift from one foot to the other. I thought he'd been lost or given away. Soggy's appearance is both welcome and annoyingly inconvenient – just as I was starting to feel properly organized, he comes back with his droopy, bitten ears and turns me into a baby.

'I haven't seen this for years,' I say coolly. I can see my mum's eyes welling up with sentimental tears and the worst thing to do now would be to join her. 'Soggy needs a good wash.'

'Oh no, don't,' Charlotte cries. 'He's lovely just the way he is. Anyway, I thought you'd like to have him.'

She gives me a drippy look, her bottom lip going. 'Wee Eveieeee,' she whines.

'I'm not "wee". I'm an adult now,' I tell her, not very convincingly.

'Yes, yes, I know,' she says, squeezing my hand and pulling herself together. 'So you've got everything you need, have you?'

'Yes,' I say, clearing my throat.

'Right, I'll leave you to it, then. Go forth and conquer! You're going to do fantastically well.' She plonks a kiss on my cheek and leaves me holding Soggy, who looks as limp and pathetic as I feel.

'Oh, and when you make your bed, don't forget to do hospital corners!' she trills from the hallway. 'You never know when there might be an inspection. Remember Clause 257 – stand by your beds! Oh hello, Lorna, didn't see you there!'

All I can hear is the sound of rapid-fire machine-gun sneezing coming from a startled Lorna. Oh God, no. I quickly hide Soggy in a drawer, check again for any glimmers of metal in the carpet, push the remaining bed packaging out of sight, and shove the contract into my coat pocket. When the front door is shut, and the sneezes subside, I put my head round. Lorna is standing in the hallway, simultaneously spraying an anti-bacterial into the air and chuffing on an asthma inhaler.

'Hi, Lorna,' I say. 'Are you OK? I'm really, really sorry about my mum. I didn't realize you were allergic. It's probably the cat.'

'No, it's fine,' she wheezes. 'But FYI, I'm allergic to all animal hair, pollen and dust.' She walks past my room into the kitchen, throwing me a watery-eyed glare, and slams the door. I consider going in and attempting a reconciliation, perhaps suggest that bottle of wine Mum was talking about, but I don't want to disturb her while she's gasping for breath. Instead, I go back into my room and make my bed. When it's done, though, I'm so tired I just climb into it and lie there for an hour, unable to uphold Clause 24 – disposal of waste – or behave anything like an independent adult with a normal life.

'If you put a bathroom and utility down here and knock that wall down to make the kitchen bigger, then you would add value . . .'

On the Homes and Interiors channel, Phil and Kirsty are laying into a humourless, fussy couple who want two homes in Devon for £300,000. Thankfully, Lorna has recovered, order has been restored, and I feel much better. I had visions of a lonely night in my new room, with Lorna not daring to come near me in case I was infected with cat hair, dust, pollen and airborne nasties, but she asked me if I was going to be in for dinner, and cooked a veggie chilli, which she prepared with great care – she weighed everything accurately, washed up several times as she went along, and even put a small sprig of coriander in a puddle of sour cream on top. I felt quite flattered – surely the garnish was for my benefit? Or maybe she does it all the time. I suppose it's possible. Lorna is quite unlike anyone I've met, and certainly nothing like other students I've seen round here, who tack bed sheets to their windows instead of curtains and look like they've never seen a hairbrush in their lives. This is like living with someone much older. She's amazingly well equipped, with all manner of posh pans and garlic presses and dangerous-looking knives in blocks. In the bathroom, she uses Clarins products and Lancôme, stuff I've seen in *Vogue* with extortionate price tags. I find myself wanting to rifle through her cupboards, to see how she could possibly get her hair looking so sleek and her shirts so crisp. It must take her hours to get ready in the morning. Even with all my efforts to make sure I'm presentable, she makes me feel like I've just climbed out of a skip.

So here I am. My first night in my new house. Saturday night. After stacking the dishwasher, Lorna is curled up on the opposite sofa, a look of blank contentment on her face. She's in her PJs, but still looks as if she might be ready to go out, with tiny pearlescent toenails and a lace-trimmed top with thin silky straps. I notice she hasn't really touched her wine (is she allergic to £8.99 Merlot?). I sip mine extra slowly – after all, we don't have to finish the bottle, we can appreciate it and savour the flavour. I take the tiniest sip and let it linger in my mouth – oh yes, it's robust and cheeky, with blackcurrants and a hint of vanilla. At home with my mum and her friends around, it wouldn't even touch the sides, and a wine stopper would be about as much use as a chocolate teapot. But here it feels sophisticated to just have one small glass and put the rest away for later.

Yes, this is nice. Quiet. Cosy. I think of the alternative – jammed up against the 'Utopia' mural in Alice's flat, finding bits of bicycle repair kit in my socks, while lurking men in duvets and taxidermy reign supreme and the dishes get up and walk out on their own. This is heaven compared to that.

An ad break comes on, but still the silence lingers. I begin to wonder whether Lorna is still in a mood with me. Then the programme starts again, and the fussy woman, who bears a striking resemblance to the receptionist at the Travelstyle Hotel, is complaining because a perfectly good house she is being shown is too small.

'What makes these people think they deserve two houses anyway?' I say, just to start a conversation. 'Can't they just have one?'

Lorna clears her throat and tosses her hair, but doesn't reply.

'My parents have two houses,' she says eventually, still looking at the TV. 'Actually, three, if you count this one.'

'Oh, I'm sorry. I didn't mean you.'

Shit. That was probably the wrong thing to say to an aspiring property magnate. I take an overly huge gulp of wine and concentrate on not doing or saying the wrong thing all the time. It seems that since my mother arrived with her slapping sandal straps and her aura of careless hygiene, I'm not proving to be the model flatmate.

'It's not like I wouldn't like two houses myself, though,' I backtrack. 'So where do your parents have their second home?'

'Spain.' She says the name of the place, but I don't catch it.

The conversation fades away. She doesn't seem to be in the mood for talking – maybe I should leave her alone or something. Then I remember, Charlie usually comes at weekends. She must have cancelled so that I could have a chance to settle in. It's very thoughtful of her, but even so, I don't want her to feel she has to babysit me.

'I hope I'm not stopping you from doing anything this weekend,' I begin, trying to be tactful. 'You did say that Charlie usually visits, and I don't want to be a nuisance . . .'

'Oh no, he's coming,' she says, breezily. 'In fact, he'll be here in a minute.'

'Oh, OK. That's fine then.'

Silence. All I have in my glass now is a tiny crimson circle at the bottom, but if I have another one she might think I'm an alcoholic, and I don't want to get too settled in the living room in case I get in the way. So I sit there for a while until the programme finishes, feeling awkward, waiting for the buzzer to sound. 'Should I Stay Or Should I Go?' by the Clash is bouncing around in my brain. Would it be rude to make my exit before Charlie arrives?

In answer to the Clash, the buzzer goes almost immediately, leaving me with no option but to stay and say hello. Lorna bounds off the sofa in a cloud of perfume while I straighten myself up and put the glass down. I feel like I need a book to tell me what to do. I know, I'll just meet him then gracefully slip away – it'll be like I'm not here. On the TV, the presenter is getting pissed off with the picky clients. *You're going to have to make compromises, I'm afraid, and just accept that you can't always get what you want.*

There's a deep burbling voice in the hall and Lorna, who has perked up considerably, appears in the doorway, with a faint rash on her chest and a lovestruck look on her face.

'Charlie, I want you to meet Evie, my new flatmate.'

'Oh right. Hi there,' says Charlie, not very enthusiastically. He's a thick-set, rosy-cheeked lad in a pink pinstripe open-necked shirt who suddenly seems to take up half the room. He looks overconfident and cruel – I imagine he likes to shoot small animals at weekends and brag about it to his friends. Although five seconds ago I was ready to warmly receive him, I hate him on sight.

'Hello,' I say, standing up and trying to be gracious.

'Charlie, would you like a drink?' she twitters. 'Evie brought some red wine, but I don't really like it much. Do you want me to open a bottle of white?'

'Yeah, that'd be great,' Charlie drawls, plonking himself down and fixing his eyes on the TV. Lorna leaves the room and I stare at my painstakingly selected, four-star Oddbins-approved Merlot. If she didn't like it, why didn't she just say? Although my every nerve and sinew is telling me to leave the lovebirds to their own devices, I pour a big glug of it into my glass and stubbornly sit down again.

'So where did she find you?' Charlie says, looking me up and down in disbelief.

'What do you mean?'

'I mean, are you new, or do you know her already?' he asks suspiciously. He spreads himself out all over the sofa, sitting splay-legged as if his enormous manhood couldn't possibly be accommodated any other way. He seems to be trying to point it in my direction, too.

'Oh, I answered her advert.'

'Right. Thought so. You don't seem like her type,' he remarks condescendingly, scooping up the remote and flicking to a sports channel. 'I told her to be careful – there's a lot of weirdos out there. I hope you're not one of them.'

'OK, here we are,' Lorna chirps, coming in with two glasses and a bottle of cheap Chardonnay, the same brand Mona always gets because they're three for a tenner at the off-licence. 'Have you eaten, Charlie? I made chilli if you want me to put it in the microwave.'

'No, I had some grub on the road,' he says, thudding his belly. 'You look sexy tonight,' he says, pinging the waistband of her silky pyjamas while she bends over to pour the wine. I wouldn't be at all surprised if he started humping her over the coffee table while keeping his eyes glued to the rugby highlights. What an obnoxious sod. I decide it's time for me to go, but I can't think of a way to disentangle myself without seeming either bad-mannered or ridiculous. Shall I say, 'I'll leave you to it'? Or start yawning?

Lorna gives him the wine glass and they have a loud, squelchy snog. Yeeeuch. She lies down at the other end of the sofa, with her legs over his, and he shifts and adjusts the crotch of his chinos. Neither of them speak. I've become welded to the seat like a statue.

Five minutes later and we're all still here, as if we've been cryogenically frozen. As the football scores scroll past at the bottom of the TV screen and everybody sits motionless, I have to pinch myself to check whether I'm still alive.

'I think I'll go and sort out a few more things in my room,' I say, rousing myself and picking up my glass. 'I'll just put this bottle in the kitchen. Nice to meet you, Charlie.'

'Yeah, blah blah, and all that stuff,' says Charlie, still staring at the TV. I stand there marvelling at his rudeness, but Lorna just gives him a watery smile, as if she's forgotten who I am.

'Night – see you tomorrow,' she says, giving me a half-hearted, disinterested wave. The last thing I see is Charlie lazily putting his hand on her knee. Once I'm in my room, I feel a cool wave of relief, and run my fingers over the mottled case of my sewing machine, the only thing that seems to have any personality in this snow-white guest room. All that sitting in front of the TV has made me restless, and it's only about ten o'clock, so I reach into my sewing bag and spread out the pieces I've cut out for my dress project. I run the dark satin through my fingers, the same colour as the Merlot. I can't believe Lorna was so dismissive about the wine. Still, I suppose I should be grateful for her other efforts – she doesn't know me from Adam, after all, and she didn't have to make me dinner on my first night.

When I switch on the machine and attach the foot pedal, I can feel the blood returning to my brain, as if I've slept on my arm and it's coming back to life. This dress is going to be the best thing I've ever done. For extra inspiration, I spread out a book called *Hollywood Greats* that I got from the second-hand bookshop in Kirkness, leaving it open on a picture of Carole Lombard wearing a silvery silk dress to a party in 1938, a vision of old-time glamour with Clark Gable on her arm. Going through my box of cotton, I thread the machine and start to sew, losing myself in the rhythmic, fluid movement of the needle. It's not long, though, before there's a sharp knock.

'What's that noise?' asks a bleary Lorna, pushing her way in and standing over me with her arms folded. 'You never said anything about a sewing machine.'

'I said I was doing fashion and made clothes,' I reply, a little surprised. I notice she's got a brand-new, blossoming love bite on her neck. Charlie is such a charmer. 'I didn't think it would bother you.'

'Yeah, well it's really loud and we're trying to watch the telly. Can you keep it down, please?'

She leaves, but not before she has a good look around my room, then shuts my door rather too firmly. I feel stung and ashamed and unwelcome. It's not like I'm playing death metal or anything. Even so, I don't want to tread on anyone's toes, so I unplug the foot pedal, tidy my bits and pieces away. Maybe tomorrow I'll measure up to her high expectations. I can't bring myself to cut the half-sewn thread though, and leave the fabric trailing out of the machine like a defiant red tongue.

Step Five – Give an Inch, Run a Mile

> There is no sight more discouraging than a poorly-made frock. A woman can be made a laughing stock by a rogue seam, so stick to some hard and fast rules. The seam allowance on a standard pattern is 5/8ths of an inch, so it is vital to check that your machine settings are the same. Otherwise the only admiring glances your outfit will attract will be from the organizers of the local jumble sale.

'We don't want people who toe the line, we want people who cross it,' says Duncan Howitson, pacing the wood-panelled assembly room at MetroTech College. In a checked shirt and workman's jeans, Duncan would look like a plumber, not a fashion lecturer, if it weren't for the completely out-of-place diamanté stud earring and the belt buckle that says 'DIVA'. At the interview he was much more subdued, studying my work with intense scrutiny and asking me pointed questions. Now he seems aggressive and swaggering and full of himself.

'You're going to have to work your arses off here,' he says, in gravelly Glaswegian. 'This isn't an excuse to ponce around thinking you're Kate Moss and worrying about what you're going to wear to fucking college every day. This is hard graft – comprendo?'

There's a reluctant murmur of agreement amongst my fellow students, who are all dressed in their finest outfits. There's a skinny boy in a floppy checked cap and three girls wearing the same Marc Jacobs copy dress, accessorized with various scarves and tweedy jackets. One guy has gone completely over the top – wearing a canary-yellow puffa jacket and neon-orange footless tights. I opted for businesslike black, thinking it would make me blend into the background, but I stick out like a sore thumb.

'Every day, I want you in and I want you grafting,' he continues, as if he's putting us to work down a mine. 'If you want to be a serious contender, you have to be serious about your craft. The catwalk is a competitive and intense place and you will be lucky to go near one in your lifetime. I've been teaching here for ten years and let me tell you, very few people make it in the industry, and the ones that do are the ones that work their asses off. So if there's anyone here under any illusions . . . if there's anyone here because they dream about being famous and having cokey-dokey nights out with models . . . then leave now.'

There is a slight bristle amongst the crowd. The girl sitting in front of me, who has two blond bunches of hair pinned to her head like fairy cakes, looks round curiously, but nobody leaves. Someone mutters 'Cokey-dokey?' under their breath and there's a stifled giggle, but Duncan doesn't notice.

'OK. We're going to teach you about tailoring, pattern cutting, CAD and fabric technologies and by the end of term I expect you to have shown vision and initiative and some original ideas or you may as well go and get a job in a bank.'

He pauses for effect, points at the ceiling, and we all look, half expecting to see an insect, or God, or Karl Lagerfeld dangling there on a wire, before realizing he means we have to follow him upstairs. Thirty-two strangers scrape their chairs back and dutifully file out of the room, which smells rubbery and stale, just like my old school gym. I feel as scared as I did on my first day at school. MetroTech College is not the buzzing, focused seat of higher learning I imagined it to be. It looks different filled with students, as tatty as Kirkness High, with orange curtains and varnished wooden doors and the disinfectant stink of a hospital, and there are the same kind of tribes here as at school: bunches of neds, goths, and high-street trendies. I'm in the most ridiculous tribe of all, the fashion folk, the demographic most likely to get beaten up and have their lunch money nicked. Duncan, however, seems to have developed a thick skin, and leads the way past vending machines and gangs of hard-looking guys in tracksuits, up a never-ending flight of stairs past the library and finally into our spiritual home, the Fashion and Textiles department, on what feels like Floor 386. All the way up the stairs, people are having breathless conversations, small talk about the college, but I stay silent. I'm so filled with dread, it's all I can do to keep moving upwards.

'Come on,' Duncan barks. 'Get a move on.'

Duncan hustles us all to the workroom, B14, with benches and high chairs and dressmaking dummies huddled up in the corner as if they're gossiping at a party. The room is cold, with draughty, aged windows, perforated, crumbling pinboards and anglepoise lamps fixed to each workbench. Outside there's a brilliant view of Glasgow I want to go and look at, but unfortunately Duncan's wheezing, strawberry-coloured face is the only thing we're supposed to be paying attention to at the moment.

'This is where you'll be spending all your time,' he says, with a theatrical sweep of his arms. 'The hub of all creativity. Theory classes are in the lecture room across the hall, B17, but here the magic will happen. Or it will if you put your back into it. Now, do you know how to use a computer, Mary Quant, or didn't you know they'd been invented?' he asks, and I realize he's talking to me.

'Yes, I do know,' I stammer. Suddenly everyone is looking at me, and I note a faint glimmer of amusement from the guy in the neon footless tights. How he can laugh at my outfit when he looks like Big Bird in Space is beyond me. I glare at the floor and feel my confidence shrivel.

'For those who don't know, CAD stands for Computer Aided Design and you'll be doing a lot of it in here,' he says, flinging open a door to reveal a room as big as the one we're standing in, full of monitors and workstations. 'We'll be using it to design patterns, sketch out ideas and realize them in 3D – easy when you know how.'

I think about my sketchbook, and how drawing designs by hand is my favourite part.

'Next week, we'll start with a few CAD tutorials followed by some sessions of drawing and pattern design. Then we're going to do a group project followed by an individual assessment. Write this down.'

Everyone reaches into their bags for notebooks. The skinny boy in the floppy cap has a PDA. Poseur. Duncan then reels off a list of expensive-sounding items we need to buy from a nearby haberdashery department.

'Inspiration can come from the past, but fashion is about the future,' he lectures. 'It's about anticipating the next moment, being open to juxtaposition and suggestion and taking creative vision to its limit.' Duncan looks at me as he says this, his big thumbs stuck in his 'DIVA' belt like a gay cowboy. 'We are not just dressmakers,' he spits. 'We are artists. See you on Monday.'

I'm not sure I'm going to like this course.

'Evie, I very much want to see you and your flat,' barked my dad the other day. 'Charlotte says it's very nice.'

'You can't come here,' I hissed, going over to the other side of my room in case any sounds travelled through the paper-thin walls. 'My flatmate is allergic to animal hair. When Mum came she nearly died of asphyxiation.'

'OK, well you show me the outside then. Come on, I'll buy you dinner, right? You like food. I don't want you to starve.'

The prospect of a night somewhere other than Lorna's (I still can't quite get my head round the phrase 'my flat') is tempting. Every night we have watched countless property programmes. For the past two weekends horrible Charlie has come over and I have had to go to my room. I mean, I love that it's so quiet, and there are no loud parties, I really do. But Lorna will only talk when she feels like it. It's as if sometimes she can't wait to see me, and other times she doesn't even recall why I'm there. When we have spoken though, it's been fine. We've had conversations about the miraculous properties of Febreze and the merits of certain styling products, she's told me her theory of dishwasher stacking, and she gets very animated when she talks about the wedding, the big event of 2008. She buys slabs of bridal magazines and asks me my opinion, which I find quite endearing, even though sometimes I have to lie. The dress she wants is this awful confection of lace and taffeta, which looks like Barbara Cartland's toilet roll holder, but when I suggest something she agrees with, and she writes it down in her special spiral-bound wedding notebook with 'FOREVER' embossed on the cover in flowery script, I feel a flush of pride to be involved in the elaborate proceedings, despite not approving of her obnoxious future husband. Or perhaps I was wrong about Charlie. Perhaps he has great depths I know nothing about, and I'm just being judgemental. After all, he only knows me as this stranger who turned up one day with red-wine teeth and a flushed face and sat on the sofa while he was trying to get it on with his girlfriend.

So anyway, it's Thursday night and I'm going out to meet my father; big Anton, destroyer of bedrooms. The cat-hair incident proved a good deterrent in the end – at least he won't be barging into the flat, knocking things over, spreading the smell of metal and turpentine around the place and trampling WD40 into the floor. Lorna is in the kitchen, furiously scrubbing the inside of the cutlery drawer, singing a James Blunt song over and over again in a thin voice. If she came face to face with Anton, she might never recover. I sit on the edge of the bed, facing the blank cream wall that separates my bedroom from Lorna's. On first viewing, I didn't notice, but my room contains the flat's only flaw, a hollow dent in the wall where a socket once was. I stare at it as I figure out what I'm going to wear and how I'm going to behave tonight. My dad and I rarely sit down together as adults without shouting at each other and stomping off to separate areas of the house. Can we get through two hours in a restaurant without tipping plates of spaghetti over each other's heads? Of course we can. This is my chance to show how grown up I am, to prove that I've made the correct choice. I will even rise above the Victor McDougall debacle, and all the other debacles, even though a layer of resentment still lies heavy on me, like the skin on a rice pudding. I put on a high-collared black minidress and red Sixties raincoat, with high-heeled black boots, and make sure my bob hasn't got any kinks in it. I can't find my crocheted tights, though – they must have got lost in the move. I want to look sleek, confident and together, a real lady about town, rather than a wee daft lassie waiting in the queue at the chip shop, or nipping down to the Spar for a packet of ciggies. Popping my lip gloss into my bag it dawns on me why I'm so excited – tragically, this is my first proper night out in Glasgow.

'See you later, Lorna,' I say, heading out, and she comes padding into the hall, hair in a ponytail, holding a bright yellow sponge.

'Is that what you're wearing?'

I look down at my ensemble – the boots and mini-skirt. Very 1966. Cool, metropolitan, lots of eyeliner and attitude, a bit foxy.

'Yes,' I squeak, withering under her incredulous gaze, suddenly feeling like a twenty-stone wrestler in drag. 'Why? Do you think it's too much?'

Lorna looks stricken. 'Well, yeah, a bit. Don't you? I thought you said you were going to meet your dad.'

She's probably right. Dads and restaurants perhaps call for something slightly more demure. I return to my room to put on a cardigan and flat shoes.

'Jesus Christ, Evgeniya, what happened to you? You're dressed like my grandmother,' says Anton, who emerges from a black cab like King Kong getting out of a Mini. I see he's really glammed up for the occasion in a jumper with an enormous hole in the sleeve and a pair of trousers that look like they've been wrestled out of the jaws of a bin lorry.

'What?' I snap, irritated that suddenly everyone has an opinion about the way I dress. You'd think that as I'm about to be a fashion student I would know at least something about the subject. 'Look at the state of you – I said we were visiting a restaurant, not a pig farm.'

Dad laughs heartily and puts what I think is supposed to be an affectionate arm round my shoulder, but it's more like a headlock. The restaurant is across the road, a square white door with a bouncer/security guard standing outside in a black suit that doesn't fit him. I hope they let Dad in. Perhaps they'll think he's an eccentric millionaire.

'How're you getting on, angel?' he shouts, as I try to pretend I'm not with him. 'How is college? Got a boyfriend yet?'

I ignore him and try to navigate the traffic. This cardigan is really itchy lurex, a charity shop bargain that wasn't even worth the £2.99. I just want to get him in there, preferably in a corner, away from the eyes of respectable diners. After all, my dad doesn't go to many restaurants, and seems to treat the whole idea of a dress code as some kind of foolish game. The last time we all went out for a meal together was three years ago, when we were celebrating my mum's first solo show at the Wobbly Wheel. We went to a place in Kingsferry called the Red Barn, where, dressed in an orange boiler suit covered in oily stains, he proceeded to get roaring drunk, pick his teeth with the menu and chat up the waitress, who was someone I knew from school. I hope he behaves himself this time. I say a quiet hello to the bouncer and he steps aside to welcome us in, a hint of fear on his face when he sees the Incredible Hulk come in behind me. We go down some tiled, narrow steps into the basement. It's a far cry from the Anchor Hotel, every surface shining white antique tiles, with mahogany booths and dancing candlelight and shadowy faces lost in intense, important conversations.

'Looks like a public toilet,' booms my father, just as the maître d' approaches. She reminds me of Lorna, with a mane of poker-straight hair and a groomed self-confidence.

'I booked a table for two,' I say, trying not to fall over my words. 'Kaminsky.'

'Oh, yes.' The immaculate maître d' smiles. 'Follow me.'

Anton raises an eyebrow.

'What?'

'You are such a big shot now,' he says. 'What is this place called again? Pobombo? Pompompo?'

'Pomodoro,' I whisper.

'Ah, that means tomato!' he states delightedly, shoving himself into a spindly chair that seems ready to collapse. 'Cheers, love,' he says to the maître d', as if she's someone who works at the supermarket. 'We'll be needing a bottle of your house red.'

'And some water, please.' I smile weakly.

There's a flutter of menus and a reading of specials as we get ourselves settled in our seats. It feels odd sitting across from my dad, observing the little details of his face. I thought I knew it well but he looks weird. He's greyer and more whiskery than I remembered, the dead tooth – broken in shady circumstances as a youth in St Petersburg – is turning black from all the fags and coffee, giving him the look of a maladjusted pirate. He does look like me, though, somehow, a fact I try to distract myself from by looking at the menu. Linguine allo scoglio, crespella con verdure, insalata di pancetta e rucola . . . in my quest to be grown up and cosmopolitan I didn't realize I might not know what anything is on the à la carte, or how to pronounce it.

'So, Evie, I want to know why are you here, and what you hope for in your life,' he says, getting a bashed tobacco tin out and placing it by his side.

'Dad, I don't think you can smoke in here.'

'Oh, I'm sure they'll arrest me,' he agrees conversationally, his thick fingers opening the tin anyway. 'So? Tell me your strategy.'

I close the menu and survey the room. The couple at the next table seem to be engaged in a vicious argument. It's probably only a matter of time before we are too.

'I'm starting my course on Monday. It seems like it might be hard work. The course leader, Duncan, doesn't put up with any nonsense,' I say, trying to sound chirpy, but secretly dreading my first day in front of their CAT monitors, or whatever they're called, with Duncan calling me Mary Quant and being snide.

'Anyway, that's it. I'm doing that for two years, then I want to work as a professional dressmaker.'

'Hmm. And you like Glasgow?'

'Yeah.'

'Better than London?'

I don't answer.

'I know you think we destroyed your portfolio on purpose, but it was an accident and that's the truth. We only desire the best for you. Even if we couldn't have afforded it we would have found a way.'

'Mm.' I squirm in my seat, embarrassed. 'I don't want to talk about it.'

'Well, it's true. But I think this place will be the best for you.'

He would say that. The old injustice starts to sting again and I watch him rolling his fag, yellow fingered. A bit of lemon juice would get rid of the nicotine stains in a second, but naturally, he can't be bothered.

'This Lorna – Charlotte says she is not very much like you.'

Yes, there it is. I knew it. I knew as soon as she got home that Mum would start laying into Lorna.

'Look, Lorna is nice,' I say, as if telling him for the millionth time. 'She's got high standards, and she's neat and tidy, and we both have a desire to live in an uncluttered environment,' I say, sounding like a press release. 'We've got more in common than you think. She's normal, at least.'

'Ha!' he says. 'Normal. What an ugly word. What a dreadful thing to be!'

I wouldn't expect him to understand. He has no idea why it would upset me to get up in the morning in a place that's freezing because someone forgot to pay the bills, or why I would want to sit quietly on a sofa that isn't smelly and old and occupied by an unwashed dog.

He doesn't get why I want to be able to reach into a fridge and not have my hand devoured by The Blob, or have food in the house that's not so old that it should be in the Museum of Natural History, or need to get away from the constant banging and the endless babble of artists and neighbours who just wander in through open back doors and stay there for days. Instantly fuming, I turn my attentions to the menu.

A waiter comes to the table and presents my dad with the wine.

'Yes. It's a green bottle with a label on it – very good,' he says with a smile.

'Dad!' I snap.

He ignores me. 'No need to taste it – I'm sure it will be fine. I can smoke in here, yes?' he asks, about to light up.

'I'm afraid not, sir,' says the waiter, giving him a pally 'what can you do?' shrug. He doesn't seem at all embarrassed to have this scruffy geezer cluttering up the place, giving him cheek.

'Oh shame. I shall have to sit on my hands and face the wall.'

The waiter laughs. I smile along with them, hoping it means they won't chuck my dad out. I'm amazed by how little Anton cares about his behaviour in public. He's just sitting there in this posh restaurant, his elbow sticking out of his jumper, trading stupid jokes as if he lives here, and nobody seems to care. Perhaps if he takes his shoes off and puts his feet on the table they'll give him a free pudding.

'So, Evie – here's to you,' he says, raising his glass.

'And your normal life.' He gives me a sideways look and I reluctantly clink glasses.

'And I hope you will be happy. You are a skilled dressmaker, but more than that, remember, while you're busy being normal, that you are also an artist.'

'Oh God, no. That's the last thing I want to be.'

'Tough tits,' he barks. 'I see the pieces you have made – they are the product of intense deliberation, a careful deconstruction of tradition. They just need to be more expressive, and then they will shine. I believe that when you have truly found your voice, there'll be no stopping you.'

Blah blah blah – what a load of old bollocks. I think of Duncan Howitson's thumbs in his belt buckles saying, 'We are artists,' and shudder.

'That's very interesting,' I reply, disinterestedly. 'So what are you having?'

'I'm going to have antipasti, followed by veal Parmigiana,' he says, with a passable Italian flourish, necking his wine. 'What about you?'

'I don't know.'

'I tell you what,' he begins, leaning forward conspiratorially. 'Close your eyes and pick something.'

'Oh, don't be silly,' I say, combing carefully through a section of the menu called 'Il Primo Piatto'.

'Go on, I dare you – be spontaneous – let fate take you where it may!' He makes a wild, flailing arc with his arm, straight from the *Handbook of Extravagant Russian Gestures*, and slams his fist down on the table, causing the dainty cut flower in the centre of the table to quiver.

I'm about to protest but then realize it might help to keep him quiet, so I indulge him in his wee game. I close my eyes, whirl my finger in the air a couple of times and let it fall on the laminate surface.

'Penne con salvia e burro,' he says, his face full of mischief. 'Now again.'

'OK, OK . . . for God's sake.' I do it again, feeling stupid. I'm probably ordering donkey stew, knowing him. The couple at the next table have finished their argument and are now watching us with vague curiosity. I hope they don't think we're boyfriend and girlfriend. I bring my finger down once more and open my eyes.

'What does it say?' he asks.

'Fishi al proscuitto?' I say, stumbling over the words.

'Ah, the sensuous combination of figs and Parma ham! An excellent choice, madam.' He grins. 'Now where is my friend the waiter? He'd better not be in the back having a fag when I'm sitting out here with nothing.'

I close the menu. Even here, Dad is calling the shots as if we're still at home. I can't even order without him interfering. So much for being a fabulous girl about town who knows how to handle herself in the big city. I wonder whether I should bring up the small matter of my destroyed glass collection, and present him with a bill. But Anton is on a mission, too consumed with the idea of having a good time to listen to my wheedling. When the food arrives, he orders another bottle of wine.

'Well, this is wonderful – a night out with my

daughter,' he says, topping up my glass. 'We should do this more often.'

The figs look gross, like shrivelled, blackened internal organs. Ugh. I gingerly prod them with my fork.

'Eat, Evie, eat!' Dad says, shovelling what looks like an entire pig into his mouth. 'That's the food of love, y'know.'

I take a bite. The figs actually turn out to be delicious and sweet, but I don't let on.

'Now I will tell you my news. You know that the Arts Council have finally given me permission for *Windscape*?'

The wind thing? I think back to the scribbled notes on the back of the unpaid electricity bill I found from 1995. The pole with the propeller on it. Surely he scrapped that years ago?

'It has come not a moment too soon. I was just about ready to give up and be normal myself. There is only so much rejection that a man can take before it starts to eat away at his self-worth,' he continues, scarfing down another slice of pig. 'No doubt it will be controversial, and all the little people in Kirkness will miss the point of the exercise. They will be up in arms about this latest blot on the landscape and call me all kinds of names in the paper. But after eleven years of changes and frustrations the project has been approved. I don't care what anyone says about me now. It will be wonderful and be there long after we have all gone. It has taught me to have the courage of my convictions. You must always listen to yourself, not other people. Trust your instincts.'

'Is it definitely going ahead?' I ask, aware that quite a few of his grand designs have fallen by the wayside in the past.

'Oh yes, the council has approved a lottery grant of £750,000 so that I can build it.'

'£750,000? Really?' It seems like an astronomical amount of money to give to my dad, who, as far as I know, doesn't even have a bank account and keeps his loose change in a large pickling jar that once contained gherkins.

'Yes,' he says, triumphantly stabbing an olive. 'Really. So our financial hardship may be over one day soon. And I can pay you back for the unfortunate accident. All of the accidents.'

'Oh right, well. Wow, well done,' I say. I didn't realize he'd been working on it for so long. I just thought he was upstairs randomly welding bits of piano wire to radiators. Amazingly, though, it seems that my dad is going to build a monument. I look at the hole in his jumper, trying to compute.

'Really, that's great,' I repeat.

'So, another toast. To me! One day I might even be able to afford to pay for this meal!' he laughs, and our clinking glasses ring festively in mid air. I look down at the remains of the £9.50 figs and ham, and hope to God that he's joking.

I honestly didn't want to but I've had a few. My tongue feels big and dry in my mouth, like I'm swallowing a Muppet, and my hand/eye co-ordination isn't what it could be. I'm completely squiffy. The streets are practically empty, save for a few groups of drunk people and a line of slick black taxis, one of which is taking my pie-eyed father to the station right now. This isn't how I wanted the night to go, but it seems too late to worry about that, and the meal was delicious and rich, a welcome change to the watery tomato sauces and bland ready meals Lorna insists on serving. Not that I'm ungrateful, of course.

'Hello, Evie!' says a voice from behind me. I almost jump out of my skin, and turn painfully on my heel, dizzy and unbalanced. The city is full of murderers and rapists and it would be just my luck to bump into one – I try to remember what you have to do, but all I can think of is nuts. You have to kick them in the nuts. But if it was a rapist, why would it be female and know my name?

'Alice!' I yelp.

'We seem to be bumping into each other everywhere!' she says. Alice is dressed up to the nines. Her hair is beautiful, a cascade of glossy black curls, and with make-up on, she looks quite unlike the harassed girl on the bike with the green socks.

'Oh God, I thought you were a rapist!' I gasp.

'Sorry, I didn't mean to startle you. How are you, anyway?'

I mean to just say a nonchalant 'Fine', but my mouth doesn't seem to be connected to my brain.

'Well, I've just been to dinner with my dad – Pomodoro – have you ever been? It's lovely. I had figs. They were amazing. Anyway, he's a sculptor and he's been given permission to build a thing . . . a sculpture.

It's going to be a monument about wind energy,' I finish, running out of breath.

'That's cool!' she says, apparently delighted. 'And how's your mum?'

I wonder for a moment how Alice would know anything about my mum, and then I remember.

'Oh, I'm sorry about her. She's a bit mental,' I mumble, vaguely aware that I'm slurring my words.

'Not at all, I thought she was great. Are you going home?'

'Yeah. Back to Lorna's. She's very neat and tidy.'

'Hmm.'

'I'm sorry I turned down the room in your flat, it's no reflection on you,' I begin clumsily, before wishing I hadn't even started.

'Oh, don't worry about that!' Alice replies, easily. 'To be honest, I'm having trouble getting rid of it. Must be that mural. It's cursed.' She laughs. I laugh too, a brief honk like a drain being emptied, and have to conclude that I'm practically legless. Not for the first time, I'm embarrassing myself in front of her. I try to straighten myself up and stop gibbering but my mouth is still racing ahead.

'How's Mickey?' I ask.

'Oh, he's all right. He's always all right,' she says, offering me a tab of chewing gum. Do I smell of booze? I bet I stink of garlic too. I take it and chew it heartily.

'Oh, yeah. He is definitely all right,' I say, involuntarily, thinking of his shoulders wrapped in that duvet. Oh my God, what am I . . . ? 'I mean, you know, I didn't mean to sound . . .'

'That's OK,' Alice giggles, digging her hands into her coat pockets. 'Look, Evie, I've got to go and get the bus,' she says, nodding to a double-decker trundling slowly up the hill. 'Here – take this.' She pulls out a mysteriously small piece of photocopied paper. On it is a little drawing of a bottle, with 'Drink Me' written on it. Underneath that it says, *Friday 3 September, from 10 p.m., Alice's Party*.

'You should come along. I think you'd enjoy yourself,' she says, and before I've had a chance to respond, she's skipping up the street after the bus, curls flying. She looks proud and agile, like an Olympic torch bearer, and, dizzy with wine, all I want to do is follow her. But in that instant my feet are welded to the spot, and after the bus pulls away I turn and trudge back to Lorna's. The blank, darkened windows and quiet hallway bring me back to earth. Alice seems nice, but what would be the point? I've had enough parties with artists to last me a lifetime. It would just be more of the same, so why look back? My new friends need to be different somehow, more ambitious and successful. People who have dinner parties, not drunken free-for-alls in rented hovels – all loud music and penniless art students snogging on the stairs.

In the cool of the hallway, I stop and gather my thoughts – what's left of them – but getting in without making a noise in the echoing stairwell is practically impossible. I try to tiptoe, but my shoes make even gentle steps sound like a tap routine. Once I'm outside the door, I take out my key, my vision blurred round the edges, and attempt to connect it with the brass lock.

The key is sticky. Dad would know what to do in this situation, he'd probably kick the door off its hinges with his big boot and Lorna would come out in the Snoopy nightshirt she sometimes plods around in and chase him down the street with a Flash duster on a telescopic stick. Shhhh. Shhhh. Be quiet. I look at her proud brass nameplate, the one she polishes religiously, with her surname, McHastie, stamped on it in Mackintosh font. Mackintosh's mackintosh. Honestly, that stuff is everywhere. What's the big deal? Wonder what my boyfriend Johnny's up to? He said I was a firecracker! What a silly boy. Now Mickey on the other hand . . . I giggle merrily, then stop, clamping my hand over my mouth. Shhh, Evie, sshhhh. Disturbing Lorna would be bad. Very bad. Very very very. Oh, but did I really say that to Alice? Maybe they're more than just friends and she thinks I'm trying to crack onto him? Oh God, it's probably best to keep my distance from them – every time I meet them, I say something totally ridiculous. Best to file that under Forget It. He's an arty-farty party boy, anyway. And his hair could do with a good brush.

I rattle the key in the lock, as gently as I can, but there's no give, and my hand hurts to push it any further and then it might break, which would mean hell to pay and a twenty-four-hour locksmith and Lorna not speaking to me for a week. Instead I try to turn and push, turn and push, turn and—

Clunk!

Shoooom!

The door suddenly opens up, draught excluder strips

tearing apart like a terrible wound. There's Lorna, her hair not so well groomed now, face greasy with £50 Lancôme night cream she doesn't even need, glaring at me with absolute disgust. The wine is making my head spin, and any attempt to seem sober is made worse by the fact that it's obvious, even to me, that I'm trying not to fall face down on the welcome mat. I need to get it together. The rational part of my brain knows I've messed up, but the drunk part thinks it's hilarious. She looks so funny!

'Hello, I'm sorry, sorry, sorry . . . couldn't get the key . . . didn't mean to wake you up,' I blurt, words tumbling this way and that. This is not going to look good on my flatmate CV. Lorna says nothing, just steps aside to let me in, making me horribly aware that I stink of garlic and booze, which I've fruitlessly tried to cover up with chewing gum, and my demure cardigan is decorated with a wilting red flower, which was poked into the material by my dad, stolen from the tiny glass vase on the table during the forty-fifth glass of Valpolicella. I concentrate on my feet, getting from here to my room without creating a scene, all the while breathing 'sorry' in a haze of fumes.

'So you had a good time, did you, Evie?' she snaps. 'In the future, could you please be more quiet when you come home steaming? If you need to refresh your memory, I suggest you read Clause 13 of the contract you signed.'

'Sorry, Lorna,' I squeak, making myself scarce.

When I open my bedroom door I fall on the bed, clothes still on. Struggling up to take off my shoes, I blearily look across at my sewing table. From here the red material looks crumpled, but it's probably just the angle I'm at, halfway off the edge of the bed with my foot in the air. Clean up your act, Kaminsky – it's time you got serious.

Step Six – Darts Have a Point

> The body is not rigid, composed of right angles and straight lines. As the contours of the figure must be accommodated, it will often be necessary to make folds and tucks within your material. These folds are called 'darts' and will help provide ease of movement.

Our first college project is a 'funky top'. When Duncan said the word 'funky' my whole body just collapsed in on itself – I thought of backless, strapless, glittery things you can get on the sale rail in Top Shop for a fiver, of *Hollyoaks* and *Footballers' Wives*. 'You're not designing for yourself!' Duncan told everyone, slamming down his coffee cup on the desk; but if you don't like what you're designing, what's the point? So I decided I would make something more feminine and respectable, with a glitzy 1920s feel to it, but I can't quite get the hang of the stupid mouse. My computer screen is a confusing array of squiggly lines that I have no hope of turning into a real item of clothing. It would be so much quicker and easier to just do this on a piece of paper and scan it in.

'Interesting,' says Duncan, breathing coffee and stale cigarette fumes into my ear. 'Is this a top or a map of Scandinavia?'

'It's a top,' I growl.

'Remember your seam allowance,' he says. 'And remember what year it is.'

What a cheeky bastard he is. Duncan has had it in for me ever since he saw me again at the induction day. He has me down as a retro loser, with no new ideas. I have no idea why. Maybe I'm his mascot. Does he take on one student a year that he can humiliate in front of everyone else? I look at him leaning on the desk, arms folded over his not insubstantial belly, and wonder again why he keeps singling me out.

As for Big Bird in Space, whose name is actually Neil, he seems to have settled into the role of Duncan's gimp. Today he's wearing a bandanna and a dollar sign necklace, proving to one and all that he's ridiculous. But the girl with the fairy-cake hair, Flossy, has attached herself to me and seems OK, even though she spends a large amount of time talking about how many drugs she's taken and how many she's planning to take in the future. Apart from that, nobody has really talked to me much. But it doesn't bother me that I'm not the most popular girl in the class. I'm not here to make loads of friends, I'm here to learn with as few distractions as possible, to find out more about the process. I'm going to be a top-class hotshot couturier, and nobody's going to be able to stop me, not even Big Bird.

'Right, I've done enough for one day,' says Duncan, putting on a flamboyant furry-edged coat and slinging a satchel over his shoulder. He must be nearing his forties. What kind of an outfit is that for a grown man?

'Anyone want to come to the Sub for a drink?' he adds, rubbing his hands together.

I keep my eyes fixed on the confusing rainbow of lines on my screen, waiting to see what kind of people would volunteer to spend an evening listening to him talk about 'fashion, passion and innovation' when they could be out having a good time. Unsurprisingly, Neil starts packing up, as well as Jezebel, an unsmiling, dark-haired gypsy temptress who impressed everyone very early on with a story about meeting Alexander McQueen in a nightclub in Shoreditch, wherever that is.

'Fancy going?' shrugs Flossy, reaching into a Sanrio rucksack covered in Japanese writing. 'I need to get messy. I haven't worked this hard in ages.'

'I can't. I promised my flatmate I'd go out with her.'

This isn't exactly true. Lorna wouldn't go out on a school night, or any other night for that matter, especially not to the Sub, a student shed that sells lurid-coloured alcohol for discount prices and shows football on giant screens. But I've got this horrible feeling that she's been avoiding me after my faux pas last weekend. The house has been even quieter than usual, and she has started leaving notes on my door saying things like 'Please can you not leave wet umbrellas in the umbrella stand as water collects at the base' and 'It's your turn to replace the milk!!!!' She tries to be lighthearted by putting smiley faces at the end, but they look more like grimacing babies. I think I might have some making up to do.

So tonight, I thought I'd surprise her with a meal. I figured I'd play safe and cook pasta, and ask her some more about the wedding. Then we'll undoubtedly watch ancient repeats of *Changing Rooms*. OK, so not exactly thrilling, but I'd rather do that than have this atmosphere going on.

I turn my computer off, straighten my skirt and reach for my vinyl raincoat, happy to get away from this cheesy room and all its confusing, infuriating difficulties. Flossy accompanies me down the stairs.

'Do you have a clue what's going on?' she sniffs, blowing her nose with a shredded tissue.

'Not really. I don't know how to work that computer thing, it's horrible.' I look at Flossy and smile. Thank God, someone who's as hopeless with technology as I am. She's a strange wee girl – snub nosed and cute, but with dark circles under her eyes and a murky social life, like a baby Drew Barrymore during her wilderness years.

'Oh, I know how to work it, I just don't know what I'm doing. I mean, the patterns are so confusing. All these technical terms and rules and regulations and being accurate and shit. And what the hell is selvedge anyway?'

'It's just the edge of a piece of fabric,' I begin, happy to at least have some fashion expertise under my retro Sixties belt, but Flossy's attention span is exhausted and she's talking to someone else about going to a club later, where they're supposed to play really good music, and does anyone know any dealers?

At the bottom of the stairs, we go our separate ways: Duncan's cronies, me and the rest. While they're off getting high as kites and drinking the bars dry, I head for the bright orange lights of Sainsbury's.

'I'm not really in the mood for pasta,' says Lorna, primly, writing a 'To Do' list on her wipe-clean board. 'Anyway, unless it's wheat free, I can't have it. I'm allergic.'

'Oh,' I say, putting the shopping bags on the counter. With the garlic bread and salad and Wickedly Indulgent Chocolate Cappuccino Ice Cream, plus a few extra things for the house (Lorna gets through cleaning products like nobody's business), the bill came to £20. And now she doesn't want it. Is she punishing me?

'I just thought it could be a treat,' I say, wiping the drops of rain off my sleeve, careful not to let them land anywhere on the precious laminate flooring. My hair is soaking wet – I couldn't hold an umbrella and two shopping bags at the same time.

'Ugh! Can you not get a towel? You're dripping everywhere!' shrieks Lorna, turning round to see the state of me. I watch her as she flaps about, feeling remarkably calm. In contrast, she seems ready to explode. Do I irritate her that much? Her neck looks pinched and stretched, lines of tension round her mouth making her look older than she is, and she swoops to the bathroom for a towel, throwing it to me as if I'm in a boxing ring with three seconds before the next round.

'I'm sorry,' I say, but she's too busy with her Vileda supermop, catching drips.

'Yes well, it's fine,' she lies, 'but I can't be doing with this disruption. I'm a very busy person.'

'That's why I wanted to cook you a meal,' I protest, making sure my hair is thoroughly dry. 'I thought it would be a nice surprise. Don't worry – I'll clean that up—'

'No!' she squeaks. 'I'm doing it! And just so you know, I'm not a big fan of surprises. I've already planned what I'm going to have for dinner, and after that I'm going to watch some TV and then have a bath and go to bed.' I'm sure I can see a vein throbbing in her temple. 'I appreciate that you got some shopping in, but also I would ask you to observe the rules of the house and try to consider my needs. And not make the kitchen floor all wet.'

I don't understand what she means. Apart from accidentally dripping one or two splashes of water on her floor, surely I was considering her needs? As she skitters about with the mop, swinging its limp fronds this way and that, I briefly wonder whether I should take the ice cream out before it melts, but I'm too terrified to move.

'What needs?' I enquire, feeling pissed off.

'I am a stressed person!' she shouts, suddenly ferocious, ceasing her mopping and leaning on the handle for dear life. 'And I need calm. I need serenity.

I need to avoid stress! I don't need surprises! I need my space, OK?'

'OK,' I whisper.

'So if you wouldn't mind, I'd like to have my dinner in peace this evening.'

Right on cue, the microwave pings, and she hustles on a pair of oven gloves. With her back to me, she carefully extracts a ready meal in a black plastic tray. I could swear it's pasta.

Not knowing whether to leave the room or stay and wait for her to leave, I stand there idiotically, running the Egyptian cotton towel through my fingers. Lorna seems very highly strung. Perhaps she's had a bad day, or an argument with Charlie, or something catastrophic has happened. The wedding might be off. That would leave her devastated, with nothing to focus upon, and make her fly into a rage, wouldn't it? Or is she just bonkers? I wonder if I should say something.

'Are you OK, Lorna?' I ask, barely audible above the vicious scraping of ready meal onto plate. She says nothing, but I can see even from here that she's vibrating with tension. 'Something terrible hasn't happened, has it?'

Still nothing. She reaches for a fork (not a knife, thank God), shoots me a black look – as if I'm the something terrible that's happened – and stomps out of the room.

Great.

Well, that's the last time I suggest a nice night in. I'm damned if I do, and damned if I don't.

She slams the living-room door, just to underline

that I should never, never spring any awful surprises like dinner on her again, and I'm alone, listening to the tick tick tick of the kitchen clock, which I notice is a cheap antique reproduction with roman numerals that looks like it should be in someone's mum's house. I'm instantly bored. The weekend stretches out before me, featuring, no doubt, Charlie, who'll come barging in here at about half past nine with his overfilled chinos and all the charm of a pit bull, and I'll have to retire to my room like a nun. This wasn't part of the plan.

Now I'm allowed to move freely again, I reach into the bag and pick out the tub of ice cream. I should install it in the freezer, for a special occasion, perpendicular to the frozen peas, but instead I open it and stick in my finger, scooping a large glob into my mouth and letting it melt on my tongue. It's delicious. I have some more, pleased I'm not even using a spoon, even though my finger is so cold that it's ready to snap off. I can hear the inane music to *Changing Rooms* next door, and eat a bigger bit. She's perched there, napkin on her knee, elbows at right angles to her tray, and I'm shovelling ice cream into my face with my hands. Ha! Before I know it, I'm scoffing it as if I haven't eaten for a week, almost dying of chocolate-related pleasure, and carry on until most of it has gone. Sugar is racing through my veins and I feel unhinged. In this mood, I could go mad. I could do anything. I could wipe off her To Do list and put 'Move to Mozambique' on it instead! I stand there for a bit, and realize that while I was eating, ice cream has splattered muddily onto the counter, collecting in gloopy pools of sugar and cocoa.

Then I do something that I would never do at home. In fact, I don't know what's come over me, but I . . . write my name in it.

E . . . V . . . I . . . E.

As soon as I finish the 'E', though, my giddiness gives way to a terrible pang of guilt. Behaving in such an uncontrolled manner feels like an outrageous thing to be doing in the House of Lorna, and I try to get rid of the evidence. I put the pasta and the sauce in the cupboard, and the cleaning products (labels facing front) under the sink, nerves shredded. I tidy away the bags and clean up the ice-cream drips, making damn sure that the surface is restored to its shining former glory. Then I go to my room, still absent-mindedly holding the ice-cream tub, but before I can backtrack to put it in the bin, Lorna comes out of the living room to wash up her plate, and I hover by my door, frozen in fear, listening to her opening cupboards and muttering under her breath. The absence of blood-curdling screams must mean that she hasn't found anything untoward in there, but moments later I hear footsteps advancing towards me, the swish of her work trousers, and the barely perceptible breath she takes before she knocks.

'Evie?' she calls in a sweet voice. I dive to the bed and shove the empty carton under there, straightening my duvet as I do so.

'Yes?'

She comes in and peers at me suspiciously.

'Just for future reference, you got the wrong kind of washing-up liquid – it's Lemon Burst, not Ocean Fresh.'

'Oh, OK.'

'But thanks anyway,' she says, unconvincingly, closing the door and heading back into the kitchen.

I suppose that's her idea of an apology. I sit for a while, catching my breath, and realize that I can't face a Friday night in my room, with my lone ashtray and the outlawed sewing machine with the fabric pouring out of it and the dent in the wall. I look at that dent, wondering how such an obvious imperfection was overlooked. I can relate to it, actually – that's me – the unwelcome human imperfection, the blot on the landscape. While Lorna is temporarily deafened by the running water in the kitchen sink I get my coat and leave the house, stomping up the glistening path and into the street. Outside it's no longer raining, but a damp blanket of moisture hangs heavily. Something is buzzing in my head, propelling me towards the main road, towards the lights of the cafés and the pubs. I feel like going on the subway, round and round in a circle on the Clockwork Orange until I get dizzy or someone tells me to get off. I feel like climbing up to the top of a hill in the park and standing on a bench and howling at the moon. Right now I could go and sit on my own in a pub and introduce myself to a bunch of strangers and do karaoke all night. I could dance to Led Zeppelin like my mum does! Perhaps I'm allergic to dairy products.

I walk and walk, wondering where to go and how I can get rid of all this excess energy that's building up inside me. I'm going spare. Is this what I wanted? A clean room, nothing to do, no distractions? A quiet life,

I told Charlotte. I wish she were here. She'd liven the place up a bit. (I can't believe I actually just thought that.) I go to the shop and buy a pack of cigarettes, even though smoking is disgusting – it feels good to have them, a bit rebellious and James Deany – the brand is American Spirit, with a drawing of a Navajo tribesman on the front and they cost almost as much as dinner in a restaurant – a wilful waste of money and bad for you to boot. I buy a quarter bottle of vodka too, just because it's something Lorna wouldn't dream of doing, not because I really want to drink it. But I take a slug anyway. The vodka burns in my stomach, spurring me on. I'm a rebel without a cause. I want some action. All I need is a leather jacket and I'd be Johnny, a thought that makes me laugh out loud. I reach into my damp pocket and find a crumpled piece of paper, a receipt or something.

It says 'Drink Me'.

Alice's party. Alice's party is tonight. I head off automatically, as if pulled along by an invisible leash, in the direction of Copeland Street.

'Yeeeeah! Evie!' she says, enveloping me in a warm, slightly musty embrace. Alice is dressed in bottle green, like a glorious insect, her throat white against antique black lace trimmings, waving a long cigarette holder as if it's a magic wand. I look terrible in comparison to her and the rest of the female guests, who appear to be dressed for Saturday night on the *Titanic*. But despite the fact that the dress code is more upmarket than Kirkness parties, there's something homely about the place, with the familiar stink of cigarette smoke and booze and frozen ready-to-bake party snacks slammed drunkenly into the oven. In the kitchen, a gaggle of riotous art school girls in black evening dresses are trying to mix cocktails, spilling a pinky red cranberry juice goo all over the floor and cackling. In my vodka-and-caffeine haze it all seems very exciting.

'Come and have a drink,' Alice says, grabbing my arm. 'This is Nadine, Tracy and Eleanor. This is Evie – she came to see the flat and she's new to Glasgow, so we have to look after her. Evie makes clothes.'

'Do you now?' says one – Nadine, I think – who is sporting two perfect swooshes of liquid eyeliner that make her look like a cat. I notice that her eyelashes are false, studded with sparkles.

'Well, I'm not a designer or anything . . .' I begin.

'Yeah, you are!' Alice says. 'When I met her she was wearing this amazing skirt, and she was just like "I made it myself".' She shrugs, mimicking me quite badly. 'Honestly, it was so good. Will you make me one?'

'Yeah, maybe . . .' I reply.

'OK, but do you know how to make a Tom Collins?' asks Nadine, who has finished examining me and has moved back to her drinks recipe. 'Nobody seems to be able to remember.'

Pleased for a distraction from my mythical fashion designer status, I have a think, and remember I once looked it up in a book about cocktails (the most well-thumbed recipe book in the house) because Marilyn

Monroe drank it in *The Seven Year Itch*. It seemed such a glamorous drink, old fashioned and strong and feisty, and here I am amongst people who actually drink it.

'It's gin, lemon juice, soda and some sugar,' I say, with a glint of pride.

'Och, check you!' says Tracy, a big girl with a stripe of white in her dark hair like the bride of Frankenstein. 'You're like Tom Cruise in *Cocktail*, except you're no a Scientologist . . . What did you say again? I cannae remember.'

Soon I've dumped my coat in the bedroom and I'm mangling lemons with a blunt knife, having been taken on as a bartender, while Nadine, Tracy and Eleanor (a very drunk, tall and skinny person with a thick brown fringe that goes halfway down to her nose) gossip about people they know. The latest scandal is that Caroline is a bitch, Alex spreads sexual diseases, and Eleanor is angry with her tutor, who recently rejected her suggestion of a ten foot by ten foot painting of a fallen Eighties celebrity.

'I said to him, the scale and detail of it is intended as a comment on how obscure Corey Haim has become, as well as the nature of celebrity. I mean, the guy's selling his teeth on eBay. How bad can it get? And so Tony says' – she adopts a posh Edinburgh brogue – '"I HARDLY think that someone so profoundly obscure is worth wasting paint on." I mean, that's the fucking point! What a dick . . .'

I don't even care that I don't know them, or understand what they're talking about. This is just like being at home, but without the Led Zep and the old people.

Tracy and Eleanor are particularly attentive, while Nadine hangs back, watching me closely but without malice, occasionally asking me where I got my dress, or what kind of clothes I make. Elsewhere, Alice's favourite squeaky bedspring music, angular art school rock played by moody boys with wonky haircuts, is blaring out of the living room. It's not so bad – not my kind of thing, but quite adventurous, really. Better than the music in my house, anyway. Lorna buys those supermarket CD compilations called *Careless Love* and *Acoustic Rock Anthems* and puts them on repeat until they lodge in my head all day long.

'Cheers, Evie,' says Nadine, when the cocktail is satisfactorily mixed. She looks at me over the glass, and I notice that her luxuriantly fringed eyes are an exotic violet colour that I've never encountered in the Kirkness gene pool. She's very beautiful, an Audrey, or a young Elizabeth Taylor, all poise and alabaster skin.

I clink glasses and take a sip of the sour–sweet mixture, which tastes great. I feel rather pleased with myself. These people seem nice, sophisticated but not snobs – not like the fashion people at college, who despite being nineteen-year-olds from Kilmarnock and East Kilbride seem to think they're superstars already, nurturing drug addictions, having hissyfits, sucking in their cheeks. With every sip, I can feel my inhibitions gleefully sliding away.

'Better make another batch, though, eh?' says skinny Eleanor. 'Just to be on the safe side. Or, hey, let's make our own signature beverage. Evie, what's your favourite kind of booze?'

'Ooh, I dunno. I haven't really got one. Let's say . . . whisky.'

'Oh Mickey,' breathes Tracy, who has cut the top off some lemons and is sporting them as nipples under her dress. 'I am erect.'

Mickey, who has appeared holding a bottle of beer, mooches into view, still looking like he just got out of bed.

'Hi, Mick! Look at the state of you,' Nadine says, reaching her hand out to ruffle his hair. 'Don't you have a tuxedo?' He gives her a wry smile and she throws one back at him.

'What are you witches brewing?' he croaks, looking at me. I feel instantly unable to function and try to hide my bright pink cheeks in my cocktail glass.

'We're making our own drink. It will be the best drink known to humanity,' says Eleanor, pouring half a pint of Jack Daniels into a blender. 'What goes with whisky?'

'Lemons,' says Tracy, fondling her ends and prancing about.

We watch in mild horror as Eleanor mixes whisky with orange juice, own-brand cola, more Cointreau, lemon juice and a shot (or seven) of vodka. Mickey stands next to me, a giant next to a shuddering wee mouse. I'm so shaken and stirred that I simultaneously want to stand here for ever and get as far away from him as possible.

'How do you know Alice again?' he asks casually, flipping the top off a new bottle of beer.

'Oh, er, I came to see the flat. The spare room.'

'Oh yeah, I remember. So how come you didn't move in?' He smiles pleasantly.

My mind, which isn't exactly working on full power anyway, goes completely blank. Something to do with puncture repair kits in the hall.

'Check it out!' shrieks Eleanor, holding up a jug of swamp water. 'It's called Keef's Teef. It's sheer rock-and-roll badness. Drink it and you will turn into a rock monster!'

Everyone reluctantly takes a sip of the sludgy brown liquid and makes the same tortured expressions.

'Cor, that's magic,' says Tracy, taking another gulp. 'It's like raw sewage.'

'Alice says you're a fashion designer,' Mickey says, as we drink the deadly stuff. My entire body is humming with toxins and a kind of fiendish excitement, but I hope I look like I'm keeping it together.

'Not really. I've just started a fashion course. At MetroTech. I think it might be a bit rubbish, to tell you the truth.'

Mickey asks why, and I start wittering about Duncan and his Diva belt, and Big Bird in Space. He seems to think it's funny (although he could be humouring me). We manage to have something resembling a sparkling conversation, even though his arm is brushing against mine and distracting me immensely, and the drunken weird buzzing in my head is making me want to do things that are quite out of character for a wee girl from Kirkness. We go to sit in the hall, on the thread-bare carpet near a dusty phone socket surrounded by crumpled take-out menus and discarded items of clothing. Mickey tells me he's an English literature student and has vague desires to be a writer, he's even written a novel, although it's been rejected so much he's thinking of giving up. Even though I ask, he won't tell me what it's about. Instead he tells me where it's set, a weather-beaten village on the wild north-east coast, isolated and forgotten, with one school and leaking council housing and too many rough pubs.

'I used to live somewhere a bit like it,' he says, quietly. 'It was a real shithole. Pubs full of drunk sectarian psychos, shit football team, unemployed alkie shipyard workers and fights and in-breeding. The usual stuff.' He smiles. 'Terribly gritty.' He rolls his eyes and yawns apologetically, a picture of stoned procrastination, but tonight that suits me just fine.

'Where are you from?' he asks.

I think about my village – chocolate-box pretty, with artists instead of shipyard workers. The only rogue element is Teresa and her gold Argos finery, a testament to inbreeding if there ever was one.

'Kirkness.'

'Fancy.'

'Not really. Everyone's a lunatic.'

He raises one eyebrow and looks around the room.

'So you came here to get away from lunatics?' he drawls, incredulously.

We talk about the party and make fun of people. I feel like I could listen to him all night – his voice is quiet and I have to lean right in to hear him, while all around us, the festivities go on. Mickey seems like the only real thing in here. Everything else appears fabricated and vaguely surreal – a girl with an inflatable hammer passes by, and once Alice looms up, curls dangling, and asks 'Are you having fun?', giving me an exaggerated comic book wink, which makes me feel vaguely ashamed. I'm surprised at Alice's transformation. She seems so grown up, a mischievous glint in her eye, circulating gracefully and throwing her pale, stick-thin arms around the shoulders of her friends. There's no trace of the threadbare art student tonight. All the while, Mickey is stuck to my side, his close proximity making it impossible to concentrate on anything for very long. Or it could be the whisky. He tells me that he doesn't like anyone at university and he hasn't done any work for about a month, which makes me feel better about my unpromising start in Further Education. I tell him about Lorna and her mop freakout and he's horrified.

'Shall we go for a smoke?' Mickey eventually asks me. I don't take drugs, I'm about to say, but then it occurs to me that I would probably climb onto the roof in a chicken costume if he asked me.

'Sure,' I find myself saying, as if I do it every day.

'Have you got any fags?'

'Er, yes, I do, hang on,' I twitter, scrambling to get up and wobbling slightly.

He puts his hand on my ankle to steady me and smiles and I curse myself for not being cooler. I go into Alice's bedroom, where the coats are, and fumble in the pocket of my damp, sticky coat for the cigarettes, which feel dense and foreign in my hand. He follows me in there, inevitably, I suppose, and sits down on the bed with a tin and some Rizlas. It feels strange to be in Alice's room, with all her personal stuff. An antique dressing table is covered in objects – hairbrushes, make-up, a torch, a Chinese take-away carton customized with paper flowers and used as a jewellery box. On the glittery green walls that are, come to think of it, very much like a drag queen's eyeshadow, there's a black, white and red poster for something called the Modern Institute, the rest of it is in German. Elsewhere is a litter of postcards and photobooth strips, while polystyrene letters spelling out the word 'LOVE' hover boldly, and somewhat embarrassingly, over the bed.

'Is it OK to be in here?' I ask, ripping off the fiddly seal on the cigarette packet. My fingers feel big and useless, my whole body has happily collapsed into a kind of debauched floppiness. Somewhere there's a voice in my head screaming 'What the hell are you doing?' but it seems very far away and about as relevant as a passing car or a shout from the street. Mickey is lighting a tiny block of resin, engaged in the ritual of making a joint. I've seen it a million times before, no big deal, but I can't help feeling as if I'm on the verge of being corrupted; an innocent in a 1920s opium den.

'Me and Alice are old friends,' Mickey volunteers. 'We went to school together. She's brilliant. She's the sort of person who seems to be able to make things happen. Like Alice in Wonderland.'

'I just want to be a seamstress,' I murmur.

'Seamstress?' repeats Mickey, trying the word on for size. When he says it, it does seem preposterously old-fashioned and unimaginative, bringing to mind a spindly middle-aged woman, following instructions and pleasing others, seen and not heard. 'I can't really see it myself. I can see you in Paris, designing your collection, kicking the arse of some poor little assistant. Sitting at a pavement café with a poodle in your handbag.' He smirks. 'Called Fifi.'

I pretend I'm cross at this character assassination, but my stomach flips – apart from the poodle, I feel like he's been reading my diary.

'Excuse me?'

'Then when you're famous, maybe you can bail me out when I'm half dead from consumption and coughing up blood on my typewriter,' he adds, picturesquely. 'Anyway,' he continues, looking a bit shamefaced, 'Alice thinks you're a good designer. She thinks you're destined for great things.'

'Really? Oh . . . I don't know.'

I'm embarrassed again at Alice's admiration. It was only a skirt, nothing special. I just copied it from a pattern and changed a few things, that's all. He takes a cigarette from me and splits it open with his thumbnail. When he passes the spliff to me, I inhale, recalling nights at the bus stop smoking stolen fags with Mona, but this tastes less bitter, more like a blast of cool air. An image of me and Mickey having a baguette fight on the banks of the Seine creeps unexpectedly into my mind. Must be the drugs.

We sit there for what seems like ages. I tell him about my parents and their penchant for parties and Led Zep. He remembers my mum from Ikea, which makes me blush. 'She seemed pretty cool,' he says. (Oh well, nobody's perfect.) His parents are divorced, not into drugs or Seventies rock music. His mum still lives in the hellish, non-fictional town he grew up in, his dad moved to London when he was five and is a meteorologist. Not a very nice one, apparently. 'He's got a cold front,' he jokes bitterly, and I laugh even though it's not really meant to be funny. Mind you, at the moment I would laugh at a hat stand. But he doesn't seem to care.

The party carries on next door, its bumps and shrieks and music are soothing and continuous. When I was a kid I would go to sleep with those noises rumbling on downstairs, knowing I was safe.

I'm so tired all of a sudden and don't know how I can possibly move to ever go home. All I know is, I don't want a repeat of the stuck-key incident – dealing with Lorna after a few glasses of wine is one thing, after this, I couldn't promise not to pass out in her wardrobe. The thought of her with her mop, barging in and seeing this, makes me want to giggle.

'Are you all right?' He smiles, his gaze falling to my lips.

'I think so,' I say. My head is spinning. The green walls swell around us, and the bed is like a creaking ship, adrift somewhere, in no real hurry to reach land. The last thing I remember is him kissing me and the zip of someone's coat digging into my back.

Step Seven – Biased

If you cut your dress 'on the bias', you make a cut at a forty-five degree angle to the 'grain' of the fabric. This can be a tricky manoeuvre for a beginner, but the bias produces such stunning and unusual results that it will soon bowl you over.

The first thing I notice is sickly flesh-coloured and mushroom paint, daubed onto woodchip wallpaper. It's dark in here, but not night – it feels really absurdly late in the day – lunchtime? Three o'clock? I close my eyes again and I can hear the sound of breathing, but the breathing doesn't match the rhythm of my own. I'm in a bed, a strange bed, a single bed, not my bed; a substantially weighty arm, not mine either, is heavily draped across me, crushing my ribs. Oh dear.

Strangely, my immediate thought is for Lorna, who is probably rushing around the flat spraying things and wondering why I haven't come out of my room. Staying out all night will be a black, black mark against me. I'm sure it will probably contravene Clauses 1–42, Sub-clause 7, Paragraph B in the Lorna handbook and may involve an official warning and a smack in the face with a tea towel. My second thought is that, thankfully, I'm still wearing clothes, and that me and whoever is with me (please God let it be Mickey otherwise I'm going to have to book into a convent) are on the bed, rather than in it. The arm moves, and I freeze, then settles back and rests on my hip. My body, which is barely alive, likes that, but my head is desperately trying to recall what happened last night, snatching at scraps of information like a mechanical hand in a fairground grabbing at a bucket of stuffed toys. What did I do? I see an image of me dancing with Alice, jumping up and down on the threadbare sofa to the music, but that seems very unlikely. I remember Mickey and me on the coats (so clichéd, Jesus), smoking, kissing, but everything else is blackness.

Oh God, I've got to get out of here. I move the arm and try to wriggle free, but getting out of the tiny bed would be impossible without going on a hiking expedition over Mickey's mountainous frame. His hair has fallen into his face and he's looking annoyingly pretty for an unconscious stranger who needs a shave. The sight of his collarbone under his T-shirt is almost enough to make me stay in this godforsaken room all day. I shouldn't be here. I'm a nice girl. Edith wouldn't do this sort of thing.

'Mickey?' I whisper. I shake him, starting to get annoyed, but he doesn't respond. Wake up, you big lumbering bastard. 'Mickey – I need to go home. Move!'

He comes to, faintly annoyed, but when he sees me, a slow grin crawls across his face.

'Evgeniya, you little minx,' he says saucily, pulling me back to him so my face is in his neck. I fight to lift my head.

The barbed, theatrical sound of my real name jars in my ear. What else have I revealed?

'Why am I a minx?' I ask, struggling to sit up. Something feels wrong with my dress, like it's inside out and back to front.

'You just are . . .' he murmurs, falling back into sleep.

'Wake up! I need to know. I can't remember anything. Please, Mickey – just tell me, OK?' I sound desperate. The thought of scuttling out of here in the cold light of day, facing Lorna, and then trying to locate a morning-after pill brings tears to my eyes. What have I become?

'Shhh, it's fine,' says Mickey, suddenly wide awake. 'You were having a good time, that's all.'

'What kind of a good time? Did we . . . ? You know . . . on the coats?'

'Don't you remember?' he asks, looking a bit put out. 'Well, nothing happened. Nothing like that anyway, don't worry. It was fun though,' he recounts, his eyes closing again, looking happy to relive it. I feel temporarily annoyed that I can't remember it.

'Then what did I do?'

'You dragged me into the living room for a dance, and you kept saying, "I hate Acoustic Anthems, I wanna hear some squeaky bedsprings." Nobody knew what you were talking about, but you did this funny chicken dance and everyone thought you were hilarious. Then you showed James Warner your bra and told him it was an antique, then you and Alice did karaoke to "Since You've Been Gone", and you spent the rest of the evening playing the Rizla game with the witches from the kitchen. You were Napoleon. You ended up miming it, because Tracy couldn't guess it, and then I had to put you to bed because you passed out.' Tracy, with the white stripe in her hair, looms up in my mind like a weird sprite.

I rub my eye and try to digest it all. Not the worst news ever, but not the best. So undignified! I showed James Warner my bra, for God's sake.

'Who's James Warner?' I ask.

'Huh? He's erm, he's a friend of Alice's. He's in that band—'

He says a name I've vaguely heard of but can't place.

'Anything else I should know?'

'You're a minx,' he says, before jumping on me again.

'Nyaaaah,' I say, wrestling myself out of his grip. I didn't come here to get embroiled in all this nonsense. My life seems hopelessly muddled – a messy ball of string with no end to get hold of. 'I'm just going to get cleaned up and go home.'

'C'mon, stay . . .' he wheedles, but I manage to leave the bed and sneak into the hallway. The floor is disgusting and I wish I'd put on shoes, but I correctly locate the bathroom and lock the door. The grimy mirror confirms my worst fears – panda eyes, hair frizzed and clumpy, and a strange rash around my mouth, as if I'm in the early stages of German measles.

I look like a very low-priced Sixties hooker. I wash my face furiously, but there's no towel and no toilet paper. Then I notice the stuffed marmot, grinning viciously from its mount above the sink. I suddenly see how seedy and disgusting it all is. The sink is encrusted with the residue from different coloured soaps throughout the ages – coral, pink, slime green – and the bath is ringed with brown muck. I can't believe I came here through choice, after rejecting it so strongly before. What was I doing? Hanging around with these people – artists, writers, scenesters – all style and no substance, people with no sense of responsibility, people who are so into their oh-so-creative ideas that they can't wash a sink or clean a bath or go in to college on time. It's so depressingly familiar, I wouldn't be surprised if I bumped into my old friend Victor McDougall on my way out. I don't want to be here. This isn't me. Last night I became something else – a monster, an arty exhibitionist. I became one of them. Who could have thought that a carton of ice cream could have so much to answer for?

Back in the bedroom, which is airless and stuffy, I put on my shoes and Mickey watches me. The coat is still in Alice's room, but I'm damned if I'm going in there and getting it now – I'll go to a charity shop and buy another one.

'I've got to go,' I say, keeping my head down. Mickey lies there, looking as if he'll lie there all day, thinking about a novel that'll never get published, smoking hash. I feel twitchy and frustrated – everything in the flat now represents something I want to get away from.

UTOPIA, the vomit mural says, letters dripping down the wall like rotten custard.

'What's the matter?' he asks, but I don't want to look at him. I'm disgusted with myself for doing this. I think of my abandoned box file, Plan A, and how far I've deviated from my original goals. I must stick to what I think is right. Anyway, it's not like Mickey will be lost without me. This is just a bit of fun for him – he probably does this with a different girl every week. I think of Alice's comment when I met her on the street that night – 'He's all right – he's always all right.' He'll be all right.

'I've just got something to do for college,' I mutter, stumbling over a cardboard box marked 'GINA'S STUFF'.

'Careful.'

'Say thanks to Alice for a great party,' I announce. I'm about to add 'and it was nice to meet you', but stop myself.

'Don't be a stranger,' he says with a smile, and all my blood vessels and ventricles and cells have a wee celebratory dance, which I cut short by tugging hard at my fringe and adjusting my dress.

I walk out of there, down the wide, dusty stairs, and wrestle open the Yale, dragging the door through the pile of flyers and free newspapers. It's actually earlier than I thought, a blank canvas of a day with low clouds and no wind, so I set off back to Lorna's, hoping that I can get in silently and disappear off to my bed. This time the key slides easily into the lock, and when I come creeping through the door, the flat, in contrast to Alice's, is a calm and serene sanctuary. Nothing debauched could happen here. In my room, the white bed and the glossy paintwork soothe me. Although it's an effort, I take off my dress and fold it up into a neat rectangle; then attempt to drift off to sleep, images from last night occasionally nudging me awake.

'You shouldn't just create,' says odious Neil, who today is wearing a banana-coloured T-shirt that says 'Berlin Angels 1983' and a Tweety Pie headband. 'You should innovate. I totally agree with Duncan. I hate all those cosy designers who make clothes for unadventurous women with money, women who think glamour equals smart tailoring and silky evening dresses and all that shite. Push the envelope, man – bring in new shapes, new styles, new ways of looking at the body. I want to make a piece of clothing that people remember for decades, like the puffball skirt.'

'Maybe women want to look good,' I point out, my voice sounding too high and squeaky. 'Maybe they don't want to wear impractical clothes that make them look ridiculous.'

Neil throws me a sneer. 'Practical! Who cares about that? This is fashion, sweetie – pure haute – let the high street water it down. We're here to push things forward.'

Only tossers say things like 'pure haute'. I grind my back teeth.

'Why can't you make something new and exciting that's also wearable?' I snap, wanting to prove him wrong. His sallow skinniness and preference for wearing yellow make him look weak and liverish, as if he's in the final stages of a terrible disease. Even so, it's not enough to make me feel sorry for him.

'You can't make anything new and exciting if you're stuck in a rut, following the rules. You can't be pioneering and play it safe at the same time.'

'Yeah, but . . .'

Irritatingly, Neil is not as stupid as he looks, and I can't find my comeback. Knowing he's won, he flips open his mobile and starts talking loudly to someone called Barry about when he can 'fit him in'. Personally, I'd like to fit him into a neon-yellow jet pack and fire him off the roof.

We're sitting in the canteen, a mass of tracksuits and cold chips and plastic mouldings. I suck on a carton of orange juice, wondering whether I could suck hard enough to give myself a frontal lobotomy. It's Monday, and Lorna seemed not to suspect that I'd stayed out all night, assuming I was in my room. I spent Saturday gladly avoiding her and Sunday on the dress, making sure everything was going right with it. I bound the seams and covered up any raw edges, and switched off the foot pedal at 7 p.m., in observance of the sewing-machine curfew. On Sunday nights Lorna likes to watch an insipid drama set in the Yorkshire Dales or the Lake District, which I usually run a mile from, but this time the green scenery and undemanding situations were like ointment. This morning I felt fine, my night of shame cancelled out. Next to me, Flossy is twitching. She reeks of sweet perfume, which is intended to disguise the smell of booze leaking from her pores, but doesn't quite manage it. I don't want to sit near her, or have anything to do with that kind of thing, not now, but she's rapidly turning into a limpet. She seems to think I have access to the secrets of the universe or something, always asking me exhausting questions and following me around.

'I feel like shite,' she croaks. 'Last night we went to the Sub, and I had four double vodkas and a pint then I met this guy John who said he owned this club, what was it called . . . Product? So we went up when the Sub closed and I was drinking margaritas I think and someone had some coke and the last thing I remember I was being sick in the toilet but then I must have started drinking again because I woke up in Paisley at this guy's flat.'

She shrugs, as if she's just recounted a quiet Sunday afternoon at home. I don't want to hear it. I just want to work. The 'funky' top still only exists in virtual form, and I better get to grips with the software soon or it'll never be born. Neil has already started cutting out his pattern. Meanwhile, I'm sure that Duncan is finding my technical difficulties hilarious. What's more, we've got a group project to do in tandem with this – an exercise in marketing and promotion that will probably involve shame and humiliation on a devastating scale. I'm dreading that too.

'See you later,' Flossy mumbles, suddenly bolting for the toilet.

Neil leaves almost immediately, probably worried that he'll catch some kind of retro Sixties infection from me, but I stay, guarding the pile of debris on the table. I'm just about to start tidying up, delaying the inevitable trip back up to the 386th floor, when my mobile goes. It's Lorna.

My stomach falls. Has my ice-cream writing miraculously appeared on the counter like the face of Mother Teresa on a bread roll, or Jesus in the seeds of a tomato?

'Hello?'

'Hi!' she trills. 'How are you?'

'Oh, er, fine thanks.'

'Listen, Evie, Charlie isn't coming down next weekend because he's got a golf tournament, so I wondered whether you'd like to go on that shopping trip we talked about?'

I look at the picture of rolling hills on Neil's discarded bottle of water, temporarily stupefied. What shopping trip? Oh yes, she was going to take me on a grand tour to help me get over the horrors of Kirkness Fashions. (Poor Mrs Morrison – I should give her a ring and ask her how it's going.) But judging by the various indiscretions I've committed over the last couple of weeks, I didn't think that was ever going to happen.

'Yeah, that'd be great,' I say, glad that Charlie isn't coming, and grateful to have something to do.

'Brilliant!' she whoops, and I'm surprised at her enthusiasm. 'See you later. And don't worry about dinner tonight – I'll cook!'

Well I never.

I hike upstairs, past the vending machines and the leering guys, at least knowing I have one friend in town.

'Come in! It's been so long!' says Duncan when I get

there, and I slide into my seat. I don't know why he doesn't just make me stand in a corner in a dunce cap, occasionally throwing things at me. Jezebel, who has shaved off her long gypsy locks over the weekend and now looks like a furious Buddhist, gives me a piercing look, as if I've personally offended her.

I type in my password and click on my project. My design, which I could have drawn in about three minutes by hand but has taken nearly a week using this infuriating software, is looking particularly uninspiring. What's more, its 'funkiness' is debatable. It's turning out to be a 1960s version of a 1920s Chinese Mao jacket, a long, flowing, high-collared one-piece tunic with a brocade trim, which is supposed to be worn with wide trousers. The sleeves are bell shaped and made of a thin, transparent material. I once saw a film set in the Twenties, featuring a very glamorous lady wearing something similar, prior to being gunned down by some gangsters. I get the feeling that this rag-bag of styles and decades might be just as doomed.

'How are you getting on, Mary?' Duncan caws, breathing post-lunch beeriness in my general direction. 'Hmmm. Why don't you lop off those sleeves and live a little?' he asks. 'Girls like to show a bit of flesh these days, you know.'

I hold my breath and hope he goes away.

'Just a suggestion.'

He walks off, ready to torment someone else.

'By the way, children, there's the small matter of your group marketing project,' Duncan announces to the class, as I squint unhappily at my computer screen.

'It's not a big deal, but you've got to work together and come up with a brand for your respective projects. I'm putting you into threes and you have to pitch it to me for ten minutes. We want a logo, an ethos and a direction for the future. This is about being able to work as a team and debate ideas, as well as to visualize and promote your work in the wider world.'

I sigh heavily.

'What will probably be most challenging is that you will have to work with people whose ideas are unlike yours. It's a good process and teaches us about compromise.' I pretend to look idly round the room and see that he's eyeballing me. I turn away. 'So here are your groups.'

I tense up. I bet he puts me with Neil, I bet he puts me with Neil . . . 'Andrea, John, Daniel . . .' he drones, 'Carmen, David, Helena.'

'Evie . . . Flossy . . .' he booms, pausing for effect, his finger hovering in mid air. Together, our names sound fluffy and harmless, dolls or teddy bears at a tea party, but I know there's going to be one uninvited guest who's going to spoil it all . . . come on, you bastard, put me out of my misery . . .

'. . . and Jezebel.'

Thought as much. Across the bank of CAD monitors, Jezebel's head twitches and she turns round to me, her dark eyes flaring with resentment. For a minute I wish it had been Neil. Flossy isn't even here to hear the news – she's probably still got her head in the toilet. This is going to be an unmitigated disaster. Duncan, meanwhile, finishes his not-so-random selection and returns to looking nice and pleased with himself in his wee corner, chewing at his thumbnail and staring out of the window.

Just to spite him I spend the rest of the afternoon deliberately making the sleeves of my tunic even wider and more voluminous. (Why not experiment with your first project anyway – it's all about trial and error, surely?) I save it and send it to the colour printer in the corner, where, due to some ink cartridge error, it comes out as a black, unrecognizable stain.

I'm in a chain store with Lorna, a not very interesting one, full of plain (mostly black) work clothes and a few sparkly tops. I wish I was at a proper second-hand shop or a jumble sale – not knowing what you're going to find, and hoping to rescue a Thirties evening dress from behind a mass of old coats, or a pair of wrinkled patent leather winklepickers from a basket of dead men's ties. I yawn and finger a pair of a drab trousers made from acrylic mix.

'Ooh, that's nice,' says Lorna, picking out a forgettable black skirt. 'But I don't need a skirt, I need some shoes – let's go.'

'OK.'

I follow Lorna, fainting with hunger. Before we left the house she prepared a list of possible shops for us to go to, and I figured it'd be safer to let her be in control. So far, we've looked at bras in Marks and Spencer for longer than I've ever looked at anything, she's trawled through River Island with a fine tooth comb, distractedly asking my opinion on some jeans, and she's spent £99.99 on a power suit for college. But she's making me feel welcome, which is good. I think she must be trying to make an effort with me. Perhaps she's lonely. After all, the only people who phone the house seem to be her parents and Charlie. And unless she's got an army of friends from college who haven't appeared yet, she might need me as much as I need her.

'I need some black shoes,' she says. 'Or boots. Oh look at that pendant!'

We duck into an arcade and stop in front of a dazzling array of rings and gemstones of every kind, some revolving around on their own miniature podiums like game-show prizes. Wee black-and-white cubes show astronomical prices, thin whips of gold are draped in varying sizes on cushioned stands, and Lorna is spell-bound, her eyes twinkling with greed and glitter.

'Do you want me to show you the wedding ring I think Charlie will be getting me?' she gasps. I nod. 'There,' she says, pointing at it with trembling fingers. It's enormous, a fat white gold band with diamonds embedded into it in the shape of a butterfly. It's ghastly – like something Mariah Carey might pick if she was forced to shop at Argos – but it sits on a plinth of its very own with a helpful caption reading '£18,000'.

'Could he afford that?' I ask, innocently. If golf caddying is Charlie's only source of income, then I doubt he's got eighteen grand to burn.

Lorna stiffens. 'Of course he could. What, you think he's poor or something?' she snaps, fixing me with a dark stare.

'No, not at all, I don't—'

'Charlie's father owns a very successful car hire company and he's going to be the boss when he turns twenty-one,' she says, her mouth curling into a satisfied smirk.

'Oh, I see.'

'So he's going to get me that,' she adds with irritating smugness. For a second I feel like ramming her head through the window.

'Now – where were we? Oh yes, shoes. I saw this pair over here.'

We walk out of the arcade and into a downmarket shoe shop. While she deliberates between various shades of generic black heel, I look out of the window at the streams of people on the street. I've been here for a month and I still feel as if I just got off the bus. I wonder what's happening in Kirkness tonight – what dramas are waiting to unfold between Linda Appleby and Malcolm Chance, or Mona and Teresa. If there's not a party at our house, then Anton and Charlotte will probably be round at someone else's, having dinner and getting wasted and staggering up the beach. From nowhere, I get a pang of ridiculous nostalgia for the messy living room and its stained, dog-drool-covered furnishings, the sound of banging and the low whirr of the potter's wheel fighting each other for space.

'What do you think?' says Lorna, as if it's the second time she's had to ask. She waves a pair of nondescript shoes with a slim heel in my face.

'Very nice.'

'Do you have them in a size five?' she asks the assistant, rather snootily.

'God, the girls who work in here are so thick,' she huffs, wriggling her feet out of the shoes she's wearing, which look exactly like the ones she's about to buy. From the corner of my eye I see a boy through the window and something makes me look twice. It's Johnny, wearing his too-small leather jacket, his fringe in his face, practising his rock-and-roll swagger. I stare rigidly at a pair of brown sandals. The last thing I want is for Lorna to think I know a degenerate guy in a band – she would surely kick me out into the street in disgust. But just as he's checking his reflection in the window, he catches sight of me and presses his face and body against the glass, waving his arms in semaphore, his nose as compressed and round as a slice of banana.

'EVIE,' he says, in a muffled Dalek voice.

'Who is that?' Lorna asks, pointedly.

'I don't know,' I say, fighting back a smile. How could anyone be so completely exhibitionist as to hump the front of a shoe shop?

Go away, I mouth, furiously, but this just makes Johnny act up more.

'We're playing tonight! Come and see us! Temperance Hotel!' he booms.

'He seems to know you,' Lorna adds suspiciously.

'He might have me mixed up with someone else,' I say.

'Called Evie? Who is he?'

'I really don't know . . . I've ever seen him before . . .'

I mumble, feeling slightly treacherous. Poor Johnny. He never did me any harm. 'Lots of people look like me. Anyway, I don't think he said Evie. I think he said, "EEEEE!"'

I turn away from the window and hope to God he doesn't come into the shop. Lorna is thankfully too preoccupied with shoes to give Johnny much thought, and when I turn back, I note with some relief that he's disappeared.

'Are these a size five?' she asks the assistant, a sixteen-year-old who probably makes the minimum wage and couldn't afford anything in this shop. The assistant checks.

'Oh sorry, they're a six . . .' she begins, smiling. 'I'll just . . .'

There's a dreadful pause, and a cold viciousness descends on Lorna that takes me right back to the Night of the Dripping Mop.

'Can't you do your job properly?' she storms, folding her arms like a spoiled child. 'I mean, the word "five" sounds nothing like "six", does it?'

The assistant says nothing, holding a shoe uselessly in mid air.

'I said five, didn't I? Are you deaf?'

I move back from the scene, trying to disassociate myself from the brattish Lorna, who seems to have morphed into a horrendous diva. The assistant looks ready to cry.

'You know what? Forget it. Just forget it,' she says, putting her shoes back on and getting ready to flounce out. 'Due to your complete incompetence, you have just lost a customer.' Lorna breezes past me in a gust of citrus shampoo, expecting me to follow slavishly behind.

'I'm really sorry about her,' I whisper, before I go. 'I think she might have some issues.'

The assistant, whose badge says 'Kerry', straightens herself up and gives me a defiant look.

'She's a bitch,' she says, matter-of-factly, and walks away.

Back in the flat, I sit on my bed in silence, watching the light fade. The nights are drawing in, but the tail end of summer is still hanging around, forming a stagnant space between the seasons. In the bathroom, Lorna is embarking on one of her marathon bubble baths. I'm full of food – we had a late lunch in a soulless restaurant in an overpriced shopping mall surrounded by girls like Lorna, with caramel-coloured hair streaked with blond and families of different-sized carrier bags and a high opinion of themselves – but I still feel empty. By way of explanation for her behaviour in the shoe shop, Lorna told me about her management training, and how it's very important to instil high standards in staff by having zero tolerance for slackness. She said it was a test of the girl's ability to deal with customers. I didn't like to point out that she doesn't even work there.

I get my Plan A box file out and leaf through its disjointed contents, as if to remind myself what I'm doing here. I don't know what I'm looking for – some proof of my aims, some indication that I'm on the right track, but all I can find is a bunch of maps and leaflets advertising the Scotland Street School and the Lighthouse and other places I have yet to set foot in. Half of it seems to be missing (did I throw some of it out?) and the life I so meticulously planned doesn't seem remotely reminiscent of the life I've ended up with. What's the solution? I close the file, none the wiser.

As for Lorna, I can't decide whether to pity her, feel grateful for what she's done for me, or drive a stake through her heart. She certainly isn't the ally I thought she was. Her moods are terrifying – to cross her would surely mean death. But then she sometimes seems to want to be my friend so badly, and I feel sorry for her, alone watching TV every night.

A bit of work might cheer me up. According to my prospectus, by the end of term we have to complete a personal project that's apparently a really big deal, and could mean the chop if we mess it up. I'll prove Duncan and Neil wrong – women want perfection, not puffballs. My funky top might be heading towards the fashion graveyard before it's even been started, but how can Duncan mark me down if I turn in something perfect that would make everyone who wears it feel great?

I take the dark scarlet material and start to finish the neckline, but three minutes in and Lorna pipes up, just as I've reached a tricky bit.

'Evie!' she trills from the bathroom. 'Can you keep it down, please? I'm trying to relax.'

The interruption startles me, and I accidentally push my foot down on the pedal: the needle zigzags all over the delicate satin. Shit shit shit! Bitch bitch bitch! I can feel my blood pressure flying through the roof. Can't she just mind her own business? What does she need to relax for? As far as I can see she does bugger all apart from wallow about in her knickers all night every night, painting her prissy wee toenails and indulging herself and talking about her stupid wedding to that big arrogant idiot. I fling myself on the bed, and claw at the covers with my nails. My stomach feels leaden, I want to cry, I want to kick the door in. I want to go home.

I want to go home, where people let you use your sewing machine and don't mind if you don't leave your shoes at a perfect right angle to the wall when you come in. But that would be defeat, and soon I would be stomping around Kirkness in the same pathetic state. I go to the drawer and take out Soggy, my battered, chewed, flattened rabbit with more personality than Lorna could ever have, and clutch it to my chest. For good measure, I throw a cotton reel on the floor and don't bother to pick it up. Crazy! Oh, let it lie there, contravening Clause 27 of the Lorna Code – no personal possessions to be left on the floor. Poo to you.

After my temper tantrum, I feel chastened, glad that Lorna didn't witness it. Instead of flinging myself about with my wee bunny rabbit like a spoilt child, I decide to take the night into my own hands. I go to the wardrobe and select the most ill-conceived outfit I can think of. I put on a charity shop floral skirt that I trimmed with lace and match it with a fitted velvet jacket, a 'Come to Kirkness' T-shirt and a neckscarf. I put my hair into pigtails and wear knee-length socks and a pair of regulation school pumps. Pleasingly, I look like a deranged bag lady. The buzzing in my head is back, making me think about Alice and Mickey, Mickey who told me not to be a stranger. I try to stop it, but these thoughts are whizzing about like bees in a hive, busy busy busy. Whatever that night was, I suddenly want more, even though I know it probably won't do me any good, that it's much better to make sensible friends and concentrate on my career and responsibilities and getting my act together. After all, I don't want to be like my parents, growing cultures in the fridge, wearing jumpers with holes in them, putting sausages under the grill and leaving the house. But I can't live like this either.

I deliberately make lots of noise getting ready, throwing tubes of mascara noisily down on the table when I've finished with them, then opening drawers and slamming them shut. I can hear the delicate splish-splash of Lorna vacating the bath, presumably to give me a stern telling off about decibel levels. Sure enough, as I'm about to leave she pokes her towel-wrapped head round the bathroom door in a cloud of fragrant steam and glares at me.

'What are you doing?' she demands.

'Going out,' I tell her, simply.

'In that outfit?' she says, adopting an amused sneer. 'You're joking.'

'Have a nice night in, Lorna. I hope you enjoy *Location Location Location*!' I say, cheerily, and as I close it, the front door makes a satisfying smack.

* * *

The Temperance Hotel is on the first floor of a disused building, which is none too hygienic or structurally sound. It's entirely painted a deathly white, apart from the beams, which are encrusted in pigeon shit. The whole place is packed with bodies. What a bunch of oddballs. The crowd consists of young girls with blackened eyes and older types who look like they might run record labels or be vaguely important in some way. The guys are like Johnny or Mickey, leather-clad wasters or hippies with lumberjack beards, or skinny junior Bob Dylans with wiry hair and jumpy demeanours. Over in the corner is a guy with thick black hair and a yellow coat that flares brightly in the dim light. Everyone seems to be wildly drunk, talking loudly like a bunch of chattering chipmunks. The backdrop of the stage (which isn't a stage at all, just a tiny area strewn with musical equipment) is a large grubby sheet with 'TEMPERANCE IS A VIRTUE' daubed onto it. It's like something Andy Warhol might have concocted when he wasn't really concentrating – completely home-made and falling apart. I spy Johnny by the bar, talking to someone who looks oddly familiar. In this environment he seems to make sense – a dark streak of nothing crowned with a mop of greasy hair and a confident stance that doesn't quite disguise his nerves. Further away to his side a gaggle of girls, obviously dying to speak to him but too shy, are standing looking vacantly outwards, twizzling straws in half-empty plastic cups.

'Hi, Johnny,' I say, feeling bold.

'Well, if it isn't Little Miss Prim herself,' he says in

his goofy high voice, propping a pointy elbow onto the bar.

'Hey,' says the other one, a lank blond-haired boy who looks like a Roman soldier, but is dressed in the snazzy suit jacket of a snooker player or a bingo caller. He seems a bit over-friendly for a stranger, his pale eyes lingering too long over me.

'Jamesy, this is the one I was telling you about – Evie.'

'Yeah, I know Evie.' He smiles, and I realize he's James Warner, and he's seen my bra. Oh God. I try to look somewhere else, hoping to catch the eye of the barman, but he's busy pouring a pint in slow motion, gazing off into the distance.

Johnny asks James how he knows me and he mutters something, to which Johnny replies, 'No shit!'

Suddenly Johnny is right with me, hot leathery arm slithering around my shoulder, humming with gossipy glee.

'You been showing your bra off at Alice White's party? I don't believe it. I can't believe you'd do such a thing. Man, I knew it – lib-er-teeeeeeen!'

'Shut up, Johnny. I was just drunk, that's all.'

'Bet you were. So what were you doing with that shiny girlie girl at that loser-ass shoe shop? I saw you pretending you didn't know me.'

'She's my friend,' I say, doubting the words as soon as they exit my mouth. I'm distracted by the fact that Johnny is behaving like an annoying little brother after too much Sunny Delight and next door to him there's a guy who seems to think my bra is public property.

'She ain't no friend of yours,' Johnny announces. 'She's the devil in disguise, honey.'

'Oh stop talking like you're American,' I snap, losing patience with his antics. 'And there's no such word as loser-ass,' I add, about to call to the barman just as he disappears for ever to change a barrel.

'HA!' Johnny squeals. 'I love you, Evie. You're a schoolteacher gone BAAAD.' He wraps his arms around me and picks me up, twirling me about.

'Get off!'

'You know, when I'm famous, you'll want me,' he says, plonking me down. 'But I'll be too busy with supermodels to give you the time of day. Hey, watch out for this song I wrote. Think ya gonna like it!' He points at me and does a stupid Wild West manoeuvre, which involves whirling his thumbs and forefinger around and sticking them in his belt. As he does so, he stumbles and stands on the toe of one of the girls.

'Och, sorry,' he mutters, and I can't help but smile. The girl in question looks outraged until she realizes it's the guy from the band, then she goes all twinkly and starts giggling, holding onto his arm too long. The whole performance makes me feel immensely cheered.

'Catch ya later, Johnny.' I grin, and he waves and ambles away, limping as if he's twisted his ankle. What a dozy boy. Now the barman is back too. I order a beer in a plastic cup and stand at the side as the rest of Johnny's band trickle to the stage and start twiddling knobs on amps. The drummer is wearing a top hat and wraparound shades, blowing pink bubblegum bubbles at intermittent intervals with a stoned look on his face.

'All right, doll!' says a gruff voice. I peer through the murk to see a big girl advancing towards me, followed by a tall, skinny one with a long fringe. It takes me a minute to realize that it's Tracy, minus the white streak in her hair, and Eleanor, who out of a cocktail dress looks mannish and imposing, her wide shoulders made wider by a black-and-white-striped vest.

'Hello! I didn't think you'd be here!' Tracy says, plonking a kiss on my cheek, which almost makes me spill my drink. Eleanor peers towards the bar.

'What we having?' she says. 'But don't let her choose, for fuck's sake,' she says, gesturing towards me and raising an eyebrow.

'I'll have a pint of cider. Has Johnny's band been on yet?'

'No,' I say. 'In a minute. How do you know Johnny?'

'I'm puttin' the gig on, more fool me,' she says. 'And everyone knows Johnny. He's a wee bit of a handful. Actually, he's a total pain. But we love him. Our wee Johnny. When he's no being a dick, of course.' Tracy waves to someone across the room and sticks her finger to her ear in a 'call me' gesture, before giving them the Vicky sign and dissolving into cackles.

'That's Malky. Don't get involved with him – he's a tool!' she says, still smiling gaily. 'So, you recovered from the other night? Man, you sure can drink. Great impression of Napoleon, by the way. I never did history at school so you know, it really brought it all to life for me.'

I squirm, feeling awkward that everyone but me seems to be able to remember my ridiculous behaviour.

'I didn't do anything really bad, did I?'

'Nah. I'm only messing about.'

Tracy smiles, her large eyes creasing with kindly amusement. She's very glamorous and curvaceous, like a raven-haired burlesque model of the Fifties, with perfectly drawn red lips and a cleavage that you could probably lose your dinner in. On her bare shoulder is a tattoo of a mermaid with red hair, holding a chainsaw.

SKRRRRRREEEEEEEEEEEEEEEEEEEEEEEEEEEEE!!!!!

The piercing wail of Johnny's guitar cuts through the chatter, causing a few whoops and cheers. Someone bellows something loud but inaudible and a handful of people near the front snigger.

'Hello-ladies-and-gentlemen-we-are-Bottle-Rocket-ahhhh!' he announces, making sure his hair is just-so over his face and tweaking the mic. Next to him James Warner stands like a sentry, his bass slung low on his hips. The other member, aside from the loony drummer, is a girl with blond hair, who is holding a tambourine and looking as if she'd rather be anywhere else.

'One two three four!'

They launch into a lurching, twangy racket, punctuated by the rock moves of Johnny, who is flinging himself around as if he's lost control of his mind and gurning as if he's lost control of his bowels.

'Oh Stella Stella what you done to me?' he wails. 'My bed is wet and my woman won't talk to me!'

My mouth is buckling and I can't hold back a smile.

'They're great, aren't they?' Eleanor grins, holding two full pints. 'It's total genius.'

'Hmm,' considers Tracy, sarcastically scratching her

chin. 'If the words "rubbish" and "genius" were one and the same.'

The three-minute song clatters to a halt and Johnny is somewhere down on the floor, bathed in fresh sweat, violating his microphone cable and saying 'WOMAN!' over and over again while an unseen cheesy keyboard tinkles out what sounds like the theme to a gardening programme.

There is rapturous applause. I'm finding this all unbelievably amusing. I sip my pint and let the tiny bubbles dance around in my mouth.

'OK . . .' Johnny drawls, getting up. His lip is bleeding, which he ignores. 'This one's called "Little Miss Prim",' he says, pronouncing 'little' as 'liddle'. 'It's for you, Evie!'

I gulp and duck down.

'Whooo-hooo! Johnny's written you a SONG!' Eleanor and Tracy screech, shoving me and jumping up and down. 'My God, he's never written a song for me, not the whole time I've known him, the bastard,' Tracy snarls.

'You must have captivated him,' Eleanor adds, pretending to swoon.

'Go JOHNNY!' they both start chanting.

'Go Johnny!' I find myself yelling, swept along by the tide as he crashes headlong into another blundering, trashy 'masterpiece'. It seems to have a lot of words, this one, something about 'she likes the fashions' rhymed with 'hidden passions'. My toes are curling in my shoes.

'I can't believe this,' I squeal, utterly mortified. 'It's terrifying.'

‘What d’ye mean, doll? This is one of his best yet!’ booms Tracy, beside herself with laughter. ‘You know, this is gonnae go to number one.’

‘What’s he talking about? You’re not prim! How did you meet him anyway?’ asks Eleanor.

‘In a café,’ I shout over the din. ‘He told me I was a “firecracker”.’

‘Oh Jeeee-so!’ Tracy screams.

‘He said we were destined to meet and that it happened for a reason, and that I was just like him, and that I was a libertine.’

‘What did you say?’

‘I told him I wasn’t.’ I shrug.

‘Man, that’s the worst chat-up line I’ve ever heard,’ Tracy concludes. ‘Hey, Johnny! You’re a firecracker!’ she yells, but he doesn’t hear, too busy tipping his head back and pouting. He’s actually really good at the whole rock-star thing, a scrawny, charismatic sewer rat with no regard for his personal safety. At one point he climbs on top of a wobbly stack of amps and stands there, back to the audience, head tilted towards the rafters. People are taking pictures of him, the flashes bouncing off the back of his leather jacket. He turns, looks down for a split second, then hurls himself down into the scrum at the front, disappearing into a sea of outstretched arms. Eventually he reappears, jacket falling off one shoulder, grinning like a madman, ecstatic at being molested by gangs of giddy girls.

‘He’s such a show-off . . .’ Eleanor drawls, rolling her eyes and lighting a cigarette. ‘So, have you seen Mickey?’

'Er, no,' I say.

'He's in here somewhere.' Tracy winks, conspiratorially.

'Oh.' My chest tightens.

'Just saying.'

'Hmm.' I carry on watching Johnny, but he's lost a bit of his stardust. He's just a fuzzy silhouette, making knuckle-scraping monkey moves.

'I'm just going to the loo,' I say quietly and Tracy gives me a sideways glance.

I wander towards where I think the toilet is, and see him in the corner. There he is, arm draped over the side of a booth, talking closely with Nadine. She's all in black, purring, wearing pearls, of all things, and looking fabulously out of place. A muddle of feelings surface – lust, uncertainty, anxiety and what the hell is Nadine doing practically sitting on his knee? Perhaps they're going out and I've totally misjudged Mickey's intentions. Maybe he's a 1969er, a swapper of bodily fluids. Maybe his bedpost is so whittled away to nothing that it's just a tiny matchstick. *Don't be a stranger*, he said, with a twinkle. Perhaps he's said it a million times before.

He sees me, and I'm expecting that slow burn of a smile, but it doesn't come. My cheeks zinging, I decide to duck down the peeling stairwell to the toilet, a cupboard with raw brick walls and the sparsest of amenities. There are no mirrors, only a crappy, faded print of *The Hay Wain*, tacked clumsily to the wall and defaced with marker pen, and a leaking sink with handfuls of tissue clogging it up.

I hole myself up in a rickety cubicle with no lock, and try to figure out what's going on. There's a flurry of graffiti on the back of the toilet door, a tidal wave of hormones from people who think so-and-so is sexy or want to shag thingumabob from some band or other – everyone grabbing at a piece of someone else or wishing they could. All the while, Johnny's music booms through the thin ceiling, causing plaster to splutter onto the floor, and I can hear the words he's singing, if singing is the right word. It's not exactly Shakespeare, that's for sure, but it's naggingly insistent and unnervingly appropriate – 'Little Miss Prim, where are you going?'

I think I'd better go. Maybe I'm just too prim for all this. The image of Mickey and Nadine sitting there like some hot-shot rock-star couple is still stinging as I straighten myself up and make for the door. I brush fallen plaster off my T-shirt and leave the bathroom, wishing I had somewhere to go: a plan of some kind. I want to go home and make my dress and make something of myself, but that would be impossible with Lorna on the warpath. Racking my brains for other alternatives, I draw a blank.

'Evie? Are you leaving?'

Mickey's quiet voice barely carries down the vacant, booming stairway, but somehow it reaches my ears more effectively than if he had a megaphone.

I turn round and he looks at me, hands in pockets, hair everywhere, same pose as usual – as if he's slept in his clothes and is shambling to the kitchen to put the kettle on. His terminally laid-back demeanour irritates me, while also bringing on some kind of biological circus under my bag lady outfit – an extravaganza of backflips and somersaults and party poppers.

'I think so,' I mumble, hoping I seem detached and disinterested, cool about everything, like they are. But I can't resist it. 'How's Nadine?'

He mishears me.

'OK. How've you been?' he asks, awkwardly. Despite his relaxed posture, I notice that his face is pinched. He doesn't seem like the easygoing person I met at the party. Upstairs, Johnny's music has dissolved into random wails of deafening feedback.

'I have to go outside,' I say.

We stand on the street, opposite a fast food restaurant. Across the road someone is being sick.

'Did you like the song?' he asks, looking at his shoes.

'What? Oh. Yeah.' I giggle stupidly and my face turns crimson. 'I think Johnny might be a bit mad.'

'Yeah,' he says, flatly.

'How's your erm . . . book?' I ask, trying to pull myself together.

'Still not a bestseller.' He shrugs.

Silence. Faint retching from over the road.

Well, this is awkward. If he's written a book, why doesn't he know what to say?

I wonder what Mickey thinks of me now. I'm not the unbridled little minx I was at the party. I'm shy, sullen and sober, wearing a 'Come to Kirkness' T-shirt. Maybe Nadine is more his thing – cut-glass and glamorous and refined. A lady. If he ever finished his book (and it was any good), I could just see them at some literary awards dinner, him in a rented tux with his tie askew, Nadine playing Audrey Hepburn to his bumbling writer.

'I might go home,' I say.

'What, now?'

'Yeah . . . you know.'

'Evie! You missed the encore! Johnny fell off the amps and nearly broke his arm! Och sorry, were you two snoggin' or somethin'?' Tracy comes battering down the stairs, a flailing blur of black hair and tattoos.

'No,' I tell her.

Mickey clears his throat and stares off down the street. I fix my eyes on a piece of old chewing gum on the pavement.

'Anyway, c'mon – we're going to Maximo.' Tracy grabs my arm with a super-strong grip and drags me along with her. I assume Mickey is shambling along behind but I don't get time to look. Streetlights, bus shelters and traffic lights whizz past me and I'm powerless to do anything but move away from him.

Maximo is a black hole, a total sweatbox under the ground. Tracy leads me in, past a small booth staffed by a girl with black hair and grey-framed glasses. Inside the dance floor is heaving, and the music is discordant – at the moment it sounds like a speeded-up Russian peasant song. The booming darkness is disorientating and I suddenly feel completely out of my depth. Kirkness doesn't have a club, unless you count the social club, where they have ceilidhs and an antique fair on Saturday mornings. And this is a long way from Kirkness. Again, the feeling dawns on me that I'm about to be corrupted, initiated into a group of people with interests that verge on the obscene.

'Hey look! There's Alice!' says Tracy, gesticulating wildly. Alice advances through the crowd, a vision of jet black hair and white skin, dressed in her trademark green. Men turn to stare at her quite openly, but she doesn't notice, just pulls silly faces at us and pretends to be running in slow motion towards us.

'HELLOOO!!' she booms. 'Evie! This is a surprise!' she says, turning to Tracy. 'Have these girls been leading you astray?'

'You know Johnny wrote a song for her?' says Tracy. 'She's all like, "Oh, I met him at a café, blah blah." He dedicated it to her and everything!'

'Really?' gasps Alice. 'Johnny? Wow. You're a real dark horse!' She seems mightily impressed. Alice's attention somehow makes me feel ridiculously flattered. I stand there beaming like a shy child in a big frilly dress at a wedding, embarrassed at the clucking aunties, but secretly pleased at the attention.

'Well, aren't you making a big impression in this town?' she chirps, taking me by the arm to the bar while Tracy and Eleanor, who has made the walk to the club intact, queue for the cloakroom.

At the bar I get a vodka, which I hope won't make me too drunk. I wouldn't want a repeat of the last time. There's no way I'm waking up in a strange bed again, not knowing what I've done. Beating a path through the crowd of people – a ragged selection of trendy Top Shop girls, beered-up guys and vaguely sleazy older men, all of whom seem completely off their heads on something – Alice finds a half-empty booth. We squeeze in and I take a good gulp of the vodka. I feel out of place. I should go home and go to bed. The music has switched to pounding industrial techno, and each slashing, metallic beat threatens to splinter in my head, which feels soft and vulnerable and full of fluid – more like a watermelon than a skull.

'Hey, Nadine!' Alice calls, waving her over. Nadine shimmies across the dance floor, a timeless vision in black. She holds herself upright, the pearls loosely piled up round her neck announcing her otherness to the rest of the girls in the club. It occurs to me that she's trying too hard. However, she's also holding Mickey's hand – he tags along obediently, a big aimless puppy who'll go after anyone who'll throw him a bone. I slump into my seat. Then I sit up and I have some more vodka.

'Hello,' Nadine says, as graciously as the decibel levels allow, still holding onto Mickey's hand.

'Oh, I love this song!' Alice says, leaping to her feet to the leaden strains of 'Love Will Tear Us Apart'. 'Come and dance with me, Nadine.'

'Aw, do I have to?' whines Nadine, with a tortured expression. 'I've only just got here!' But Alice ignores her protestations and drags her to the dance floor, leaving me and Mickey conspicuously alone. He hangs around for a little while then he sits down, slightly reluctantly. I wish I knew what to say, but even if I did, he probably wouldn't be able to hear me.

Mickey glances at me and raises one eyebrow. I can't really tell what that's supposed to mean. It's so dark it's difficult to see, and breathing is no mean feat either – the air is a wall of stifling perspiration. I wish I had a whole bottle of vodka, so I could be transformed into the girl he remembers in Alice's flat, clambering on furniture and exposing myself. At the moment, I feel completely bemused by the modern world and all its complex social etiquette – I may as well be a Victorian handmaiden at an orgy.

I look out at the dancers, and see Alice's curly hair amongst the throng, stretching out its black tentacles like some strange sea anemone. I wish he'd stop being so weird. To think I woke up in his arms and now I'm stiffly perched at the end of the booth as if awaiting the results of a chlamydia test, and he's on the other side like he's waiting for a bus.

'Are you OK?' I ask. He seems agitated about something, and gives a tight nod.

'Nice outfit, by the way,' he adds. I blink at him through the flashing lights, to see whether he's being sincere, but he's gazing into the middle distance, a sour expression on his face. I want to shake him and ask him what the matter is, but I don't know him well enough. What's his problem? I take an enormous drink and he looks my way just as half of it dribbles down my chin.

'I'm thirsty,' I shrug, by way of explanation, wiping my mouth. Something seems to give way in him and he smiles, edging up the seat in my direction.

'So how's your mate Lorna?' he asks. I tense up as his thigh grazes mine under the table. Over on the other side of the room Nadine's head is swivelling around like a submarine periscope, trying to find our booth through the crowd of bobbing heads.

'She's . . . er . . . she's OK. Actually, she's nice . . .' I start to say, brain cells annoyingly refusing to co-operate and form sentences. Then I remember I told him all about her. 'Well, no, actually she's a bitch who shouts at people in shoe shops.'

'Why's that?' I think he says, so I carry on regardless, unable to hear even myself properly, but it seems better than not speaking at all. I tell him that she dragged me around all day, crucified a shoe-shop employee and then shouted at me for using the sewing machine, before finally criticizing my clothes. He's watching my lips, but I can't be sure he can hear anything I'm saying, which is probably a good thing.

'Yoooschoomat,' he says, looking concerned.

'What?'

'You should move out!'

'Oh, it's not that bad,' I say, trying to convince myself that I haven't just moaned about how rubbish it is for the last fifteen minutes. 'I can't really imagine myself living anywhere else at the moment.'

'You should live in Utopia.' He smiles, and the memory of waking up under his arm under the terrible mural makes my face burn for the second time. I curse myself and briefly wonder whether I should get that operation to cut your blushing glands, or whatever they're called.

'Are you blushing?' he whispers, making it worse.

'No.'

'Evie?' he says.

'What?' I yell.

'Would it be possible for you to . . . ?' He frowns and looks desperately at the table, as if his next line is written there. 'Would you . . . ?'

I stare at the side of his face, a picture of inner turmoil.

'Would I what?'

'Come on, Mickey – you should come and dance!' blares Nadine, who has materialized beside us. She's doing rather well at carrying off the cool swan-necked look while everyone around her is slowly dissolving into a puddle of sweat. But even if we weren't in here, she'd look better than me. Next to her I look like an extra in *Oliver*, queuing for gruel.

'Maybe later,' he says, straightening up and coming out of his own world. His thigh springs away from mine like a catapult.

'Well, I'm bored,' she says, plonking herself down on Mickey's side. 'I want to go somewhere classy. What about that private club in the West End for a nightcap? I know the girl who works on reception.'

Mickey nods slowly, while Nadine crosses her leg over towards him. Meanwhile, I toy with my empty glass.

'I'll get you another drink,' he says suddenly. 'What is it?'

'Vodka and cranberry. Thanks,' I say, and as he passes me, he puts his hand on my shoulder for an instant, a move that makes my skin twitch. He points at Nadine and mimes the word 'drink', to which she shakes her head.

Once he's gone, Nadine smiles coyly at me, her lips shimmering with some expensive gloss.

'How are you, Evie?' she asks politely.

'Fine,' I say. 'Did you have a good time at the party the other week?'

Either she can't hear me, or she's ignoring me.

'You're a new face round here, so I don't expect you to know . . .' she begins, rooting in a small black evening bag for a pack of cigarettes. I realize she's quite drunk. 'Mickey, you see, me and Mickey – we went out. Well, we go back years, really. It's one of those things. You know, it's complicated.'

'Oh,' I say.

'You see, for a while now, we've been getting closer, if you know what I mean . . .'

I look at her. I may be a country girl but I wasn't born yesterday.

'That's funny,' I breeze. 'Mickey didn't mention it.'

'No, well, he's shy,' she says, shifting in her seat.

'Not always,' I mumble.

'I spoke to him the night after the party and it was a total shock, but I realized I'd never got over him.' She pauses, as if she's struggling to find the words. 'He said he wasn't sure but that he did have feelings for me too. I know it looks bad, and you probably feel a bit misled, but he's confused at the moment. So am I, to tell you the truth. It hasn't been easy.'

Some instinct directly inherited from my dad flares up and I fix her with a glare.

'Yeah, it must be terrible for you,' I snap. But when I see her expression I don't feel so certain. She looks at me, seemingly tormented, the two ticks of liquid eyeliner creasing at the corners. Her eyes look watery and anguished.

'I'm sorry,' she implores. 'I really am. It's just totally bad timing. But some things just happen when you're not expecting them. I didn't set out to hurt your feelings.

'Mickey is so kind,' she continues, hurriedly. 'He wouldn't want to hurt you, but I thought it'd be better in the long run to let you know what the situation was. Before you got . . . too attached.'

I glance over to find Mickey through the gloom, to get him to back up her version of events, but there's no sign of him.

Nadine stares at the floor and glumly lights her cigarette, the soft flame illuminating her face. She's beautiful, almost flawless, with a perfectly defined bone structure and softly padded lips. Why wouldn't he want her? I suppose if it were the truth, it would make sense. After all, he goes to Johnny's gig with her and acts weird when I show up. Maybe he's changed his mind. And it was just a snog at a party, not *Gone with the Wind*. I search Nadine's face for any signs of deviousness, but there's no trace.

'I'm sorry,' she says again.

Nadine looks at me solemnly. Her face suddenly looks puffy and waterlogged, as if she's about to cry. If she isn't telling the truth, she's a great actress. I'm having difficulty breathing and the club seems to shrink and contract around me, a murky, suffocating hole in the ground filling with earth.

I grip my glass tightly.

'I'm just going to the toilet,' I say, following my usual get-out procedure. She gives me a regretful look and mouths 'sorry'. I walk away from her, wading through a swamp of heat and dread, weaving my way through the dancers, whose faces look demonic and contorted. I should be grown up about this, I should be modern. This is how modern relationships work. They're light-hearted, pleasurable transactions between enlightened mature people, and until anything concrete is established, then a person is single, free to do whatever they want. I feel sick. Alice comes towards me and asks me what the matter is. I tell her I don't feel well and that I should go home. She puts her arms around my shoulders and tells me to take care. I drift away, separating myself from the group, slowly disengaging myself. Finally, I glance around the bar area, but Mickey is nowhere to be seen. Even if he was around, I wouldn't know where to start.

So I choose the best option, the only practical option, and get as far away from them as I can, running up the stairs and past the booth and onto the street. When I leave this building, I say to myself, they'll all disappear. It'll be like none of it ever happened.

Step Eight – Do not Flatter to Deceive

It is crucial that you now look at your dress with the sharp eye of a professional. If you encounter an imperfection at this stage, do not make excuses for yourself or your creation. This is no time for self-deception. Do not imagine that tightness at the waist will be solved by dieting, or that nobody will notice the fabric straining over a voluminous derriere. Deal with problems immediately, or you may find yourself literally coming undone.

In dressmaking, when something is wrong, it has to be identified early, otherwise everything gets ruined, and you might as well have not bothered at all. I think about that while I'm unpicking the spoiled seam of my dress project and wishing Monday would come so I can go to college and immerse myself in work. I have to get back on the straight and narrow. I have to tidy up my life, tie up all the loose thread, and concentrate. All I want to see in front of me are train tracks of stitches, smooth and uncomplicated, everything fitting together as if by magic. At least everything is peaceful here. Charlie is hanging around in the living room, watching TV. Apparently he turned up late last night to surprise Lorna, who is now crooning to herself in the kitchen. She's making him a Sunday dinner before he gets into his car and drives home, a ritual I'm never included in, even though the smell of roasted chicken wafts under my door and makes me half mad with hunger. Their lives are so predictable and ordinary, based on routine and the ultimate pursuit of making money, but they seem happy enough, don't they? It's so easy. Go to work, come home, read catalogues, plan for the future, build up a nest egg, make a life with someone, fit into the world, have children, buy houses and go on holiday. A normal life. Instead, though, I'm apparently obsessed with deliberately seeking out drama and chaos, chasing flaky characters who inhabit darkened cellars and live like there's no tomorrow. What's wrong with me?

I look at my postcard of Edith, which leans against the orange ashtray on the shelf. (Blu Tack is forbidden due to its greasy residue.) But today, instead of being a kind and guiding light, she just looks like a funny-looking bloke, too manly and intense, too strange.

'Evie!' Lorna trills from outside my door.

'Yes?' I say, as sweetly as I can. After last night's door-slamming performance she's probably not my biggest fan.

'Would you like some dinner? I've set a place if you'd care to join us!'

Huh?

'Er . . . oh, OK, thank you! I'll be out in a sec!'

Wonders will never cease. I can't quite believe what I'm hearing – usually her time with Charlie is so sacred that I'm not permitted within a two-metre radius of the living room. Now, I'm the guest of honour at their feast. I put down the dress and make sure I'm presentable, wondering if there's a hidden agenda or an announcement she's going to make. But that would be cynical, wouldn't it?

In the living room, the table is set up in the window, a folding one that is brought out for occasions such as this, complete with starched tablecloth and a peculiar centrepiece made of pine cones and woodchips sprayed with gold paint. Charlie is slumped in a striped polo shirt and jeans on the sofa, watching golf. As I come in, I hear the minute tap of a ball and a polite ripple of applause.

'Yes!' he yells, punching the air. 'You beauty!' He turns round and sees me, his expression waning.

'Montgomery's winning,' he explains, turning back to the TV.

'Oh right,' I say, trying to smile. Maybe Charlie and I could be great friends if I took the time to nurture an interest in golf. But all that interminable walking about and knocking balls into holes is so mind-numbingly tedious I'd rather watch fourteen-hour repeats of Carol Smillie stencilling a dado rail.

'Excuse me!' Lorna shouts, appearing behind me with a sizzling dish of roast potatoes, which she clutches onto for dear life. I leap out of the way and she marches towards the table.

'Do you want a hand?' I ask, seeing as Charlie is in no hurry to help out.

'No, Evie, it's all fine – you sit down,' she says, her cheeks flushed from being in the hot kitchen. Next she brings in a glistening chicken, a steaming bowl of broccoli and carrots, and a little gravy boat filled with pale brown goo, studded in the middle with a star of drowning parsley. I sit upright in the middle chair and hope that's the right place to sit. Charlie is still motionless on the other side of the room, seemingly oblivious to all the trouble she's gone to.

'Help yourself!' Lorna practically screams at me, and I automatically reach for a spoon and start piling some vegetables onto my plate, in what I hope is a refined manner. Charlie gets up slowly and stretches, padding towards the table. I watch him out of the corner of my eye as he prods the chicken with his fat finger.

'What a sorry-looking bird!' he says, picking up a carving knife. 'Looks like it's been circuit training.' He laughs uproariously at his own joke and plunges the blade directly into its breast, as if re-enacting a scene from *King Arthur*. I wince, feeling its pain. I'm suddenly not hungry at all.

'Want a bit of skin?' he leers, glancing up at me.

'You all tuck in!' Lorna interrupts loudly as she takes her seat. She's still flushed though she's out of the heat of the kitchen. She tucks a piece of hair behind her ear, which I can see is faintly damp with sweat.

‘Thanks for this, Lorna,’ I say, attempting cheerfulness. ‘It’s really great.’

‘It’s just the usual. Nothing fancy,’ she replies, her voice clipped, holding both sides of her plate like a steering wheel. ‘Nothing is too much trouble for my wonderful boyfriend.’ She gives Charlie a pointed, vinegary smile, but he’s too busy tearing the chicken carcass apart. Is there trouble in paradise?

‘I just thought that as you seemed to be very socially active recently, going out till all hours and sleeping in late, you might be in need of a good meal,’ Lorna adds, gazing benevolently in the direction of the gravy.

Ah, there it is. Strike one. I should have known.

‘Thank you,’ I say, trying to stay calm.

‘Charlie,’ she says, in a horrendous baby voice, ‘can I have just white meat, please? You know I don’t like the icky brown stuff.’

‘Yes, dear,’ he fires back sarcastically, lobbing a junkyard of assorted wings and tendons on my plate. It’s as if he’s deliberately chosen the worst parts. I thank him anyway, wondering what time he has to go home.

‘So have you decided on the church?’ I ask, referring to a conversation Lorna and I had a couple of days before. She said she was hoping that they could get Skibo Castle, where Madonna was married, but couldn’t decide between that or the pretty parish church near her parents’ house. My secret hope is that whatever weird dysfunctional atmosphere is going on will be diffused by some upbeat wedding banter. If it gets any worse, maybe later I'll start a fascinating discussion about napkin rings.

'What church?' Lorna asks, looking at me as if I'm from space. 'Nobody goes to church on Sundays any more, do they? I really have no idea what you're talking about.'

'But, I—'

'Have some more vegetables, Evie. They'll do your complexion no end of good,' she interrupts, ladling more pale-looking broccoli on my plate.

Once the chicken has been served, we sit in silence; the clink of cutlery on plates and the sound of Charlie chewing with his mouth open are the only evidence that we're all here. The food is an illusion – apart from my hideous array of scrag-ends it all looks delicious, but in reality it's flavourless. I'm loath to reach for the salt in case Lorna takes it as a criticism of her cooking, but it's definitely in need of something. It's as if everything has been boiled and bleached, a plastic doll's house version of the traditional Sunday roast.

'This is delicious,' I lie. Nobody replies. Lorna seems lost in a reverie, chewing mechanically, occasionally sipping, zombie-like, from a wine glass full of water.

Well, this is fun.

'What's the name of that girl who works at the nineteenth hole?' Lorna suddenly asks, nudging a baby carrot – tiny and bald and stripped entirely of its carrotness – with her fork.

Charlie looks up distractedly. 'Eh? Oh, er . . . I don't know. Justine? Jenny? I'm terrible with names. Some tart.'

'It's Jenny and well you know,' she says quickly, with a killer finality.

'Just drop it.'

'Jenny with the big tits,' she goads.

What on earth . . . ?

'Oh shut up, will you? You're like a stuck record!' Charlie snaps, his face a blur of anger. I stare down at my plate, wishing I could vanish and reappear somewhere else.

'Evie?' Lorna enquires conversationally, tilting her head playfully in my direction. 'I'm curious. If your boyfriend, assuming you've ever had one, spent an awful lot of time with another girl, would you be jealous?'

I clear my throat, which seems to have half a potato lodged in it, pretending I didn't hear the bit about never having a boyfriend.

'Well, it would depend who she was . . . and who he was . . . and in what way . . .' I say lamely.

'Hmm, let's see,' Lorna says, considering each point. 'He's away all week, and she's working behind the bar with fake blond hair and her big tits hanging out all over the place serving him drinks, and HE fancies her. Oh, and she fancies HIM. That's what way.' She pushes her plate away, glaring at Charlie.

'Well . . .' I stutter, looking nervously between them. 'Erm, that doesn't mean anything's going on—'

'EXACTLY!' Charlie explodes, cutlery falling to the floor. 'And I don't think that I should have to listen to your whining and complaining when I should be relaxing and eating my dinner, which, by the way, tastes like someone put it in the fucking washing machine!'

Charlie pushes his plate away too, and nobody moves. A horrible silence descends. Lorna looks as if she might be in need of the Heimlich manoeuvre, her head tilted downwards and her neck outstretched like a bird looking for scraps.

With a dreadful clatter she springs to her feet and tips over her plate, baby carrots catapulting into the air.

'I slaved to make this dinner, you bastard!' she growls, as I drop my fork. 'You're a pig! My mum was right about you – you're mean, and you're selfish, and you shag anything that moves!'

'I haven't shagged anyone!' he screams, matching her anger. 'And your mum never said that!'

'You liar!' she bawls. 'I bet you're at it every night! I bet they're crawling all over you!' Spittle is collecting at the side of her mouth and any minute now her head could swivel 360 degrees.

'You're a bastard! Fucker! I bet you've even shagged her!' She points at me.

'Hey, wait a minute,' I say, reasonably, but Charlie's laugh drowns me out.

'As if! She's a freak! And so are you!' He gets up and moves slowly and threateningly towards her, an imposing, stocky, ape-like presence, but Lorna doesn't seem at all fazed, in fact, she looks as if she's more than ready for a fist fight.

'Get out!' she yells, pointing at the door. 'I never want to see you again! Go on! Get out!' Amazingly, for someone who tells me off for leaving five microscopic crumbs on the chopping board, she throws a roast potato at him, which hits his barrel chest with a thud and plops onto the floor.

'Calm down!' He grabs her and shakes her, trying to get her to stop, but using all her strength, she untangles herself and shoves him in the chest, causing him to stagger back and hit the couch. As he lies there, beached on the spotless cushions, a look of resignation crosses his face, as if this happens every day and he's about to go back to watching the golf. Lorna has her hands on her hips and her back to me, a flap of white shirt hanging limply over the waistband of her trousers. I can't see her face, but she's shaking.

'Lorna, calm down,' he says, not looking at her.

'I'll calm down when you're out of my life,' she breathes, murderously. 'I don't know why you're even here – I can manage perfectly well on my own. I'm fine. You're all making it worse.' She starts picking the potato off the carpet and seems to become entirely absorbed. I try to catch Charlie's eye, but he's too busy trying to prise something out of his teeth with his tongue, grimly staring at the TV.

'I'd better go to my room,' I whisper, quietly getting to my feet.

Lorna turns round and they both seem surprised I'm still there. I fix my eyes to the floor and scoot out as quickly as I can.

'She's got to go,' I think I hear him say as I scurry back down the hall with my eyes on stalks.

* * *

'So this brand . . .' Jezebel drawls in an affected London accent, toying with her necklace, a massive locket with spikes all over it, like a metal conker. It probably contains something really pretentious – a bird's wing, or myrrh, or the heart of a Himalayan mountain goat. 'S'gotta be really out there. Edgy. You know, like . . . real edge.'

Flossy nods fervently, self-consciously tweaking the waxed ends of her blond hair. I can tell that Jezebel despises me by the flare of her nostrils and the fact that her head is tilted away from me, and when her eyes do slide reluctantly my way, she makes me feel about as welcome as a leprous dog. The canteen is empty, apart from workers who wheel clattering trolleys to the kitchen and noisily pull down metal shutters. I sit there, waiting for Jezebel's amazing idea, but she just stares into space. On the bright side, though, it gives me a chance to notice, with a small wrinkle of satisfaction, that her top lip is quite hairy.

'I've had a few thoughts,' I quietly volunteer. In fact, I spent the best part of yesterday holed up in my room, sketching out ideas. Racking my brain for inspiration, I drew different fonts and colour combinations until my hand was sore, thankful to have something else to concentrate on apart from Lorna vs Charlie. Jezebel looks annoyed and starts flicking at the corners of her notebook, but I carry on regardless.

'I thought that maybe it could be classic looking. A lot of big, established brands are white and another colour, to be eye-catching, so I thought we could maybe use a deep aquamarine blue and white, or a crimson . . . the names are words I randomly picked from the dictionary, to give an idea of what a logo might look like. But these are just suggestions.'

Jezebel fingers the edges of the paper like she's holding a flaming cowpat, her coal-black eyes flitting over the drawings that took so much time and effort. She snorts.

'Yeah whatever,' she says concisely, handing them to Flossy with a dismissive flourish. Flossy eyes Jezebel and they trade a smirk.

'What'd you do all this for? We'll just do it on the computer – it'll take five minutes and then we can go home. All we need is the idea and the name,' Jezebel drawls, indicating how spectacularly bored she is with a huge, watery-eyed yawn.

I sit back, feeling stung. Flossy is lit up with admiration. I thought she was supposed to be on my side.

'What about City Traders?' Flossy squeaks.

'Too done,' Jezebel says.

'OK, then . . . um . . .' Flossy screws up her eyes determinedly. 'Fire? Water . . . ?'

'The name is everything . . . it's gotta be the dog's bollocks,' Jezebel muses, insightfully. 'Hey – wait a minute – how about God's Bollocks?'

'Pardon?' I stutter.

'Hey, it's fun, it's controversial, it's out there . . . yeah!' Jezebel frenziedly draws the logo out in bubble writing on lined notepaper, draws a few lightning bolts and daggers around it, rips it out and hands it to me.

'Play on words. Nice!' Flossy simpers. 'That's brilliant!'

It is not brilliant.

'Look, I don't think—'

'Stick that in the scanner, put it on a bag. End of,' Jezebel instructs, banging her hand onto the table top with authority.

'But aren't we supposed to develop an idea?' I ask. This little meeting is sliding into a morass of awfulness. I can't believe she's actually suggested such a thing. Is it a joke, a way to humiliate me in front of the whole class? Or is she for real?

'Here's your idea. Write this down, Miss Whateveryournameis.'

I glare at Jezebel while Flossy regards her with flushed pride.

'You know what my name is,' I growl.

'God's Bollocks isn't a brand, it's an urban reclamation collective,' she announces, ignoring me. 'It's a state of mind, a socially responsible, cutting-edge, eco-sympathetic clothing system combining recycled ideas, found objects and urban symbolism with humour and a punk rock DIY sensibility. Or something like that.' Jezebel nods encouragingly to my notebook, but my pen stays firmly resting on the table and I fold my arms. You write it down, you bald arrogant cow.

'Anyway it's totally street.' She wipes her nose with the back of her hand and gets up. 'I really think you'd better write that down before you forget it. Right, I've got to go.'

'But what about the presentation? We've got to do it tomorrow afternoon,' I say, starting to feel rather defeated. God's Bollocks . . . ? Give me strength.

'Well, you're a smart girl, you'll think of something.' Jezebel shrugs. 'Think that's got legs, though, don't you, Floss?'

Flossy, with a glowing face like a small child on Christmas Day, nods reverentially.

'You mean, we have to do all the work on our own?'

'Chill out, Evil – it won't take you a second,' Jezebel snaps, 'and I think if I can be bothered to come up with the idea then you can print out a few pieces of paper. God, this course is easy – I can do it standing on my head. See ya later, Floss!'

I watch open-mouthed as she floats off. The back of her shaved head is perfectly dark and downy, the only flaw is a clipper scar showing white scalp (probably where she puts her microchip).

'Wow, that's so cool,' says Flossy, leaning wistfully on her elbow and looking at the carelessly rendered logo.

'Do you honestly think so?' I ask, amazed.

'Yeah! It's really now.'

I look out of the creaky, floor-length windows at 'now', a grey, sodden concrete car park with an overflowing skip. MetroTech was a big mistake. Rather than feeling in control of my new life, I'm losing my grip entirely.

'I've got to go too,' Flossy suddenly announces, grabbing her bag. 'You'll be OK to scan this in and make up a few bags, won't you? It won't be really hard work. It's just that I told my friend I'd meet her and she gets mad when I'm late. Sorry!'

'But you can't—'

'Oh come on, Evie – lighten up, will ya?'

Flossy leaps up and scuttles out of the canteen, leaving me with a few scraps of paper, a stupid idea and a presentation to write. With little choice in the matter, I shuffle off to the 386th floor and do what I'm told, raiding the pile of white paper carrier bags Duncan has procured for our mythical, ridiculous brand, scanning in Jezebel's half-arsed logo and desperately trying to think of ways to make 'God's Bollocks' seem less terminally, unbelievably stupid. But just like everything else at the moment, it's impossible.

By 7 p.m., I'm exhausted. Nudged out of the workroom by a night class, I pack up my materials and print-outs and throw away all the mistakes and mangled carrier bags that have wedged themselves in the laser jet. What has this got to do with making clothes anyway? I feel lost, not to mention hungry. But the prospect of going to Lorna's is weighing more heavily on me than Flossy and Jezebel's complete lack of consideration. Her crazy roast-potato-throwing antics haven't exactly made me feel secure, and now the flat, with all its sterile cleanliness, seems as clinical and ominous as a morgue. But as far as Lorna is concerned, it didn't happen: the event has been erased as quickly and efficiently as a blossoming of a faint ring of limescale or a rogue speck of grease, and Charlie's suggestion that I should go has gone with it. Instead of throwing me out into the street, she even asked me to go shopping with her again next week. Even so, I have no idea whether there'll be a horse's head in my bed when I get home, with a Post-it note attached saying, 'Please can you rinse out the bin before you replace bin bag? Ta! ☺'

But I haven't got anywhere else to go, apart from back home, which isn't an option, so I head towards the tube, through the lights and traffic of George Square, watched by the silent statues of great Scotsmen who suffer the indignity of having traffic cones plonked onto their heads on a regular basis. The bright lights of pubs and restaurants are inviting, but are separated from me by invisible barriers. I don't have friends to sit with, and I've never gone to a pub on my own. Even if I wanted to, what if I bumped into Duncan, taking his troop of students out for a tedious night of fashion philosophizing? 'All right, Mary!' he'd bark. 'Fancy a Babycham? Or how about a Bovril? They loved it during the war, didn't they?'

Instead I get the subway and sit down heavily on the orange seat. The carriage is brightly lit and I have to close my eyes to stop my head from pounding. The after-image of 'God's Bollocks' seems to be engraved on my eyeballs like a secret message on the inside of a ring or the back of a watch. Maybe I should just take the day off tomorrow. That'd teach 'em. I could say I was ill and leave those tarts to it, see how they get out of that one with their urban collectives and their recycled whatnots. Not that I ever would, but it's a nice thought.

'Hello,' a voice says. My eyes snap open and I jump about three feet into the air, just as the carriage shudders and starts to move.

'Shit! Oh, sorry . . . you startled me,' I mutter, trying to pull myself together. Mickey can't be more than a few inches away from me, his attractiveness undimmed by the sickly strip lighting and the rigours of a damp day, even in the same clothes – scruffy, crumpled afterthoughts. He's carrying a large, old-fashioned leather document case, which was probably once quite fine, now battered into a scarred brown husk.

'How are you?' I blink, my brain hardly functioning. Despite sitting too close to me to be a stranger, I can tell already that he's in awkward unsmiling mode, the same as he was the other night. Moody git. For a second, I can't recall where I'm supposed to stand with him, and the whole thing makes my head ache even more. I should train myself to fancy accountants or bank clerks, not confused, vague writers with girlfriends – it'd save me a lot of hassle. But, after all this, I can't even remember whether I fancy him or not.

'Sorry I had to leave the other night,' I blurt, 'I wasn't feeling too well.' My voice is as artificial as the gluey orange-squash colour of the seats.

'Yeah, Alice told me. Are you OK? You look tired.' He peers at me with concern. It makes me feel instantly pathetic and small.

'I'm fine,' I squeak, struggling to keep up the cheerful pretence and fighting back an unwelcome urge to cry about how crap my life has become, how everyone at college hates me and my flatmate is bonkers and nothing has worked out how I wanted it to. 'College is just getting me down. It's not what I thought it would be. But I'll be fine.'

The train rattles along, and I fix on an advert for a bathroom company, promising sensual delights in the shower. I'm aware that he's looking at me like he's waiting for something, but I don't know what it is I'm supposed to do or say. Eventually, as the train jerks its way through the ground, he nods to my bag.

'Is that your next project?' he asks.

'Yeah. Unfortunately. It's terrible.' I look down at the large portfolio I'm gripping with white knuckles.

'Don't do yourself down,' he says, quietly and sincerely, making me catch his eye.

'No, really. I'm not being modest – it's terrible.' I consider taking out the sheets of paper bearing Jezebel's logo, just to show him what I have to put up with.

'Evie, can I ask you something?' he says, jolting me out of my daydream.

'Sure.' I clear my throat and shift in my seat, the uncertainty returning. It's nearly my stop. I don't know where Mickey lives – we'll probably disembark together, then stumble up the road looking at the ground, racking our brains for something to say as we make our awkward goodbyes. God, this is painful. The easy-going banter that made him (and me) such a catch at Alice's party seems to have evaporated, leaving nothing but missed eye contact, uncomfortable silences and a complete lack of social skills.

'Will you read my book?'

'What?'

The train thunders around a corner, hitting the curve in the oval of the quaint underground system.

'My book. Would you read it? I'd like to hear your opinion. I mean, you don't have to, or anything . . .' he trails away, embarrassed, two blurs of colour forming on his cheeks. I see that asking me has taken every iota of his courage. The carriage rights itself again and for a second I feel cool and calm, the one in charge.

'Yes,' I say, 'I'd love to. Is it in there?' I point to the case.

'Yeah. You really don't have to if you don't—'

'I want to. I mean, I'm not an expert, but I'd like to read it.'

'Thanks.'

He gives a tight smile and hands me the case. It's heavy and the handle is dry to the touch, and for a second our fingers meet.

'This isn't the only copy, is it?'

'No,' he says. 'So don't worry about throwing it in the river.'

'Don't do yourself down,' I tell him. He looks at me with a flicker of interest, but the train jolts to a halt at my stop, and Mickey doesn't move.

'I've got to get off here . . . I'll see you soon, OK?' I say, struggling to my feet, trying to be reassuring and cool and keep my balance at the same time. 'I'm sure it'll be great.'

He takes time out from looking at his shoes, and gives me a red-faced smile, and when the sliding doors separate us, he turns to give a little wave before sliding out of view. I wave back.

Walking up the steps into the street, and up the hill past the twinkling lights of Ashton Lane, the miserable state I was in over college is dissipating. I feel vaguely honoured to be carrying someone's life's work. It's as if

I'm carrying a delicate piece of him, like I'm one of those emergency motorcycles that have a case on the back with a recently extracted liver in it. Even though, in about two minutes' time, he might come out of the tube station up the road and deposit himself into the arms of Nadine (don't think about it), this feels like a breakthrough of some kind. Giving me the book means he respects my opinion, or at least gives a toss about me. Perhaps he's going to change his mind again, this time for good. 'Nadine means nothing to me!' he might eventually say, as we lie side by side in a post-coital haze. 'I only have eyes for you, kid. Let's move to Paris, I'll write, you'll design, we'll rule the goddamn world.'

Or maybe he gives books to all the girls.

Lorna is arranged on the sofa when I get back, toenails painted, wearing a pair of pyjamas with 'Sleepy Bear' written on them. Files are open on her knee, some homework she's got, while Jamie Oliver does something with tuna steaks on the TV.

'Hi, Lorna,' I venture.

She grunts, barely looking up from her work. There's a snot-green Post-it on my door, warning me of dwindling milk and bathroom cleaner supplies with 'think it's your turn!' written underneath, frustration oozing from every stroke. I take it off and put it in my pocket, vowing to remember, in the likely event that she decides to throw something at me for failing to come home with Lemon Ocean Fresh Burst Toilet Duck tomorrow. I consider making myself dinner, but the barely audible bubble of some tomato soup on the hob would probably disrupt Lorna's evening, and in any case, she would only come in and interfere, tidying stuff away before I've even had a chance to use it.

Instead, feeling as if I've smuggled in a secret guest, I retire to my room. It looks even cleaner than I left it. Funny, I'm pretty certain I didn't make the bed so perfectly. Sitting on the bed, I open the case. Its friendly old smell of mottled leather and mildew reminds me of being at home – in a flat as spotless as this, it seems like a shameful object, the sort of thing Lorna would banish immediately. I love it. Reaching inside, it takes some effort to grip the 350 pages of double-spaced A4 that form Mickey's manuscript, which is liberally sprinkled with scribbled notes, sentences cancelled with vicious red lines and large question marks of the sort that used to appear in the margins of my schoolbooks. It's called *The Playing Field* by Michael O'Neill, and even that facing page makes me realize how little I know about him. As I start to read, I'm even more amazed. Words flow in such great, extravagantly imaginative waves that I have trouble connecting this author with the monosyllabic boy who looks as if his main concern is where to buy Rizlas. But he's obviously the main character, a teenager with a difficult life of bullying and family upheaval, trying to fit into a small-minded town in the middle of nowhere, getting beaten up at every turn. He comes to the city to escape and ends up being swept along by hedonists and people who don't have his interests at heart (I can relate to that one, mate). I read page after page. I hear Lorna go to the bathroom to brush her teeth, flick the light off in the hall, and creak into bed next door. The night settles around me, the heating dies out, and my fingers go cold, but I still can't stop reading. It's not perfect – the character is a bit too naïve for someone who has grown up in a rough estate, and there are times when I want to shake him for being so spineless, but overall, it's incredible. I wonder if Nadine has ever seen it, or Alice. I wonder whether I'm the first. The thought makes me practically hyperventilate. I stay up most of the night greedily devouring it. At one point, hallucinating from lack of sleep, I experience a curious sensation of being watched, but I carry on, transfixed, until light starts seeping in through the gap in the curtains.

Everyone went mad over God's Bollocks. Everyone. Duncan, his piggy eyes dancing with unbridled joy, proclaimed it to be a masterpiece of 'blue-sky thinking' and for the first time I was on the receiving end of a smile. Conclusive proof that Jezebel could fart into a paper bag and tie a ribbon on it and Duncan would be beside himself. She got up and, brimming with confidence, repeated her garbled mantra about punk rock DIY urban collectives while I fixed my eyes on the table, willing it to end. As Mrs Morrison might have said, she had more front than Debenhams, and completely off the top of her head managed to convince the entire class that her lame idea was brilliant. Today, though, things are going to get even worse. It's the moment of truth for my funky top and Duncan is about to hold assessments in the workroom with our final made-up pieces, which we all have to model ourselves.

This exercise in ritual humiliation is Duncan's idea, of course. So I'm standing in the girls' toilets, surrounded by twittering people pinning themselves into their creations. Jezebel is hoiking her skinny frame into a shapeless, diagonally cut scarlet sheath, which instead of straps features a length of lethal-looking bicycle chain. It must have taken her all of five minutes to make. By the hand dryers, a dumpy girl called Andrea, with a habit of sneezing wildly in class and putting everybody off, is staring gormlessly into space while someone helps her with the catch on her big scary white bra. Everywhere there are flimsy bits of material, wisps of gauze and strips of sequins, all with various outlandish additions like clunking Egyptian-style beads, plastic vegetables and jagged necklines cut with blunt scissors. Then there's me. I look in the mirror dolefully. Despite tailoring it to my exact measurements, my confused 1920s/60s tunic gives me the look of a miserable genie, shaken prematurely from its bottle. The full sleeves aren't only stupidly large, but they're also a fire risk. Plus, the black cotton I've used was a mistake – dull and drab and not funky at all, even though I've trimmed it with glitzy red and silver brocade, which now I come to think of it, reminds me of the soft furnishings in a depressing Chinese restaurant. It's crap.

'Evie? Can you help me?' whines Flossy, who is standing next to me with a gaping back. Due to hangovers and apathy, she hasn't even finished sewing her top together, and the whole thing is a mess, trailing loose threads.

'I need to hold this together with safety pins all down the back. Could you do it for me?' she asks, handing me a box of them.

'Why should I do it?' I want to scream, but refusing seems childish.

'Didn't you get time to finish it?' I ask. I open the catch on one of the silver pins and it skewers me in the thumb.

'No . . .' she croaks. 'I had a mad one last night and when I woke up it was just sitting there and I couldn't be arsed with it. I figured I'd just make it up as I went along. Hey, Jezebel! Nice top.'

Queen Jezebel glances in her direction and gives a regal smile, fingering her bike chain admiringly.

'She's excellent, isn't she? I think she might be really famous one day,' Flossy burbles. 'I want to work in fashion, I think, but I'm not really sure I want to make clothes, y'know? Maybe I could get rich and get someone else to do it for me.'

'Maybe you could,' I sigh, wanting to slap Flossy for being such a feeble-minded waster, and wishing I could get someone else to do this, as well as model my top and do this course and live at Lorna's. Meanwhile, maybe I'll go up north and keep goats.

'It's time!' an annoying male voice screeches from the corridor. 'Hurry up, ladies!'

I hastily put in the rest of the safety pins, but it looks awful. Flossy, though, doesn't seem to care either way.

'Cheers, Evie! Hey, Jezebel, wait up!' she chirps, as we prepare to go to our doom, chasing after her special new friend like a lovesick puppy.

'Come on! Hurry up!' shouts Neil, who turns out to be the owner of the annoying male voice. The only thing that cheers me up is that his top is one of the most ridiculous things I've ever seen – a selection of white straps made of terry towelling and held together with silver mesh. He's made the shoulders into large impractical angel wings that catch on the door as he goes in, giving him the appearance of an unwieldy seagull.

'Right, you beautiful people!' says Duncan, casually draped over the front desk in his regulation checked shirt. 'What a sight! Come on – sit down and let's get on with it!'

Everyone tries to sit down without ripping their clothes or snagging them on tables, a strange little game of soundless musical chairs that has Duncan going purple with amusement. My tunic is easy to sit down in – it's the getting up and standing in front of the entire class that upsets me.

'OK, so first, I want to say well done for completing this project. I've thrown you in at the deep end on this to show you the kind of deadlines and pressures you'll encounter should you go on to work as designers. Some of you were more diligent than others . . .' he adds, pausing for effect. 'But overall, you've impressed me. So hopefully this is going to be a fun day and we can all go to the pub and get pissed later!' A ragged cheer goes up. 'Now, each student will come up to the front in alphabetical order, give us a twirl, and explain the ideas behind their work, and I'll put my two shillin' in, for what it's worth, OK? While we're doing this, feel free to make comments, but please . . . be constructive. Right then . . .'

I can't believe this is actually happening, a free-for-all abuse session at the hands of these people. I look around the group and see that Flossy is squeezed up next to her new friend Jezebel, displaying the kind of weak-minded spirit that made the Nazi Party such a popular bunch. Now I have no allies, this is going to be even more difficult than I anticipated. Flossy is up first, and takes to the stage in her tatty top held together with pins, messing about with the back as she models it.

'So what do you call this?' says Duncan, looking bemused.

'It's a reworking of the famous Liz Hurley Versace safety pin dress,' she replies, bold as brass. 'By creating a deliberately unfinished look, I'm taking the form back to its punk roots.' She smiles, such a beaming, giddy, aren't-I-clever smile that even I'm impressed. Duncan inspects it closely.

'Well, it's certainly unfinished,' he says, pacing around her. 'Maybe that's because . . . YOU DIDN'T FINISH IT!' he shouts, making the windowpanes rattle.

Flossy shrinks, petrified, her smugness turning to glassy-eyed horror.

'Don't take the piss out of me, young lady,' he continues, fuming. 'I've watched you for two weeks and you've done nothing but sit on your fat arse gossiping – that's when you're here at all. I'm giving you zero out of ten!' He is incandescent with rage, the vein in his temple twitching. Flossy, too shocked to cry or reply, bolts back to her chair, her top flapping hopelessly. Everyone in the room is silent, looking at the floor or examining something fascinating under their nails.

I glare at Duncan. Despite Flossy's weaknesses, that was really harsh. Her special friend Jezebel, however, doesn't look remotely fazed, and Duncan's expression suddenly turns from one of thunder to one of delight as she floats up to the front with the grace of a swan, fanning the bottom of the scarlet slip with her hand. She demonstrates the front with a brief shimmy, and turns, in catwalk style, to show the back. Someone wolf whistles.

'OK, Jezebel – very nice,' Duncan says. 'I like the way you've combined this very thin, feminine material with hard, urban metallic detail. What was the thinking behind that?'

Jezebel, who towers over Duncan, gazes down at him, her shaven head and perfect posture like that of a Shaolin monk.

'It's a comment on pollution and globalization,' she deadpans, in a monotonous low voice. 'The bicycle chains represent the need to use alternative methods of transport. It's intended to put funky clubwear into the realm of the political.'

Oh, give me strength.

'Good, good,' says Duncan, all of a dither, scribbling something down on a notebook. 'Now, everyone, Jezebel has done something very interesting here, in that she's taken a conceptual approach, turning an ideology into really cool fashion. What do we think?'

The audience, who seem to be awestruck, applaud, making me wonder whether Duncan is going to judge our merits with a Clap-o-meter. Outside, Glasgow is veiled under damp mist, making everything look dismal and thwarted. Perhaps it's not too late to jump out of the window.

The alphabet winds slowly by, with most people getting less of a rapturous response. Helena Crolla is deemed promising, causing a great deal of excitement with her plastic broccoli and corn on the cobs, even though they look ready to fall off. Andrea Harris, of the big scary bra, models what could be a corset, except it hovers around her waist and is sorely in need of elastic. It'll be me soon. I get more and more sweaty-palmed as the roll-call creeps up to K for Kaminsky. Eventually, the moment of truth arrives.

'Right,' Duncan sighs, looking at something in his book. 'Who's next? Ah yes, Evie Kaminsky – live and direct from 1953.'

I try to get out of my chair but my legs aren't working. Jezebel is finding it hard not to burst out in demonic cackles. My second attempt to get up is successful, but I'm so rattled I can barely navigate my way around the chairs in front of me. One of Neil's wings sticks into my side as I pass and he moves sharply away, tending to his wounded felt-covered feathers. Conscious of Duncan only as a blurred entity at my side, I dutifully model the tunic, hoping to mimic Jezebel's graceful movements, if nothing else. As I turn my back, nobody claps, and when I face the front, I just see a sea of blank, bored faces. They remind me of the cows in Kirkness, slowly chewing, staring blandly and without curiosity as you go past on your bike. Duncan examines my top mercilessly, hugging himself and slowly rocking backwards and forwards.

'Turn round,' he orders, impatiently spinning his finger in a clockwise direction. I do, feeling like a slave or a prize pig he's just purchased.

'So, Evie . . .' he murmurs. 'What is it?'

'It's a tunic,' I tell him. 'I wanted to try and recreate some old-time glamour, where sexiness was about suggestion rather than showing lots of skin. I wanted to take that crisp, high-collared shape, you know, like the necklines in er . . . *Sabrina* with Audrey Hepburn and a lot of the Sixties Hitchcock heroines, and give it a glamorous, night-time feel – a sort of 1920s gangster feel.' Oh God – I sound like an idiot.

'And what are these?' he says, pointing at my sleeves.

'They're sleeves.'

There's a snigger from the class, cut short. Duncan gives them an evil stare.

'Yes, well, technically, it's the most advanced piece I've seen from a first-year student in years,' Duncan declares. 'It's a well-put-together, deftly constructed outfit. The problem is, it's rubbish. It looks like something from a bloody panto. Being technically proficient is fine and dandy but it's another thing entirely to make something wearable and stylish. It's stuck in the past, a confused mixture of styles that neither fits the brief nor looks flattering. Who would want to wear that on a night out? You look like you should be appearing in *Aladdin*.'

There's a gale of laughter at Duncan's joke, though he's not laughing. He's completely serious. I look at Neil, resplendent in his stupid wings, smirking. I wish I had some buckshot.

'It's behind you, Evgeniya!' Jezebel chirps, her voice shrill and malicious.

There's another burst of hilarity. 'Yeah! That's her real name!' I hear Flossy hissing, her eyes glinting with amusement.

'Sounds like vagina!' someone yelps.

I glare at Flossy, the little traitor. I thought she was like Mona, harmless and directionless, but she's as shallow and conniving as the rest of them. My knees are losing their ability to support me, and my chest feels hollow, a pair of invisible hands are wringing the air from my lungs. Crying is not an option – don't cry.

'Have you finished with me?' I spit, staring at Duncan through a film of welling-up tears. Oh, how I loathe him – his fat neck and his salt-of-the-earth working-class-hero bullshit, his camp diamond earring and arrogant big ideas. What's he ever done with his life? Stuck on the 386th floor of a run-down technical college. What a star.

'Yes. Thank you, Evie.' He bows, with mock politeness, and I go back to my seat. He writes something down, but I can't figure out what it is by the movement of his hand. Probably 'CRAP' with a capital C. Someone else steps to the front, a guy called Jack or Jim or something, but Duncan's voice is an indistinct burble and all I want to do is leave the room. The brocade on the collar is itching and I just want to get changed and throw the whole thing in the bin and get away from all my enemies. What I'd really like to do more than anything, right now, is get the bus home to Kirkness and sit at the kitchen table with my mum as she sketches out designs on bits of paper and I do the same, while the sea, just visible through the grubby, tiny panes of the kitchen window, carries on with its eternal comings and goings. Then at five o'clock we could watch a film like we used to do when I was small, something featuring Bette Davis or Ingrid Bergman, some pot-boiling old melodrama about evil governesses or silk-clad temptresses, getting their comeuppance in the end. I get a pang of homesickness that almost makes me dizzy.

After an excruciating half hour, Duncan calls lunch and I go to the downstairs toilet to change out of my stupid tunic. Andrea, of the drooping corset, gives me a baleful look on my way out, as if to say 'Keep your pecker up, you'll do better next time' and I return it with a tight smile. I can't let them see that Duncan's comments or those bitches in the class have got to me. At least the toilets here on the graphic design floor are cool and mercifully empty. I stuff the tunic in a carrier bag and change back into a black jumper and skirt. Staying here, listening to Duncan praise Neil's seagull outfit to the heavens, is not an option.

The bus smells of damp umbrellas and old ladies, but I swing myself onto it like a woman possessed, counting the revs of the rumbling engine as they take me away from MetroTurd College. Installed in my seat, carrier bag on my knee, I watch the city slip by, and as the bus follows its circuitous route to the West End, I feel better, the motion of the wheels offering a temporary respite from thinking. I'm nearly home by the time I come to, and I shuffle down the aisle to get off with the rest of the skiving students and young mothers and pensioners who travel around on buses in the afternoon. Through the blur of diesel and dirt on the window a couple of passers-by catch my eye. They're a picture of togetherness. She's dark, slim, elegant and dressed in velvet, a little over the top for a wet Friday afternoon, and he's tall and scruffy, wearing a padded jacket, hair everywhere. Carrying a red polka-dot umbrella, Nadine looks up at him, as if she's squinting against the sun, and laughs, putting her arm easily around Mickey's back. Mickey happily lets it rest there as they stroll round the corner.

Step Nine – Picking up Mistakes

Even the best dressmakers can occasionally fudge a seam or tear a lining. However, if you find yourself unpicking until your fingers are raw and wondering what compelled you to begin, then you have failed to follow your pattern correctly. In the most extreme cases, it may be necessary to start again from the beginning.

Back at the flat, all is still. I've never really been home when Lorna isn't around, and it makes me feel as if I'm trespassing. Everything is just-so, the remote controls neatly lined up on the coffee table, the sofa cushions plumped up and arranged, the kitchen so unnaturally ordered that the coffee and tea jars and various utensils look like props on a film set. It's all so uniformly miserable and uncomfortable that I want to cry.

I take the opportunity to poke my head around Lorna's door. I've never been officially invited in there, but I get a sneaking feeling that she doesn't mind having a good look in my room. There aren't many surprises – a smooth plump duvet encased in cream and beige checked fabric, a few pictures of Charlie, and a gleaming bank of mirrored wardrobes that show several versions of me, a small, flushed and desperate-looking person, lurking around in someone else's bedroom. I stand there for a while nervously, not knowing what I expect to find.

Vaguely ashamed, I return to my tomb, I mean room, and hold the red, trailing dress I've been working on against my body. It's not fully pressed and finished, but most of the seams have been expertly bound, the neckline is classically curved, the skirt cut on the bias. It's a dead on size 10. It's perfect. Technically.

I slump onto the bed.

Perfectly boring. It's a truss. Restricting, old-fashioned, unsexy. Infuriatingly, Duncan has seen something I couldn't see, not until now. Like the tunic, the dress does nothing for me. It has no magic properties. It's a pathetic echo of the past, nothing but a cheap copy of a dress that suited Carole Lombard but doesn't suit me. Nothing suits me. This house, college, this town, with its clans of arty, music, fashion people, all somehow connected in a million obscure ways, all swimming around pointlessly together at parties and clubs. A lead weight settles in my stomach when I think of the indignities and humiliations I've suffered today. Could being at home be worse than this?

I glare at Edith, straightforward bespectacled Miss Head, who with the power of persuasion and visual flair won seven Oscars and the admiration of her peers.

My hero. She gazes downwards, imperious, totally self-contained. She once said that you can have anything you want in life if you dress for it.

Anything.

But what do I want? Frustration rises inside me, a furious force that makes my hands shake. I want to be good. I want to be great. I cast it aside, and go back out to the kitchen, my footsteps breaking the silence of Lorna's empty flat. What I need are my scissors. I search the kitchen drawers. Lorna, I've recently discovered, uses my scissors to cut chives (a herb she appears to be obsessed with, for no other reason apart from the fact you can snip them up into pretty little bits and sprinkle them everywhere). I've been too afraid she might snap and come running after me with them to point out that stealing my scissors and blunting them on food is a cardinal sin. I look in the usual places – the cutlery drawer, the drawer she keeps cake cutters and corkscrews in – but I can't find them. I open every drawer in the room, ones for tea towels, ones for kitchen timers and strange time-saving devices from the Lakeland catalogue. Nothing. There's a drawer under the sink, but I've always assumed it was a fake one, just for decoration. But I pull at the handle and it actually moves, and there are my scissors, the long blades glinting ominously. Looking closer, I can see that this shallow, narrow little drawer is unlike the rest. It's a complete mess, a tangle of crumpled envelopes, squished boxes and little brown pill bottles. The labels say, 'Eskalith – 300mg – take one three times daily. DO NOT EXCEED DOSE. In the event of adverse effects seek immediate medical advice. Miss Lorna McHastie.' The mysterious capsules are grey and yellow – some bottles are half empty, some are untouched. I look at one of the envelopes – stamped with NHS in red, but I daren't open them.

'ZZZZZZZZZ!'

The buzzer makes me leap backwards and smack my hip on the work surface, leaving me winded. It couldn't be Lorna, she would have a key, she would never forget her key . . . maybe it's a double-glazing salesman or something. Breathing heavily, trying to stave off a rumbling feeling of fear, I retrieve my scissors and slam the drawer shut, then shuffle through the hall to the intercom.

'Hello?'

'Evie?'

'Yes?'

'It's Alice. Can I come up?'

'Alice?' Alice. What would Alice want? 'Er, yeah. Hang on.'

I hear a buzz and a click from downstairs. My head is scrambled with new bits of information that don't fit together. I have no idea what's going on. I lean on the doorframe, trying to compose myself, the bright after-image of the pills burning on my eyeballs. Maybe they're for a back complaint – she sometimes mentions aches and pains. Maybe they're not. I open the door as Alice comes bounding up the stairs, thankfully without Mickey and Nadine in tow to give me my final slap in the face. She's holding a coat over her arm and smiling. I realize I'm pleased to see her – she's the only person I know in Glasgow who hasn't turned into some kind of monster. When she sees me, though, her face suddenly falls.

'Evie?' she says, encouragingly, as if coaxing someone down from a ledge. 'What's the matter?'

I realize I'm breathing heavily, still holding the scissors out like I'm about to stab her.

'Sorry,' I say, putting them safely down on the telephone table. 'I was just doing some sewing. Come in.'

'Are you sure you're OK? You look really spooked,' she says, moving through the hallway. I look down at her shoes, green charity-shop heels, slightly muddy.

'Take your shoes off!' I shout.

'OK!' she says, holding her hands up in surrender, and flips them off into the corner.

'I'm sorry,' I yelp, guiding her away from the hall carpet and the sacred B&Q laminate flooring. 'Come in – I'll make you a cup of tea.'

'OK . . . cool,' she says uncertainly, looking around at the gleaming paintwork and neutral decor. 'Nice place you've got here – very clean, isn't it?'

We both stand around for a second, unsure of what to say. Alice's wild-haired presence is so out of place in the controlled, polished silence of Lorna's flat that it seems as if someone just deposited a tree in the living room.

'The reason I'm here is that I brought you your coat,' she says. 'I just found it. You left it at the party.'

She hands me the vinyl raincoat and I look at it as if it's some object from another world. My coat. The party. The memory of me and Mickey cavorting on the bed suddenly comes back to me with disorientating and painful clarity, but I swat it away like a fly.

'Thanks. I forgot all about it.'

'I hope you don't think I was being nosy, but I found this in it,' she says, handing me a wad of paper. 'It had your address on it . . .' Alice seems embarrassed. 'Sorry to be nosy,' she says again.

It's the contract. Pages and pages of bizarre and unreasonable demands, with my signature at the end of it. I must have put it in my pocket.

'Thanks,' I say, even though the sight of it makes my skin crawl. 'Thanks for bringing it back. So would you like tea or coffee, or something stronger?' I breeze, sounding artificially upbeat, like someone in an advert.

'Tea's great.' She smiles, appearing to relax slightly. 'Milk, one sugar.'

'OK. I'll be back in a sec. Make yourself at home!'

I go to the kitchen and fill the kettle, skirting warily around the secret drawer under the sink. Acting normally seems to be almost impossible. Everything is falling apart, unravelling around me like so much spilled thread. But I must be focused. The medication could be anything, and what happens in Lorna's personal life is up to her. As for Mickey – he's with Nadine, she told you so herself, so get used to it. Stop overreacting.

'Evie?' I can hear Alice say from the bedroom. 'Did you make this?'

Alice drifts in, holding the dress against her. The blood-red satin goes well with her white skin and dark hair, but the smooth perfect finish of it is all wrong.

'Yes, but it's not finished.'

'It's beautiful. Do you know how clever you are?' she says. Although she's only a girl holding a piece of material, it's as if a light has been switched on and for a glorious moment I can see what I need to do with it – make a few raw edges, put some different-coloured stitching on it and some detail . . . make it breathe. *Loosen it up.* I can almost feel a pinging lightbulb over my head, with 'Idea!' emblazoned across it. It's as if Alice was the missing link in the whole process, and now it's all there, waiting to come to life.

She wanders off, seemingly mesmerized, running the material through her fingers, and I finish off the tea with trembling hands, my head rattling with inspired ideas. I remember my mum's excuse for not making the dinner – 'I can't just now, I'm gripped,' she'd say – and now I know what she meant.

As I stumble in with the mugs, perhaps not exactly being as careful as I usually am, Alice is sitting on my bed. She's found my portfolio and has it spread out on her lap.

'These are really amazing designs,' she says, leafing through it carefully, treating the pages as if they're an ancient manuscript, which could crumble into dust. 'They're exactly the kind of things I would wear. You should go into business.'

'Do you think so?'

'Yeah!'

I feel seized, like my dad when he's bashing nails into something in the middle of the night. Maybe

I'm the one who needs medication. I get my pins and start to adjust the dress, tugging this way and that.

'Sorry, you just gave me an idea for the dress,' I say, getting a seam ripper and pushing the stitches apart. 'Do you mind if I do some work?'

'Oh, OK. Sure!' says Alice brightly. 'Oh, how exciting. I've always wanted to be someone's muse!' she adds, watching me as I thread the sewing machine with green cotton, the same sea green colour as Alice's bedroom walls.

My mind is buzzing with possibilities, make a frill, stitch it, fray it, knock it about a bit. I work for a while, consumed with the process, tearing gaping wounds in the seams so I can resew them. It's almost fun to watch it come apart in my hands.

'Anyway, Mickey wanted to bring the coat, but I wanted to see you,' says Alice, putting the portfolio back on the shelf.

My hands do an involuntary spasm and stitches burst free like tiny hairs standing on end.

'Oh, right,' I say, suddenly dry mouthed. I carry on unpicking the dress. For a moment it looks like I've completely ruined it, threads unravelling everywhere. An excuse to get his manuscript back, no doubt.

'I'm not just saying this, Evie, your stuff is really special,' Alice says conversationally. 'I've never seen clothes made so well. Why don't you make up a couple of things and I'll take them around for you? I know a few people in shops round here who would love them.'

'Oh, they wouldn't . . .' I mumble, turning on the machine. 'I can't even pass a MetroTech College first-year assessment.'

I tell her about the tunic and Jezebel and Duncan's appraisal. Alice is outraged.

'No wonder you're upset! You tell 'em to stick it! Arseholes!' she cries. Her indignant fury is infectious and I rise to meet it. 'Don't you think this'd be a perfect time to strike out on your own?' she froths. 'You've got the talent – who needs an HND anyway? I bet she didn't have one!' Alice points at Edith, causing me to feel temporarily dizzy. 'You could have your own cottage industry and I could make the tea and draw the labels.'

My face flushes at the thought of it. I think of Alice's childlike handwriting on her doorbell, and the 'Drink Me' drawing she did for her party invite – her style would look good on a cardboard label or sewn into a collar. 'Kaminsky designs' . . . 'EK' . . . 'Fashions by Evie'.

'We should totally do it, even if it is only part time or whatever,' she continues, boundlessly enthusiastic. 'Sale or return, nothing for anyone to lose. If you're gonna make them you may as well try to flog 'em. What do you think? Shall I go round and pimp you to all the fabulous boutiques?'

She makes it sound easy. I look at Alice, smiling winningly, curls reverberating at the thought of it, and realize she's seriously asking for my permission.

'Do you really think they'd be interested?'

'Yes!' she says, and I see a sincerity and determination

in her that I've never noticed before. Maybe it could work. After all, Alice does seem to know everyone in town. Duncan and his gang of lame fashionistas, up in their workroom playing obscure, pointless games of one-upmanship, suddenly seem disconnected from reality. Would I really be better off toeing the line at MetroTech?

'OK,' I say quietly.

'Evie Kaminsky will be the coolest new designer in town. You'll be snowed under with commissions! You can do it!' She grabs both my shoulders and does a little joyful dance. 'It's going to be great!'

For a minute, an image of me in my studio, beavering away making patterns, comes to me as clearly as if I was already there.

'Now get to work, bitch,' Alice whoops, bouncing back onto the bed. 'You're going to wear that dress tonight and we're going to go out.'

Dizzy, I dutifully start sewing. Alice sips her tea. In the kitchen, I can hear the boiler's pilot light flaring into life and the radiator starts its slow, hopeful ticking, warmth gathering at the corners of the room. She takes out a notebook and an ink pen, and soon there's a hum of productivity of the likes never before seen in Lorna's flat, as we work in our own private worlds. Outside, rain crackles against the window. This is more like it. Screw college. For the first time in a long time, I know what I'm doing, focused, no worries, no self-consciousness. It's not so difficult. The material runs through my hands, and seems to bring itself together of its own accord, hems roughen and unravel and are stitched back into place, the green cotton runs through the sleek red satin forming a luxurious contrast – emeralds and rubies. Meanwhile, there's the almost inaudible scrape of pen nib against paper. Time passes, both of us absorbed. I don't feel in control any more, I'm just letting the machine do its work, easing my foot onto the pedal in a trance. This is easy. It just drifts by me, as if in a dream, taking my problems with it. When I feel like it's finished, I snip the thread from the machine and carefully turn it inside out, then give it its final pressing. The iron glides over the fabric – the seams fall into place. I hold it up against the light, examining it for flaws, and almost marvel at it. Even though I made it, it's as if it just landed, fully formed, in my hands, complete with supernatural powers. A pair of ruby slippers.

'Is it done? Already? Wow!' Alice stares blindly, as if jolted awake, then a look of joy crosses her face.

'It's beautiful,' she coos, leaping up. It does look much better. Rough-edged frills flop prettily like damp, blood-red rose petals, the waist is more flattering tucked in, and the skirt looks fuller with a wavy, rougher hem.

'Put it on! Put it on!' she crows. 'I want to see you in it!'

Doing what I'm told, I slip into the bathroom and get changed. Suddenly, there I am, clad in rich red satin, the wee genie in the tunic transformed into a budding Scarlett O'Hara. It's one of my better creations, even if I do say so myself.

'Let me see!' Alice shrieks from behind the bathroom

door. I square up to her in the hall, feeling like a contestant on a makeover show.

'WOW! I love it!' she squeals. 'You look perfect! Stunning! If I was a man, I'd have yer!' she laughs. 'My God, it's a dream dress . . . you're a total genius!' She gives me a surprisingly ardent hug, as if we've been reunited after years apart.

'Well, I reckon this calls for a celebration,' she says decisively. 'Get your coat, you – we're going to go out and show this off. Fancy a drink? I'll buy.'

'OK,' I say.

'Oh, by the way – this is for you,' she says, going back into the bedroom and ripping a leaf from her sketchbook. It's a pen and ink drawing of me looking determined, working at the sewing machine in a thoroughly professional and absorbed pose. It doesn't look unlike my postcard of Edith.

'Can I have it?'

'Duh. Yeah.' She smiles, plonking onto the bed and adjusting her sock.

'Thanks,' I whisper, feeling flattered.

Bypassing the scattered threads and the empty cotton reel on the floor, past the tea that has formed a brown ring on the worktop, I tack it to the wall with a pin, Clause 17 – no holes in wallpaper – be damned.

On the way out, having grabbed my bag and coat and put on matching red shoes, I look again in the full-length mirror, just to check it all fits. On the glass is a Post-it note, in Lorna's tight handwriting, saying, 'SMILE! Everything is going to be fine!'

'Alice?'

'What?' she says, her reflection a dark blur behind me.

'Do you know what Eskalith is?'

'Eskalith? No.'

Turning away from the mirror, my eye catches the front door just as it opens, and in comes Lorna, face like thunder, cursing the raindrops that have dared to spatter her Gap trenchcoat. We stand stock still, as if we've done something terribly wrong. I'm suddenly spectacularly overdressed for this encounter. Lorna shakes her umbrella three distinct times before placing it in the umbrella stand, then removes her shoes, bending down to place them square against the wall. The fact that we're only a metre away doesn't seem to distract her from the ritual.

'Hi, Lorna,' I say, gently.

'Christ!' she yells, her hand flying to her chest. 'You scared me to death!'

'Sorry, sorry,' I say in a flap. 'I didn't mean to frighten you. I'm just on my way out. Lorna, this is Alice – Alice, this is Lorna, my flatmate.'

Lorna gives Alice a look of annoyed confusion.

'Oh,' she says eventually, as if confronted with a dog turd. 'Hello.'

'Hello,' Alice replies, smiling regardless, still full of dress-related fizziness.

'Evie, what on earth have you got on?' Lorna notes.

'It's a dress. We're just on our way out,' I tell her, hoping she won't notice any mud on the carpet or tea stains on the floor. 'Is Charlie coming over this weekend?'

'Hmm,' she says, not really listening, looking at a distant point in the kitchen as if trying to figure something out.

'OK, well, see you later.' I guide Alice gently out of the door. She shoots me a look, which I shoot right back.

'You'd better not make a noise when you come in,' Lorna says with a smile, her bland features spreading into a saccharine grimace.

'No, I won't,' I reply uncertainly. 'See you later.' I carefully pass her, trying not to look her in the eye. Sure enough, just as Alice is halfway down to the next floor, Lorna stops me.

'Can I just have a quick word?' she trills politely, but her eyes are cold and her expression defiant.

'Sure,' I whimper.

'You are starting to test my patience,' she urgently hisses, her manicured nails digging painfully into my arm and dragging me inside. 'Don't mess with me, Evie. You've been violating clauses in my contract since you arrived. I don't like visitors and I don't like your attitude, or the way you embarrass me in front of my boyfriend at the dinner table. And I don't like this!'

She runs to her bedroom and returns, brandishing an empty brown cardboard cup. On the side it says 'Wickedly Indulgent Chocolate Cappuccino Ice Cream'. She waves it in the air as if it's a severed head.

'I found this in your room,' she spits. 'What do you think you're doing?'

I knew it. I knew she was in my room.

'Get your act together, or you're out.' She unhooks

her nails, pushes me back, and with a powerful wrist she lobs the door shut in my face. I end up looking at the wood panels, just as I did when she turfed me out after the interview, but now I'm shaking uncontrollably.

'Is everything OK?' Alice whispers from the landing below. I follow her down the stairs, past the flats of people who are allowed to laugh and shout and move around in their houses without the thought police coming to get them.

'Let's just go,' I say. The skin on my arm is stinging as if it's been stabbed with five hot pins.

Step Ten – To Thine Own Self Be True

> Imagine yourself in your ideal dress. Perhaps it has stylish bows at the décolletage, or Parisian bindings. But is it really right for your shape? What looks ravishing on a slender model may not flatter those with a matronly bust. You must know what suits you in order to dazzle your expectant crowd – it is the key to presenting an attractive package to others. Get it wrong, and your dress will be wearing *you*.

Alice sets a glass of wine in front of me, and I take a large swig. The pub is busy but friendly, at least. We sit in a corner, at a large table, the hum of conversation around us. It feels good to be somewhere warm and well populated, the oak panelling and the glittering mirrored bar form a cocoon I'm glad to hide in, away from the white, creepy wasteland of the flat.

'Lorna is really starting to freak me out,' I tell her.

'She does seem a little bit . . . intense.'

'That's one way of putting it.'

'I read the contract . . .' ventures Alice. 'And that was very weird. All these rules and regulations . . . and I mean, some of them were deranged. "Do not put your feet on the coffee table; do not mix up the kitchen filing system; no phone calls after eight o'clock" . . . Why did you sign it?'

'I don't know,' I say, and now I really don't know. I felt so clever, so lucky to have found a neat and tidy flat. It was a triumph. I thought Lorna and I were similar, but that's now so ludicrous I can't even begin to explain it to Alice. Who would volunteer for this? It's insane.

'You could come and stay at mine,' Alice offers.

'Yeah, I suppose,' I say uncertainly. But for all of Alice's kindness, I get the sinking feeling that the alternative wouldn't be ideal either. The mural and the boxes and the stuffy smell, combined with the memory of Mickey's arm, lying heavy and suffocatingly across my body. Nadine in the kitchen, sly eyes like a cat, stuff strewn across the floor, lost hours doing God knows what. There just doesn't seem to be a happy medium.

'The thing is, it's not as if Lorna hasn't been nice to me,' I splutter, backtracking. 'She's taken me shopping, she cooked me meals. It's as if she needs me more than I need her, and I can't let her down. As far as I know, she hasn't got any other friends.'

'I'm not surprised.'

'Maybe I should just talk to her,' I venture, nervously running my finger around the rim of the glass. The truth of the matter is that I'm scared what she'll do next. 'I think I need to have a chat with her, straighten a few things out . . .' I rub my skin where her nail marks are still stinging. 'It'll be fine.'

I look around the twinkling bar, filled with the accelerated glee of the Friday-night boozers, and get that buzzing feeling again, the will to escape. Except this time it's more urgent than before.

'Anyway, what do you want to do tonight?'

'Well,' Alice sighs, propping her elbows up on the table, 'the world is our oyster. We could go on a tour of fine eating and drinking establishments, take in a couple of shows and art galleries, dance the night away. Or we could just see where the mood takes us.'

I look down at the dress. It looks so much better now it's let itself go a bit.

'Let's be spontaneous,' I say, remembering my dad in Pomodoro, forcing me to choose food with my eyes closed. I wouldn't have chosen it myself, but it turned out to be delicious in the end.

'Sounds good to me. So here's to tonight! Hey, and here's to your fabulous business, Evie Kaminsky Designs!' she says grandly. She clinks glasses with me and I see her knowing look is back again, the glinting, mischievous fairy. I realize I don't know anything about Alice – it's like she sprang from the bushes covered in pixie dust and has decided to take me on a journey. Alice in Wonderland. Maybe if I just shut up and follow her, everything will turn out all right.

'Hey, did you hear about Johnny?' she asks, as if she's remembered something earth-shatteringly important.

'No – what about him?'

She takes a magazine from her bag – a music magazine – and flicks to a page. There he is, pouting outrageously, leather jacket and cheekbones, hair carefully sculpted over one eye. Behind him are the other members, anonymous and out of focus, sitting moodily on a bench in the park.

'Can you believe it? They got signed about a month ago and he didn't say a word. And look!'

Alice points to a paragraph of over-excited blurb, featuring a quote from Johnny. It reads: '"Little Miss Prim" is about this really cool girl I know called Evie – I met her in a café underneath some plastic onions on a rainy day in Glasgow and I just had to write that song. We did it in about five minutes. We just wanna write songs about situations and characters around us, because everybody is a star.'

'Oh please,' I murmur, secretly chuffed, my eyes wandering over the headline: 'Up And Coming: Bottle Rocket – Best New Band in Britain?'

'Is this for real? Or has Johnny written it all himself?'

'It's for real. Apparently it's a really big deal. Everyone is saying they're going to be huge. Isn't it weird?'

I feel a rush of fondness for Johnny, his gangly, clumsy awkwardness and too-tight leather jacket, and can't help feeling flattered. But to think that I could be his muse is too ridiculous to contemplate, let alone that he might actually be a rock star one day.

'You must have turned his head,' Alice grins. 'Get a load of this.'

She points at the picture of the cover of their new

single. It's a girl in a café with a supernaturally straight black fringe, looking stern and caught off guard. It doesn't look like me, but it is, it's the photo he took without my permission, just before I got the call from Lorna that led me to where I am now.

'Oh God, I look awful . . .' I start to say, wondering how I could have possibly got myself into this position. My world is upside down and back to front, packed to the gills with jolts and surprises.

'I think you look pretty. Just think . . . a hot fashion designer with rock star connections! Rawwwr!' She licks her finger and makes a sizzling noise.

'Oh God!' I yelp again. I look away towards the fruit machine, where a man is staring at me, a look of blank approval on his face. 'I can't believe he'd do that.'

Alice sucks on her bottom lip and makes a kind of raspberry noise.

'Anyway, seeing as you're such a FABULOUS icon all of a sudden,' she says, rolling her eyes, 'are you up for an arty-farty party? There's an opening in town – this guy I know is having an exhibition.'

'An exhibition?'

Something jars and I shift uncomfortably in my seat. My festive feeling has gone. Going home to Lorna would be like throwing myself to the lions, and the other option is to go to a gallery, where people like my parents will be gathered around a wine box, talking crap.

'Mm, I dunno,' I say, feeling lost. 'I'm not a big fan.'

'Come on – we can always leave if it's shit. We're

being spontaneous, right?' She downs her glass and gets up.

'Hmm. Right,' I say with some reluctance, getting up from my chair. I suddenly don't want to go. Spontaneity is tiring. What if I wake up one day with squirrels in my hair like my mother?

'Everyone's going to be there.' Alice winks.

'Who?'

Please don't say it. Don't.

'Mickey?' suggests Alice.

On cue, the backs of my knees threaten to buckle and snap like elastic bands. Damn him. But I suppose I have to tell him I've read his book. It might be good for me to free myself from this particular tangle right now. Maybe it'll be character building, and I can move on and hang out with someone who doesn't carry on with girls behind my back and mess with my head all the time and write fantastically insightful and sensitive novels that make me want to marry him.

'Come on,' she says, giving that look, and I can tell she's not going to take no for an answer anyway.

The work of Tomas Jankowski is not the kind of thing you will ever see in Kirkness library, Sheila Warren's gallery or the Wobbly Wheel. It appears to be made up of large and not very subtle protrusions sticking out of chairs and walls. One piece is a small wooden box, set low by a plug socket. If you open it, a big thing comes out at you, like Pinocchio's nose, or something else belonging to Pinocchio, and when you close the door, it goes back in. Tracy, who is currently crouched on the floor beside it almost crying with laughter, keeps opening the door and touching it, until someone, a tall pointy man, possibly Tomas Jankowski himself, tells her off. There are no watercolours, and no wine boxes, only a mountain of ravaged carry-outs from the off-licence and a haphazard sensation that this party has been going on since last week and is just about to get out of hand. Over in the corner is a man in a suit with a pair of black-framed glasses, roaring drunkenly, while his friend, a dissolute-looking chap with a red shirt and an unruly black quiff, laughs blearily along. Next to them is a girl in an Afghan coat, dancing to the music being pumped out from an invisible source, which sounds like someone plucking a shoebox with elastic bands stretched across it. All the while, a small white Highland terrier licks up beer spillages and wobbles in between the legs of the crowd.

'That guy wouldn't let me touch his pole,' says Tracy, seeming put out, a big sweaty cup of white wine in her hand. 'Ah been here hours. What time is it?'

'It's half past seven,' I say, picking a foreign object, possibly cheese, out of her hair. I stand there stupidly, not knowing what to do with my hands, wishing I had a drink or a cigarette, and wishing that the entire room wasn't filled with lurid, phallic-looking objects. *Changing Rooms* and a quiet night in wearing a pair of pyjamas keeps getting more and more attractive, and it's exactly where I'd be right now if it wasn't for the dragon at home. Alice, meanwhile, is a picture of composure, skittering around the room, talking to an expensively dressed woman with a perky blond ponytail. The woman eyes me with suave interest, and I smile and look away. I'm totally overdressed and not for the first time today, I feel exposed and subject to a lot of potential ridicule. When I turn back to Tracy, she puts her cup of wine in my hand and stumbles off, going headfirst through a door that is either the toilet or a broom cupboard. I set it delicately down on a ledge.

'HEEEEEY! EVIE!' comes a roar from behind me. Johnny. And he's pissed – rubbery black-clad arms and legs flapping like a deranged spider. These people stick to each other like glue. How do they all know where to find each other? He slams into me, hugs me to his bony frame and lifts me off my feet, forcing me to grab at his neck with my free hand. His skin feels as if it's made of the same leathery substance as his jacket, cool and slithery. Over his shoulder I notice Mickey loitering in the far corner. He's wearing the big, padded, fur-collared jacket he was wearing earlier, when I saw him from the bus, and a faded T-shirt that looks as if it was last washed in 1974. I extricate myself from Johnny, embarrassed. Everyone's looking at us with a mixture of horror and awe.

'Hey, Johnny.'

'Don't "hey, Johnny" me, Prim – I'm a fucking rock star. What do you think of that?' He grins, putting his thumbs in his belt loops and holding his chin aloft, one of his standard Mick Jagger moves.

'Yeah, I heard. Well done.' I smile at the ridiculousness of his pose. He looks like a chicken.

'Goin' on tour tomorrow. Wanna come and be my number-one groupie?'

I briefly close my eyes and pick up Tracy's drink. I think I need it.

'No, you're all right.'

'You love it, really,' he says lasciviously, looking at my cleavage. 'When I'm famous you're gonna come running, mark my words.'

'Is that right?'

'That's right, doll. And Johnny's gonna make you sweat for it.'

I roll my eyes. He's already talking in the third person and there seems to be something suspiciously powdery around his left nostril. Johnny waves his finger in front of me as if to hypnotize me, and lands it on the end of my nose, which annoys me immensely.

'Hey, DOUGIE BOY!' he yells, spying one of his cronies behind me and buggering off. I try to act casually, and fixate on one of the protrusions, but out of the corner of my eye I'm watching Mickey. Best to get this over with. Great book, blah blah, see you around. I take a deep breath, trying to conquer the sensation of losing my balance, and move towards him, clutching Tracy's wine. He isn't smiling, or looking particularly welcoming. Then I notice Nadine is with him, hanging a few paces behind, as if she's been standing outside waiting to pounce. She's powdered and prodded herself into a thoroughly immaculate state, wearing a black sheath dress and a fake mink wrap accessorized with a fancy diamanté brooch. Nadine bleedin' Hepburn, back to claim her prize. I wonder whether it's too late to do a quick U-turn, but she spots me and sends me a lukewarm smile, her feline eyes unchanging. Instead of whisking her boyfriend away, though, she decorously moves away towards the drinks table, where she starts talking to some girl in a blue jacket with what looks like a dinner plate on the lapel.

'Hi,' I say, delivering myself in front of him.

'Hi,' he says nonchalantly.

'I read your book,' I say boldly. Now it's his turn to lose his balance. I watch him flinch, a barely palpable movement, and the colour spreads to his cheeks again. The fur on his collar twitches in the draught from the door like a frightened rodent.

'So . . . what did you think?' He's paying attention now, his voice no louder than a whisper.

There's a split-second pause. Oh, I could be horrible. I could mess him about like nobody's business, like he's messed me about. I casually sip Tracy's wine, which is warm and vile. But I'm a lousy liar, and I really can't be bothered to torture him.

'It was really good. Very good.'

He frowns, swaying slightly. 'You're not just saying that, are you?'

'No. You're an excellent writer.'

'Any criticisms?' he asks quickly, preparing himself.

'Well, you know . . . I'm not an expert, so don't get upset or anything, but I mean, the character was great, but—'

'But what?' His eyes are clouded, his bottom lip pursed.

I hesitate, not quite sure how to word it, or if I should say it at all.

'Come on, I can take it,' he says.

'OK . . .' I clear my throat. 'Well, it's just that . . . if he grew up on an estate, with drugs and all that, why was he so shocked and naïve when he came to the city and fell into doing similar things? The part when he's led astray didn't seem to wash somehow. He kept making excuses for himself, and not taking responsibility for his actions, and I lost my way a bit with him – he started getting on my nerves.'

Mickey's jaw clenches. 'Right,' he says, tersely.

'He just seemed slightly spineless to me. Like he needed to make up his mind what he wanted.' As I speak I'm vaguely aware that not all of this is unbiased literary criticism.

'Interesting,' he snaps, and I can see I've pissed him off.

'It's just one opinion,' I venture. 'Otherwise, it really was great.'

'You don't have to pretend you liked it to spare my feelings,' he murmurs, 'that's fine.'

'I . . .'

'I mean, some people are blessed, obviously,' he says quickly, his forehead knotted, looking around the room.

'What does that mean?'

He laughs, mirthlessly. 'I mean, it's OK for some people. They know where they're going, they know who to get in with, they're flavour of the month without even trying. All they need to do is network and go to parties and everyone thinks they're fucking geniuses.

It's not *what* you know, is it?' he says, glowering over at Johnny and bringing his eyes back to me.

I take another sip of Tracy's wine and the nail-varnish-flavoured Chardonnay coats my stomach with steel and fire. Suddenly he doesn't seem so attractive. Needy and whiny, self-obsessed, jealous, insecure, over-sensitive and dead wrong too, but I'm not going to give him the satisfaction of knowing that, not when he's parading Nadine under my nose like some mail-order Thai bride. What a cheek.

'You can think what you like,' I say, sick to the back teeth of being attacked and judged. 'You asked me to read your book and I was just trying to help. Now why don't you go and ask your girlfriend for her opinion?'

I notice, with some relief, that Alice is frantically waving me over to the woman with the ponytail, who is still observing me with an almost lustful gaze. My heart is thumping, and although I don't want to go and talk to the intimidating stranger, I need to get away from Mickey. In a state of high anxiety, and almost hyperventilating, I try to depart with the correct measure of grace and poise, but my body doesn't want to co-operate, and instead I fling myself towards them with all the force of a champion shot putter.

'Evie, this is Jess,' Alice twinkles.

'Hello, Jess,' I say, as evenly as I can. She seems important in some way, and Alice is looking at me with an expression of silent encouragement.

'Alice has been telling me all about your designs – that dress is just fantastic!' Jess immediately starts saying, her hand, heavy with jewellery, darting out to shake mine. She has a low, smoky voice and is older than us, in her forties, maybe, wearing what looks a vintage Givenchy jacket. Who is she? She certainly seems to have no qualms about staring at my cleavage.

'I've got a shop in town – Candy – have you heard of it?'

'Oh . . . right – oh, yes,' I say. My head is spinning and the cheap white wine is forming a fur on my tongue. Alice doesn't waste any time, does she? I adjust a frill, hoping to show the dress to its best advantage. 'It's in the Arcade,' she continues. 'Next to the jewellers.'

'Oh yes,' I say again. I do know the shop, I know it well. It's a fancy boutique with a dress in the window I've been coveting for a while but couldn't possibly afford. The bags are candy striped and tied with pink ribbon and the shop always appears in magazines that herald Glasgow as the glitzy shopping capital of Scotland – rumour has it that Nicole Kidman herself once went there, or at least stopped outside it to tie her shoelace. I'm sure Mickey would find it all terribly superficial, but sod him.

'It's a beautiful shop,' I tell her sincerely.

'This is really well made,' she says, examining the neckline with the sharp-eyed seriousness of a surgeon. 'Adventurous too. Are you a student?'

'Er . . . yes,' I say, remembering that I go to college, for what it's worth. Alice hangs back, wiggling her eyebrows like Groucho Marx.

'How long do they take you to make?' Jess asks, fingering a frill.

'I've made dresses in a few days. I finished this one today.' I hope I'm holding myself with the right kind of fabulous fashion designer confidence, but I can't help feeling more like a tailor's dummy. Despite myself, my eyes irresistibly slide over to the corner of the room where Mickey and Nadine must be standing, but I can't really make out anything apart from the hurried blur of the white dog, still weaving its way through the crowd.

'She's really fast, Jess,' Alice chips in. 'I watched her – she's a total whiz with the sewing machine. You won't find anyone more talented.' For a second, Alice sounds like my mother.

'Really well made,' Jess murmurs again. 'Do you think you'll be able to make another one of these by the end of the month?'

I nod.

'Great. I like that a lot – we should be able to sell that easily. Come and see me when you're done and we'll talk money. And I'd be interested to know what else you can do,' she adds, opening a flat, silver handbag and producing a card. 'You wouldn't believe how few really good young designers there are around. Do you go to MetroTech?'

'Yes,' I say breathlessly, unable to quite believe what I'm hearing. I take the card, a pink-striped slab embossed with the shop logo and number, with a tiny, thin ribbon sewn into the side. Each one must cost a fiver to make.

'Useless,' she says, rolling her eyes. 'God knows what they teach them there – they seem to think women want to wear lampshades with plastic vegetables stuck on them. Anyway, I've got to go – lovely to meet you, Evie.' She plants an expensively perfumed kiss on my cheek and does the same to Alice. 'I've got to go to a boring charity dinner, which is going to be absolutely full of arses, but I can't get out of it. You girls have a fun night! See you next week!'

And with that, Jess is off, gliding out of the room with her ponytail swinging like a horse's mane, her dainty shoes clicking across the parquet floor. I turn to Alice, who is on the verge of exploding with excitement.

'What's going on?' I ask, fiddling with the fashionably rough edges of the business card.

Alice goes off like a firework.

'Arrrrgh!!' she shrieks. 'She loves it. Honestly, she loved it . . . she was like . . . "I've never seen such strong work from someone so young, blah blah . . ." She was going crazy! You're soooo in there! You see, we've only been in business one night and already we're getting somewhere! We're a great team!'

She involves me in one of her victory dances, a jaunty wee reel, which tips the room this way and that. I go along with it, befuddled. Maybe Edith was right – you can get anything you want if you dress for it. I untangle myself from the jubilant Alice for a second, and when I do, I notice that Mickey's gone, and Nadine is nowhere to be seen.

'Hello, sir. If you could take our jackets that would be dandy,' says Tracy, struggling out of her threadbare charity shop anorak. The doorman picks it off her like it's a festering corpse, and we enter.

This fancy cocktail bar is wildly out of our price range, an old-fashioned place with 1930s plaster mouldings and the wicked smell of oysters and money, staffed by penguin-suited waiters. It's certainly not the sort of place I would expect scruffy art students to go, but Tracy and Alice don't seem at all fazed by the surroundings.

'Well, I said I'd buy you a drink!' says Alice, installing herself on a bar stool. 'I just got my student loan, and we must have Martinis – we're celebrating in style.' The barman looks at her with weary glance. 'Three. Straight up,' she says, with a winning smile, as if she's been ordering them for years. 'With olives, please.'

Tracy, who seems similarly undeterred, drags me to a booth and starts viciously attacking a porcelain bowl of nibbles. I gaze at a giant bottle of champagne – is it called a magnum? I can't believe I'm in a place like this, and keep expecting there to have been some mistake, waiting for a bouncer's arm to land on my shoulder.

'I havenae eaten for ages,' Tracy breathes. 'I'm a mess when I don't get ma tea. We should go to the Philadelphia for chips. Best chips ever . . . better than your Fifer chips. Hey, did you see Mickey at that place? He was supposed to come.'

'He was there for a while and then he left,' I say, picking up a beer mat with a picture of a cocktail on it.

'Och well, he likes to be on his own sometimes. He's from the Highlands, don't you know? They're all very serious and introverted. He probably had to rush back home and write about what he had for his tea in his next novel.'

She watches me expectantly, inserting varnished crackers in her mouth like a gambler feeding a slot machine.

'Yeah, he's really deep, isn't he?' I reply, none too sincerely. I've had it with him. He can't handle criticism so he makes cheap shots about me – how noble. Implying that I'm some kind of shallow, networking tart who knocks around with Johnny to get somewhere . . . who does he think he is? Let Nadine caress his big bloody ego and listen to his self-obsessed bullshit.

I watch as Alice walks slowly back from the bar. The Martinis are a hypnotic puddle of light and everyone is transfixed, watching the icy liquid swim perilously close to the edges of the wide-brimmed glasses.

'For you, ladies . . . and we are ladies, of course . . . a celebratory drink to toast tonight's triumph,' says Alice magnanimously.

'Hear, hear! I mean cheers. Chin-chin!' says Tracy, helping herself.

I take my glass, which has an olive bobbing perkily on the surface, and clink it against theirs. Mine sounds hollow, as if it's not made of the same dazzling substance.

'To us,' says Alice.

'To me!' says Tracy.

I take a sip of firewater and feel lightheaded. I wish I'd never mentioned the book. Perhaps I sounded too harsh. Oh, just forget it. Tracy and Alice are smiling away, friendly and warm and supportive, but the dozy girl in the tunic is back again, and the magic dress feels like it's lost its powers, petals drooping, skirt twisted, the front of it puckered and lined from sitting down. A dress can't be magic, can it? Nothing is. It's just something to wear, that's all.

'You know what you need? You need an identity,' says Alice, popping an olive into her mouth.

'What do you mean?'

'You know all that wanky stuff like marketing and packaging and image. Your brand has to be instantly recognizable. So now you're in demand, what are you going to call yourself?'

'Oh I don't know . . .' I reply listlessly, suddenly feeling uninterested in my amazing future. It's only an idea, vague and fleeting, a business card and a 'see you around'. 'How about . . . Evie Kaminsky Designs?'

'Yeah, but that just sounds like you're doing something . . . Evie Kaminsky Designs . . . Evie Kaminsky Goes To The Toilet,' says Tracy, mulling it over. 'It needs to be snappier . . .'

'Mm. EK?'

'East Kilbride?' Tracy asks.

'Fashions by Evie?'

'Hmm.' Alice frowns.

There's a pause.

'Ahhh!'

'What?'

'Little Miss Prim!' Alice yelps.

'Yesssss!' Tracy hisses. 'I knew Johnny was good for somethin'!'

'I'm . . . not so—'

'It's perfect, don't you think?'

In the candlelight, their expectant faces are glowing like carol singers and I'm touched by how much they seem to care about me and my potential wee business.

'Perfect,' I say, and it is. Why not?

'I'll design the labels – I can see it now, can't you?' I look at Alice, so pretty and full of life, so interested in helping. The overgrown, almost comical bottle of champagne behind her makes her a vision of optimism and celebration. I wish I could shake myself out of this mood. Everything should be so vital and alive – the decadent surroundings, the red dress, my new friends, Jess's calling card burning a hole in my pocket. Instead I can hardly summon the drink up to my lips. Alice dives into her bag to get a pen and starts to scratch out something on a napkin. Tracy and I watch upside down as she draws, and I'm glad for something to concentrate on. After only a few minutes, she produces a cute wee logo and a drawing of a little girl with a black bob that bears a rather striking similarity to me. It's very good, a bit old fashioned, but modern too.

'That's fuckin' spot on!' booms Tracy.

'It's quite good, isn't it?' Alice says, with some surprise. 'What do you think, Evie?'

'It's great. It's really great.'

She holds it out in front of her.

'It's a good sign,' she says. 'Every time I try hard with something it never comes off, but when something works, it's like you don't even have to try.'

I chew at my lip and wonder whether that's true. The

label is really good, as if Alice understands something about me that I don't – if I put this image on my clothes, it would give them a wholeness that they're lacking. An identity. It would actually make me look like I knew what I was doing.

'You're really clever.' I smile. I was wrong about this lot – they're such nice people. I wonder whether they would do this for Nadine. 'Thanks.'

Alice shrugs. 'No bother. As long as I get a taste of your success. I've always wanted a diamond-encrusted toilet . . .'

'And a gold-plated jacuzzi full of hoes,' Tracy chips in.

'And a butler to fold my knickers into a point.'

'How about more Martinis?' I ask, rousing myself from my stupor and heading for the bar. I need to salvage the evening and start getting into the swing of things. After all, this is for my benefit.

'Well, if that's the best you can do . . .' splutters Tracy, pretending to be put out.

The bar is awash with exotic bottles, sitting on shelves in front of a disorientating art deco mirror. A sparkling dish of blood-red maraschino cherries sits next to a silver bowl of citrus fruits so perfect that they look as if they were just painted and varnished. Everything here is fighting to impress, to be of finer quality than the thing next to it. I just want to close my eyes and go to bed, but the horrific thought of Lorna, holding the squished carton of ice cream in her claw, jolts me back into the room.

'Three more Martinis please,' I request, in my most

polite, well-brought-up voice. In the mirror, warped by time and set at a peculiar angle, I notice a man in a fedora and black suit, two booths down from ours, giving off the air of a cut-price Humphrey Bogart – oh my God, could it be . . . ? He's having an argument with a younger man, quite a furious one. I zero in on their conversation and catch a few snippets over the refined din of clinking glasses and mussel shells being up-ended into bowls. 'You've got to understand,' I hear the man say, 'this could ruin us.'

Through a dim haze of cigar smoke, the porridgy complexion and ferrety eyes are unmistakable. I should go over and punch him, bill him for my glass collection, but I don't. Instead, I quickly grab my change and dip back into the booth with the full tray of drinks.

'What's up, Evie?' Alice says. 'You look like you've just paid fifteen quid for a round.'

The highest point of his black hat is just visible over the top of our booth. I duck down, not wanting to be seen.

'It's Victor McDougall,' I whisper, 'The Painter.'

'Is it?' Alice asks with interest, craning her neck over the top. 'Where?'

'Don't look!' I hiss.

'God, so what? That tosser's in here all the time,' says Tracy, far too loudly. 'Fannying around in that stupid hat like he's a detective or somethin'. And his paintings are CRAP!'

I cup my face in my hands, mashing my palms into my ears, my face burning up.

'What do you care, anyway?' Tracy shrugs. 'Right, come on. Last one to finish this is a big jessie.'

Tracy and Alice continue our conversation, concocting increasingly bizarre visions for my future. Apparently, I will soon have my own house of couture with the world at my feet, and a line of designer items in H&M. According to them, everything will work out wonderfully when we all move into our special famous fashion designer rock star castle in the sky, and there will be a statue of me in George Square. After an hour of this, I've almost forgotten that Victor is in the room. The more they discuss my golden fantasy future, the more irrelevant he seems, a relic from a lost world. The third Martini helps me erase all my worries – Mickey's literary woes and questionable personality, Lorna's ice cream wars, the dismal weight of college, the man in the black hat.

So it's a surprise to see him still sitting there when we leave. But he's not the overconfident, shiny black slug who slimed me in my bedroom. He's on his own, his head in his hands, those shoelaces of dyed hair growing out, showing the true silver colour beneath. The backs of his hands are speckled with freckles and liver spots, and his hat lies upside down on the table, as if awaiting loose change. Is he crying?

'Come on, doll,' slurs Tracy, poking a finger in my ribs. 'I need ma bed.'

Even though I'm in the mood for a confrontation, in his state (and mine), it doesn't seem wise, and I let Tracy and Alice ease me out of the door. Besides, I have other things to think about – my imminent winter collection and smash-hit appearance at London Fashion Week, not to mention 'Temptation of Evie', my new signature perfume. I say my goodbyes to my friends, and I've almost convinced myself that everything will be all right as the taxi makes its way over the Kingston Bridge. We rise clean above a wide sweep of river, illuminated by a cheesy, almost full moon that causes showers of white sparks to dance on the surface. I like it here, I tell myself. I like it. But when we approach my street and the taxi drops me off outside Lorna's, the five faint marks she carved into my arm start to sting again, and the hallway makes me shiver. A thin whistle of frozen wind comes through the broken skylight and echoes down the stairs, and as I get to the second floor, I see that the front door is lying open, a sliver of light trailing across the doormat, which ominously spells out 'WELCOME' in thick black letters.

'Hello?' says a feeble voice – mine.

There's no answer, and I push the door open. All kinds of thoughts race through my mind – we've been broken into, Lorna is lying murdered in her favourite pyjamas, she's been kidnapped by a gang of international jewel thieves, intent on stealing her rock . . . but everything is quiet in the hallway, and nothing seems out of place – no pictures taken off the wall or shattered vases. The only thing that appears different to this afternoon are two slightly damp-looking patches on the carpet, which, I realize with a guilty jolt, are the aftermath of whatever was under Alice's green shoes, eradicated to a faint smudge with a dose of 1001 carpet shampoo.

'Lorna?' I say, my voice barely audible. Maybe she's lying in wait for me, ready to finish what she started, with that defiant look on her face, her nails filed into sharpened points.

My heart is hammering as I advance into the flat. The door to her room is closed, and when I pass the living room, it's shrouded in darkness, the black plastic army of remote controls in their usual order of size on the coffee table. Something feels dreadfully wrong. What's happening? I feel glad for the invisible armour of vodka, which seems to be protecting me from fainting with fear. Then I notice that the phone, which is usually so perfectly parallel to the wall and neatly aligned with the memo pad, is sitting at a rakish angle, the cordless handset tipped up in its cradle. Stepping towards my room, the door is ajar. Someone has definitely been in it. Is someone still in it?

'Hello?' I say again.

I hold my breath, pushing the door of my room and snapping on the light in one quick movement, like a magician removing a tablecloth without disturbing the objects on the table. As my eyes adjust to the unforgiving light, it takes me a while to figure out what has been going on. The tunic, wrenched from its carrier bag, has been cut to spidery ribbons, my silver scissors lie splayed next to them on the bed. On the floor is a small pile of cardboard boxes, forming a neat pyramid. They've been bizarrely labelled in Lorna's handwriting. 'CLOTHES', 'SHOES', 'MISCELLANEOUS'. My sewing machine has been unplugged and packed away, with a yellow Post-it note on top that says: 'Take this with you or I will bin it.' Alice's drawing, torn from its pin, has holes and crumpled identations in it, as if she's systematically stabbed it with the scissors. In its place, above the sewing machine, is the contract, Lorna's design for life, each page carelessly Sellotaped to the pristine wall, with every clause frantically underlined in red felt tip with 'violated' written in the margins. Soggy the rabbit has been thrown out of his drawer and is lying by the window, his grubby ear sticking upwards like a withered white flag. Mickey's manuscript is littered around the room like so much confetti, the battered case squashed between the bed head and the wall.

Then I see my postcard of Edith, ripped in half.

I can barely breathe. I feel like running, but I can't move, even though every hair on my skin is bristling with fear. From behind me, I think I can hear a rustling movement. Blood rushes from one part of my body to another in a great hot wave. How dare she do this? I make a grab for the scissors, and turn round, however, there's nothing behind me but the empty hall. Little by little, careful not to make a noise, and still vaguely aware that I should have taken my shoes off at the door to avoid more stains, I head towards where I think the sound came from. The tip of my nose is icy cold and my fingers are shaking uncontrollably. The scissors seem longer and more lethal than I've ever noticed before, designed for inflicting endless damage, but I daren't put them down. With my left hand, which feels wobbly and disconnected, I push the kitchen door open, half expecting to see Lorna there in a state of terrible, jangling fury, holding a weapon of her own in her manicured hands. What would she use? One of those shiny, serrated chef's knives she keeps in the woodblock by the sink?

But Lorna isn't there. The figure sitting on the kitchen counter, which is covered with utensils, tiny capsules, and the splattered remnants of a low-calorie chicken tikka masala, is a man, his broad back clad in a green and red striped rugby shirt. I step closer, just missing the broken wine bottle that lies on the laminate floor, bleeding a crimson stain that spreads all the way to the fridge.

'Charlie?' I whisper.

He twitches a bit and his fingers touch his face. As I move towards him I can see that he's shaking, and he looks tired and wrecked, his ruddy, port-stained cheeks are even redder than usual.

'Hello,' he says flatly, his face still turned towards the sink.

Where the secret drawer was, there's now just an empty slot. He wipes his nose on his sleeve and dismounts the counter, trying to regain his usual blustery rugger-bugger demeanour and create some normality, not that there's ever been much of that in this flat. As he does so, I can see his distorted reflection in the dark window, which also reflects me behind him, looking like a knife-wielding lunatic. Shocked, I put the scissors down and fold my arms tight across my chest, where my heart is still going like the clappers.

'Are you OK?' I ask. 'What happened?'

He rubs his eye with the heel of his hand and wipes at a stain – tikka masala – on his shirt. It's all over his front in a sickly, orange blur.

'Lorna had an episode,' he says quietly.

'Oh.'

I glance down at the counter and see that the capsules are all over the place, a hail of grey and yellow bullets, the ones in Lorna's drawer.

'Does she have these episodes a lot?' I ask, picking one up.

'Sometimes,' he says.

'What are these?'

'Lithium.' He smiles, embarrassed, as if I've found her birth control pills or his secret copy of *Razzle*. 'Perhaps you guessed. Lorna noticed her scissors were gone and started running around accusing you of looking in her drawer. I figured you'd seen her pills.'

I'm about to protest ownership of the scissors, but there doesn't seem much point now. I'm glad I was out when this happened. From here, I can see the full extent of Lorna's 'episode': the tea jar is broken, as is the little white dish for the used teabags, a baking tray with a waterlogged naan bread on it is lying miserably in the sink, and it looks as if she has just hooked her arm around the end of the worktop and sent the whole thing crashing down, with palette knives and wooden spoons and a broken egg timer spilling white grains of sand on the floor. The drawers are all open as if the place has been ransacked by burglars, carefully ironed tea towels burst out in messy fan shapes and there is a fish slice sticking out of the flip-top bin.

'She just snapped,' he says, standing with his arms uselessly dangling by his sides, his normally rigid, sneering face softened by total bewilderment. 'I came round at about nine as usual, and she was in your room . . .' He pauses to look under his foot. 'She'd done all the boxes, and she was calling you every name under the sun, then she went into the kitchen and started doing this. I couldn't stop her – she was wild.'

I say nothing, certain it was me who caused her to snap. I could have been more careful. I could have done more not to violate the contract. Leaving the ice cream under the bed was a stupid oversight, and I could have asked Alice to take her shoes off. Just a little bit more attention to detail might have avoided such a violent reaction. In fact, without me in the way, maybe it wouldn't have happened at all, and she would have continued her painless existence of ready meals and long baths and early nights.

'I'm sorry. I'm sorry if I caused any trouble.'

'Oh, it's not your fault,' he says with false cheer, noisily rooting through cupboards and producing a roll of bin bags. Behind me, I can hear movement, and I swivel round, fear bursting in my chest. Christ, she's here, she's still here, she's coming to get me. But in place of Lorna is a woman built just like her, but instead of caramel striped hair, she has a faded brush of greenish copper frizz. She's the older, more care-worn version, clad in tatty beige trousers and a crumpled white blouse, topped off with a pair of yellow rubber gloves, and at this very moment, she doesn't look like someone who owns three homes and can afford to stump up for a wedding at Skibo Castle.

'That's the worst of it tidied in there,' she says, in a thick Dundonian accent, before registering surprise. 'Oh, hello there. You must be Evie. I'm Linda, Lorna's mammy.'

She snaps off the glove and gives me a solemn, slippery handshake, as if she's a surgeon who has just performed a delicate operation and is about to tell me the bad news.

'Hi,' I say nervously.

'Sorry about all this.' She sighs, shaking her head. 'When she asked for a flatmate I said OK, we need the rent an that, but I dunno about that at all, I knew she wasn't ready for it.'

There's an almighty clatter as Charlie removes the baking tray from the sink and plops the bread into the bin bag, disturbing broken plates underneath, but Linda doesn't flinch.

'She wouldn't shut up about it though, and I thought, well, maybe it's better she's with someone, eh? But it's a crying shame.' She plops the rubber gloves into another bin bag and shakes her head again.

So that's why Lorna took so long to get back to me when I first came to the interview. She was trying to pitch the idea to her parents.

'I see.'

'She was diagnosed when she was fifteen,' Linda explains, more to the fridge than to me. 'We've always tried to help her, but she's an independent soul, and when she said she wanted to leave home, we couldn't stop her. For a while she was managing, and we did all we could . . . I mean we made it a palace for her.' Linda dabs her eyes with a ravaged-looking tissue. 'And you can't keep an eye on them every day, can you? I couldn't come up every five minutes to make sure she was taking her pills: I work full time at the supermarket.'

Supermarket? I stare at the floor, stupefied, as I watch Lorna's gilded life evaporate.

'It wasn't your fault, Linda,' Charlie mumbles.

'No. But you can't help but feel responsible. I don't know where we'd be without Charlie. He's been a rock.'

Charlie doesn't say anything.

'So, Evie, you're going to have to leave,' she says, decisively. 'Her brother came to get her earlier. We've got to sell the flat anyway, I mean, we couldn't afford it in the first place, and now Bill, that's my husband, now he's on the sick after his accident, the mortgage is killing us.'

'Right.'

'You can stay till the end of the week and I'll get your deposit back.'

I nod stupidly at Linda, unable to take in anything but tiny details. Her crêpey neck tanned from holidays abroad or, more likely, a sunbed in the loft, a lurid gold chain resting listlessly against her collarbone, a smashed mug lying on its side on the counter, featuring an inappropriately cheery drawing of a sunflower with a smiley face. The ordinary world gone wrong. It seems such a shame that everything Lorna was so proud of has been taken away. I imagine her being whisked back to Dundee, with a few bags in the boot and her future suddenly in doubt, watching her plans and hopes and dreams recede through the back window of her brother's car. But it was all an illusion anyway.

'Good lad, Charlie. He's a good lad, isn't he?' Linda clucks soothingly, watching him pick broken crockery from the sink. 'Stood by our Lorna through thick and thin.'

'Yeah,' I say, bending to pick up a fridge magnet that has fallen onto the floor.

'No point crying over spilt milk, eh?' Charlie shrugs. He casts his eye around the chaotic kitchen, but powerlessness seems to overwhelm him and he stands still for a minute and sighs. His bulldog neck and his exaggerated, pumped-up torso just make him look all the more pathetic in a situation like this.

'Just got to get on with it,' he adds, pulling himself together. He looks at his watch and adds: 'Linda, you should stay here tonight, it's late.' I'm surprised at Charlie's sensitivity – I didn't know he had it in him. Maybe I misjudged him. As if reading my mind, his eyes flicker warily to me.

'Och, no, I've got to drive back tonight and look after ma wee girl,' she says, already reaching for a scratchy brown woollen coat, which hangs on the back of a chair, the only upright piece of furniture in the room. 'Leave that for another time, Charlie. I'll come back and clean it up on Monday – let me get you up the road.'

I stand there uselessly, as if I've been accidentally invited to someone's family gathering and nobody knows my name to introduce me. I wish they'd take me home, too, rather than leaving me with this mess.

'I'll clean it up,' I say automatically, even though it's the last thing I want to do. And why should I, when my room has been ransacked and systematically demolished? But the gravity of the situation and the drawn, tired faces of Lorna's nearest and dearest seem to demand it somehow.

'Would you? That's awful good of you,' Linda says, struggling into her coat. 'Every little helps at a time like this.'

'Yeah, thanks,' says Charlie, quickly dropping his bin bag and wiping his hands with a tea towel.

'You know,' says Linda, 'Lorna really liked you. She was always talking about you on the phone – what clothes you wore and how you kept a good house. You did as best you could, and I'm sure she didn't mean to do all this. She's no well.'

I wouldn't be more surprised if Lorna came barging in here with a chainsaw. She talked about me? In a positive way? Then I remember she was OK sometimes, when I helped her choose party favours and napkin rings for her and Charlie's big day.

'Well, I hope she gets better soon. What about the wedding?' I ask gravely, wondering whether it might all be called off.

Charlie, his red face restored to its usual outdoor bloom, looks confused. 'What?'

Linda looks to Charlie.

'Lorna said you were getting married in 2008,' I tell them. 'She had this big notebook . . . she said you were going to get her a ring. It cost £18,000 . . .' I stutter to a halt.

'£18,000! That's as much as I make in a year!' Charlie laughs, then stops himself. Linda grimly rubs her watery eye, bruised with mascara. 'There was never any wedding,' he adds quietly, looking unnerved.

'But what about the diamond engagement ring she wore?' I say, more to myself than anything, envisaging the brilliant cluster of jewels she shoved into my face on the day I moved in.

'Diamonds?' Lorna's mum asks incredulously. 'The only ring I know she's got is the one I bought from the catalogue for her eighteenth. It's only a bit of cubic zirconia, hen. She's been telling you a pack of lies. What else did she tell you . . . ?' Her face crumples and she begins to sob uncontrollably.

'Come on, Linda,' Charlie says hurriedly. 'We'd better hit the road. Bye, Evie,' he adds curtly, ushering Lorna's mother out of the room.

I open my mouth to apologize for mentioning it, but it seems pointless to say any more. Looking down at my hand, I notice that the fridge magnet I'm holding is the one I saw on the first day I came here, back when I thought Lorna was so grown up and together, so . . . normal.

To our Special Little Girl.

Getting tikka masala off white tiles is trickier than you'd think. I abandon any hope of sleeping in this strange place, and surrender to the task of cleaning up Lorna's mess, putting on the radio to drown out the ominous silence. When everything is cleared out, I retreat into my room, but it's not my room any more, it's a horror movie, with Lorna's deranged scrawls everywhere. Looking at this, it's hard to imagine that she ever liked me. The hatred is astonishing. I sit on my bed and stare at Alice's drawing, imagining Lorna stabbing it. Maybe if I'd taken more interest in her plans for the non-existent wedding, the hunt for the best black shoes, or the importance of loft space in adding value to a property . . . But it wouldn't have mattered.

I hold onto Soggy, placing his chewed ear near my mouth, his matted towelling tickling my lip, and stare at the dent in the wall. Turns out I wasn't the aberration, after all. I look at it for a long time. It's so weird that such an obvious flaw was allowed to exist for so long in this perfect palace. Out of curiosity, I crouch down and I touch the back of the dent, wondering whether it was a socket that didn't get filled in, or whether it was caused by a foot during one of Lorna's earlier episodes. But instead of feeling the hard resistance of the wall, my finger goes right through.

It's paper. I explore it further. It's a piece of paper tacked onto the other side of the wall. Blood pounds in my ears. I go into Lorna's room next door, almost jumping out of my skin when I see my reflection in the mirrored wardrobes. Although her mum has tidied up, I can tell Lorna has been to town in here as well – there's a pile of stuff on the bed that Linda must have picked up off the floor, while a framed picture of Charlie, minus the glass, lies on its side. Going to the corner, I find the spot and lift up the paper flap. Sure enough, there's a grandstand view of my bedroom.

Reeling in the harsh yellowness of the overhead light, I stand there for a while, trying to process this new invasion. While I'm doing that, I see that in the pile of stuff on the bed, there's my missing pair of crocheted tights, a couple of reels of cotton, and a list of bullet points from my Plan A box file. 'Deadline to get flat: 19th August at the latest,' it says. 'College induction day: 22th August. Begin course: 28th August. Begin life of uncluttered serenity away from crazy people.'

I'm getting out of here.

I grab my coat and my bag and leave the flat quickly. Usually I might be scared to walk through the darkened streets on my own, but now I don't care – nowhere is as creepy as 1 left, 68 Dryden Terrace.

Advancing further and further away from the flat, I become steadily more resolved. The pavements glitter with frost, and I walk down streets and streets of tenements, all in various states of uprightness or crumbling disrepair. There's a party in one flat, still going strong, music blasting, while the neighbours probably lie in bed cursing them to hell. So many people live on top of each other around here – who could possibly have a life of uncluttered serenity? Streets lined up like soldiers, boxes filled with people, all with different jobs and ideas and stories. Even the tree roots are coming through the pavement, unpredictable, alive, too strong to be contained under a blank, boring sheet of concrete. I like it here, I repeat, like a mantra. I like it.

And now it's almost a relief to have it all fall apart. I should have known it wasn't going to work with Lorna. She was allergic to my mother, for God's sake. As I get to the corner of a street, watching a lone taxi swing by, I'm almost lightheaded, like a gambler who has lost everything but has found, to his surprise, that it's not the end of the world. Passing the bowling green and the art gallery, everything is reassuringly the same as it was the day before. Bus shelters and street lights and junction boxes plastered with colourful posters advertising bands.

Bottle Rocket the posters say, in blocky letters. *Little Miss Prim – CD and Limited Edition 7.*

Bloody hell. As if I hadn't had enough surprises tonight, here I am. Four of me. My overblown head, still damp with glue, is there for everyone to see, as if some dark family secret that's been hidden for years has finally exploded to the surface. I'm standing under a garland of plastic onions, looking every inch the daughter of two crazy artists, a Sixties throwback, an awkward teen, neither pretty nor ugly, with a geeky, too-short fringe. The girl on this poster isn't going to be getting an office job any time soon, or start listening to *Acoustic Anthems*, or build up a nest egg with a boy like Charlie. I start to laugh at myself, a deranged girl cackling at her own reflection. I'm suddenly flooded with relief. Why have I been wasting my time pretending to be something I'm not? I'm not normal. Normal! What a dreadful thing to want to be! I was brought up by Anton and Charlotte – how could I possibly be normal?

Anyway, you only have to look at Lorna to know there's no such thing. I stare at the poster, trying to piece together the day it was taken – the miserable sightseeing, waiting for Lorna's phone call, my notebook, the cappuccino foam, the feeling of being a new arrival and waiting for things to start. I remember Johnny cackling at me over the wipe-clean tablecloth, seeing me for what I really was. *Look at you, rearranging the salt pots, messing with your fringe . . .* he said. *Who do you think you're kidding?*

In dressmaking, if you follow a pattern correctly, you can't go far wrong. I haven't been following my own pattern.

Within ten minutes, I'm standing outside a peeling red door. Beside me sticky Sellotaped buzzers and doorbells hum with a disturbing electrical current. I hit the one that says 'Alice' and hope to God she's awake.

Step Eleven – A Pressing Issue

It is always preferable, when the garment is stitched, to smooth out any lumps and bumps. If there are creases that simply cannot be banished by a hot iron alone, make adjustments accordingly. Do not be discouraged: you will soon be able to step back from your creation with a sense of achievement.

MetroTech is looking particularly unappealing today. Its rubbery corridors whiff of gravy and feet, and there seems to be some kind of fight in the canteen – a full-blown *West Side Story* affair with Reebok trainers instead of dancing shoes. Jezebel is the first person I see as I reach the 386th floor. I'm expecting a barrage of snide comments, but instead she swerves to avoid me as if walking by a festering pit of silage, her superior shaved head wobbling on her spindly neck. Kicking her up the arse seems like a viable option.

'Oh hello, Evie – so nice of you to join us today,'

Duncan sneers from his usual fat Buddha position at his desk. Today he's clad in a cowboy shirt, white with red trimmings, which, instead of making him look dandy, makes him look pasty-faced and ill. It's Thursday, and I've been away almost a week. Since Friday's assessment, the workroom looks unfamiliar, smaller than it used to be, and tatty, with spindly window frames that look ready to crumble and scruffy marks on the paintwork. To think that Duncan has been here for a decade, spending his days in the same grotty rooms, with the same hopeful, hopeless students, year in year out. No wonder he's a sociopath.

'Sorry, I was away – I had some personal problems,' I reply.

'Well, we all have those. Hey, apparently, there's this great new invention called the telephone!' Duncan chirps, mostly to himself, and starts rustling some papers. I make a face and walk away, feeling suddenly and spectacularly bored of the whole thing. Despite his misplaced confidence and jazzy new shirt, he no longer seems like a hulking demigod of design, and shaven-headed Jezebel, once a slender icon of self-assured cool, just seems like a bald, obnoxious cow who needs to eat some carbohydrate. As for Neil . . .

'Hi, Evgeniya,' he says, chewing on the name like gum. 'What happened to you? You missed my crit – I got a great one. Shame about your tunic, eh? Better luck next time.'

I gaze at him through narrowed eyes and take in his latest bonkers ensemble – white trousers with a tight neon hot-pink T-shirt, accessorized with a school tie and wristbands made from belts. His eyes are blackened with kohl, giving him the appearance of a battered panda.

'What's the matter with your eyes, Neil? Did you get beaten up on the way to school?' I ask him politely, taking my seat next to where Flossy should be, but isn't. She's sitting with Jezebel now, the two of them thick as thieves.

'OK, shut up and sit down!' says Duncan charmingly. Neil, in a huff, flounces to his seat.

'Today we're going to start work on your end-of-term assessment. This is something you should have started to design already, and if you haven't you'd better pull your fingers out because this is VITAL!'

I gaze out of the window, at the glistening roofs and sharp contrasts of the frost-bitten morning. Glasgow looks so pretty when it isn't raining.

'EVIE! Do you understand the meaning of the word "vital"?' he bellows. The class turn round, peering over their shoulders en masse, like a crowd watching a tennis game.

'Yes thanks,' I yell back at him, smiling broadly.

'Good!' he shouts, but seems to lose his thread. 'OK, we're going to . . . this assessment is designed to show others how you're progressing on the course, and you MUST give it your best shot and show me what you've learned. But you're not just going to have to impress me. To up the ante, I've got a couple of very special guests coming in to have a look at how you're doing . . .'

Duncan does another one of his pauses for effect. I

wonder whether he does this at home. 'Pass me the remote . . . I want to watch . . . *EASTENDERS*!'

'David McLeod from Twenty-FiveUp, an independent Edinburgh-based design company, and Manda Bergen from Not on the Label, a Glasgow clothes shop I'm sure you're all familiar with, will also be assessing your work,' he continues, holding his hand up against a rising tide of excited murmurings. 'So you're going to learn a lot about how to cut it in the real world. Now show me the money! I want ideas and drawings by the end of the week, OK?'

There's a flurry of chatter and awestruck gasps from the rest of the class. Neil is already in full flow, talking to Andrea the sneezer about his grand plans. Feeling barely connected to my brain, my body rises from the chair and advances towards Duncan. Duncan bristles, then quickly arranges himself into a defensive position, perched on the edge of his desk.

'Sorry to hear about your problems, Evie,' he says, not appearing the slightest bit sorry and folding his arms around his gut. 'I'm glad you came over, actually. Before you start to make something from a vintage pattern from 1909, I want a word with you,' he adds, unable to resist having a pop. I look at him steadily and say nothing. His mouth seems to be going dry. Maybe he thinks I'm hiding a gun behind my back and I'm going to snap, taking out the entire department. The idea amuses me for a second.

'You know, Evie, call it what you want – a personality clash, ideological differences – I don't care,' he drawls, 'we don't have to be friends. My job is to get you people to the end of this course, in the vain hope that when you leave you might become a success. You're the most gifted dressmaker in here, but so far, you've not had the ideas. It's like you're stuck in the past. If you carry on like this, the fashion world is going to take one look at you and your old-fashioned designs and say, "NEXT!" Do you get what I'm saying?'

I nod. Yes, I know what he's saying. But he really should prune his nostril hair. I struggle to think of the name of the implement designed for that job. A fuzz-buster? A pluck-away?

'Fashion design is all about pushing the envelope and trying something new – making a visual impact . . .' he's saying.

'Hmm.' I think about the dress, lying neatly folded in my bag, the one I've been working on all week. The one I might actually sell to a real person, who might wear it for a special occasion, who might model it for a photo, whose life might be touched in some way by it.

'. . . people want drama, structure, clothes that challenge the status quo,' he spits.

'Or maybe they want something nice to wear,' I counter.

Duncan pulls back and inhales, probably wishing he was in the staff room having a fag instead of arguing with me. But I'm enjoying myself. Some strain of Dad-like rebellion is coming out, and I don't mind it one bit. After all, without a bit of healthy debate, life would be very dull. And as Duncan rightly points out, we don't have to be friends.

My eyes wander around the room and alight on Neil,

who has stopped talking to Andrea and is now eavesdropping on our 'discussion' with a face of unfettered joy.

'This is what I'm talking about,' Duncan hisses, 'your bad attitude.'

I sigh. 'If you'd listen to me, I have something to tell you. In answer to your criticisms, OK, the tunic was a bad idea,' I tell him. 'But everyone on this course is so . . . judgemental.' I glance at Neil, who shoots me a look of doom. 'Not to mention unpleasant. And I don't know, Duncan, it's like, you're up here telling students to think outside the box and push the envelope and all that, which is fine, but I think you're missing the point. People don't want to wear badly constructed lampshades with plastic corn on the cobs stuck to them.'

Duncan flinches, his arms squeezing his belly even tighter.

'Don't tell me my business, young lady,' he says.

'Oh, I wouldn't dare. But I do think you need to look a bit closer at your teaching methods. I mean, I really don't like the way that certain students are instant favourites and others are instant failures. All I want to do is design clothes that are well made and look good. I want to be good. So maybe this course isn't for me,' I finish, folding my arms to mirror Duncan's pose. My hands are shaking, but I don't let him see it. Now, as well as Neil, Andrea is watching this touching wee scene, gob open like the Clyde Tunnel.

Duncan snorts and throws up his hands.

'OK, walk away. See if I care!' he booms. 'But you, Evie Kaminsky, are never going to get anywhere.'

'I think I'll manage, thanks. I've got to go to see Jess Taylor now. You know Jess? At Candy? I've got an appointment to show her a dress I've made for her – and then we're going to discuss the collection I'm doing for her.' There. Put that in your pipe and smoke it, lardy. It's all I can do not to toss my hair and can-can out of the place.

Duncan leans back, arms still folded, trying to hide his surprise. But his face is a picture of dismay.

'So thanks for everything, Duncan,' I say (trying to stay dignified, even though this is soooo great that I want to stand on the table and cackle demonically). 'And I hope the end-of-term assessment is a roaring success.' I reach out to shake his hand, and he automatically extends his nicotine-stained paw, thoroughly bemused. Neil looks as if someone has just come up behind him and whipped off his trousers.

'By the way, Neil,' I say, turning to him. 'That look really isn't good. School ties are so last year. You look like you failed the audition for *Grange Hill*.' Miiaaaow. I walk away, past Jezebel (whose real name, now I come to look at her boring face properly, is probably Leanne) and wave a sarcastically cute goodbye to Flossy.

'Good luck with your Bollocks,' I tell them, before heading down the corridor to the lift. 'You'll need it.'

Head held high, I have to conclude that I showed 'em. Annoyingly, though, my amazing departure is marred by the fact that the lift takes ages to come, and I catch big Andrea Scary Bra poking her head round the workroom door to check whether I'm still there. So, I quickly take the stairs down to the front entrance, past the assembly hall with its dark orange curtains and smell of dust, and into the sunny street.

'Did you do it?' asks Alice, leaning against the railing, wearing her green socks.

'Yeah,' I say, as we walk to the Arcade, towards an uncertain future. 'I don't think I'm going to pass the course, though.'

Going home is the easiest thing I've had to do for ages. I've got a rucksack with me, even though I'm only going for the weekend, to pick up any remaining possessions that weren't smashed to smithereens. Kirkness is glorious in the autumn, the sea a deep and briny blue, the trees rusted with reds and golds. Freezing wind whips off the water and slashes at my face as I struggle up the hill to the house, which is chalky white against the sky and looks a little like something from one of Lorna's aspirational move-to-Spain programmes, if it wasn't for the cement mixer in the driveway, the sound of banging, and the billow of acrid smoke from the chimney. It's so big and sprawling – how come it always made me feel cramped?

'Hello!' I yell, opening the door to the tinkle of rusty Indian bells. Rothko barks and comes sliding across the stone floor in a flurry of claws and fur, his big lolling tongue trailing drool.

'Hello, Rothko,' I say, bending to scratch him behind the ears. I realize how much I've missed his undemanding doggy company. 'Poo! You need a bath.'

'Evie!' Charlotte screeches. She's got a roll-up in one

hand and an earthenware coffee cup in the other. 'The wanderer returns! Has something dreadful happened?'

She starts fussing, trying to find an ashtray, but gives up and lobs her fag end into the sink, then advances towards me with arms outstretched, threatening to cover me in wet clay, which is splattered all over the front of her work apron.

'I'm fine,' I say, avoiding a hug and kissing her on the cheek. 'I was just . . . I wanted to come home and say hello.'

Charlotte looks at me askew. 'Really? Well, that's great, darling! ANTON! STOP BANGING! Evie's home! Do you want a coffee?'

'Yeah, OK,' I say, putting my bag on the table and looking around the room. Compared to Lorna's (pre-freakout), it's in disarray, but it's funny, what I thought was a disgusting midden is actually quite a harmless array of homely clutter – the rocking chair with the threadbare crochet throw on it, the depressed sofa sagging in the middle, a dresser full of odds and ends and various misfires from Charlotte's kiln. Untidy, yes, but nothing to call environmental health about. If you cross your eyes a little bit, it's almost cosy.

'So to what do we owe this pleasure?' Charlotte croons. 'Are you pregnant?'

'No, Mother, I'm not. I just wanted to pick up some stuff and say hello.'

'And you missed us!' she gasps, gripping me round the waist and pinching my sides.

'Get off!'

'How's Lorna?' she shouts, going into the larder.

'Well . . .' I say, over a riot of clinking wine bottles.

'Well what?' she yells.

'I had to move out.'

'You had to move out?' My dad emerges like some unwieldy ghostly apparition, clanking down the stairs with his black hair covered in plaster dust.

'But why?' my mum chimes from the larder.

'Hi, Dad. Well, Lorna went a bit . . . she had an episode. It turned out she wasn't well.'

'I knew that girl wasn't right in the head!' my dad explodes, as something falls over in the cupboard, causing Rothko to start barking.

'Shit!' Charlotte yells.

'Charlotte! What are you doing? Why are you in the cupboard when your daughter is out here?'

I close my eyes, remembering why I moved out.

'Charlotte told me about the contract – you should never have gone there in the first place!' he grumbles, pulling up a chair with a piercing squeak.

Charlotte emerges with a packet of fresh coffee and a cobweb attached to her shoulder, looking rattled.

'I'll never know why you signed it,' she frets. 'It was completely bonkers.'

'And she was rude to your mother!' Anton chips in.

'And her eyes, her eyes were cold,' my mum adds, scientifically.

'Listen, it's fine,' I say. 'I have a new place to stay. Do you remember Alice?'

She looks stumped. Behind her, on one of the cupboards, there's a sticker I put on there when I was about seven – a Take That symbol, culled from the pages of *Smash Hits*. It used to annoy me, but now I'm quite glad nobody bothered to peel it off.

'Alice . . . ? I don't . . .'

'In Ikea. In the queue. You said her shoes were nice and you said I should be friends with her.' I remember the encounter, Mickey with his hands shoved in his pockets, looking amused, me a scolded chihuahua. I wonder what he thought of me then, before he decided I was a shallow little social climber. The memory of the gallery, his eyes drawing from Johnny to me, cold and accusing, still spears me in the stomach when I think of it.

'Oh ALICE! Yes! Curly hair! Yes, she seemed nice – didn't you go and see a room at her house or something?'

'I'm living there now.'

'Oh how wonderful! Oh yes, she's much more your type – that Lorna, well . . .'

'Yes, I know, her eyes were cold . . .' I repeat. 'Anyway, something else I wanted to tell you was . . . I left college. It was horrible, and I'm not going back, so don't try to make me . . .' I can't help feeling this announcement has the same hollow, desperate ring to it as my proud spiel about going to MetroTech, but I soldier on. 'But I've managed to get some commissions from a shop and according to the woman who runs it, people really like my stuff. For the past week I've been working on things for her nearly full time. So I'm going to try and set myself up in business. As a designer.'

They sit there, looking at me for a while, and I notice how I look a wee bit like both of them – I've got

Charlotte's upturned nose and Anton's dark eyes. Close up, they're not a bad-looking couple for their age, despite the fact that they're both covered in a crust of clay and plaster. Now I'm gatecrashing their lives, they both seem attractive and self-sufficient, rather than a pair of maddening eccentrics.

'How wonderful!' says Charlotte, sending an amused glance over to Anton. 'She's a chip off the old block.'

'Good for you! You're a Kaminsky, through and through! Forging ahead and to hell with the unbelievers! You will be a great success!' Dad says, thumping me on the back and nearly winding me.

'Yeah, whatever,' I mumble, embarrassed. 'I'm just going to get some stuff from my room.'

'After that, you are coming with me – I want to show you something,' my dad says decisively, rising from his chair.

'Yeah, OK.' I start dragging the rucksack up the stairs. The hallway hasn't got any tidier, I see, but the armless mannequin is still there, its expressionless face staring at nothing, as much a fixture of the house as the ceilings and the floors.

'Hello,' I say to it. I don't know what I expect it to do. Wink? Blow me a kiss? Give me two thumbs up? Predictably, it does nothing, and I open the door to my room, holding my breath, fully expecting to see the untouched shards of glass still scattered over the floor. Amazingly, though, it's tidy and clean, with new sheets and everything arranged just so. And someone has tried to salvage one yellow vase from the debris – my favourite piece. Its trunk sits squiffily on its base, a light ring of glue where the break is, but it's carefully done, and positioned to cast a buttery glow onto the wall.

I smile and put the rucksack on the bed, rooting around for what I need. A few DVDs of old movies for inspiration and an old book called *Paris Fashions the Easy Way*, which I bought from a jumble sale and which tells me exciting facts galore about basting and French seams. In its place goes the box file, Plan A. I should throw it away, but it seems like a good souvenir, an example of what not to do.

When I get downstairs, Anton and Charlotte are discussing something at the table, the much talked about coffee still unmade. When my dad sees me he straightens up and gives me a tight, almost shy smile.

'Thanks for mending the vase,' I say.

He shrugs. 'Hey, look at this. You will enjoy this immensely.' He gets up and goes to the dresser, pulling a newspaper from an overstuffed folder. Unfolding it, he finds the page and bashes it down onto the table.

> MCDOUGALL EXPOSED AS FAKE. Victor McDougall, the celebrated artist, whose most famous painting, *Brunhilde in Scarlet*, fetched £1.2m at auction in 1999, yesterday defended himself against claims that he is not responsible for the work that bears his name. McDougall, 69, of Kingsferry, whose real name is Jim Scoggie, admitted that in 1997 he 'struck a deal' with friend and business partner Mr Simon Carpenter, who painted the well-known works that make up a

£30m merchandise industry, in return for an undisclosed share of the profits. McDougall then went on to claim that this was nothing out of the ordinary. Speaking from his home, he said: 'I have done nothing wrong. It was very common for artists in Renaissance times to hire apprentices to help them produce their work. The images we create may not be executed by my own hand, but I am 100 per cent responsible for their content.' Mr Carpenter was not available for comment.

I look at the picture of Victor, a ruined old man opening the door of his house to an unforgiving flash bulb. Next to him is a smaller picture of his accomplice, the man he was with that night at the cocktail bar. What a cheat!

'I can't believe it,' I stutter.

'Aye, not only does he behave like a pig, but he gets someone else to do his homework,' my dad spits. 'I should have punched him harder when I had the chance.'

'Anton,' my mother warns. 'Those thoughts are bad for your karma.'

'Away with you, woman. Right then,' he bellows, putting an arm round my shoulder. 'Have you got sturdy boots on?'

'Why?' I ask, still reeling from Victor's spectacular comeuppance.

'The thing I want to show you! It is not far from here and then we will build up an appetite for lunch! Charlotte, what is for lunch?'

Charlotte shrugs. 'I dunno. I think I might have some cheese somewhere . . .'

'Well then – let's hurry. We can't miss that, can we?' He winks and beckons me out of the door, Rothko panting around us in a state of walkies-related excitement. Reluctantly, I follow him, back into the gale-force wind.

'Where are we going?'

'It is a secret. Shhhh!' he says, putting a giant plaster-encrusted finger to his lips and hooking his arm into mine. Wondering whether my flimsy shoes will stand the strain, I go along with him. Over on the horizon, something glints in the sunlight, and it really is a lovely brisk day, with fading vapour trails from aeroplanes scratching the sky and the smell of wood smoke in the air.

'I am glad you are starting your own thing,' he says, as we go down the hill. 'Now you have found your feet and I can see it, in your face and in the way you stand. You seem taller. You have everything you need. You are an artist.'

Here we go again. I can't be bothered to correct him. I do feel different, though, but not in the way I thought I would, not like a big-city big shot, coming back to show the yokels how it's done. The harbour, with its bleached-out front doors and shop windows etched into my memory, doesn't look as quaint and small as I expected. The chippy continues its greasy trade, the Spar is thronged with buckets of unlovely flowers, dyed outlandish colours and wrapped in spotted plastic, a handful of ancient trawlermen sit on the harbour wall, like they do every day. It's miraculous that these people tolerate each other and rely on each other, struggling to keep small businesses afloat in the bleak winter months, battling their way into work through the wind and spray and salt. Soon we're at Kirkness Fashions, where the slender, 1950s mannequins me and Mrs Morrison nicknamed Nelly and Nora are sporting itchy-looking knitwear of an indeterminate colour and standing in their eternally static poses. But even though it's lunchtime, and I know that Mrs Morrison will be in Vanelli's with her friend, slurping tepid soup and gassing about God knows what, there's no sign saying 'Back At 2 p.m.'.

Peering through the yellow pane in the door, encrusted with aged stickers advertising brands of clothing that died out during the war, I can see someone at the counter, a young girl who looks a bit familiar, disconsolately dusting the pockmarked, over-polished wood. My replacement.

'Hang on, Dad! I won't be a sec,' I call after him. He turns round, probably cursing, his hands digging deep into his jacket pockets.

The tinkle of the bell jolts the girl behind the counter out of her afternoon stupor. She smiles at me vaguely. The pink hair is gone, replaced with corn-coloured blond, and out of the black hoodie she looks pretty and grown-up, simply dressed in a V-neck and skirt.

'Hello, Evie,' Mona says. 'Long time no see.'

The well-worn comfort of the place is still overwhelming, a wee cocoon powered by woozy paraffin. But with Mona behind the counter, it's just a shop, and I'm just a customer. Going beyond that hulking, wooden partition would mean stepping onto her territory – I wouldn't be welcome to go into the tiny kitchen and make a cup of Mellow Bird's any more.

'I didn't know you worked here now. How are you?'

She smiles and casts her eye around the room, wearily. 'Not bad. How's life in the big city?'

'Oh, you know, OK,' I say, not knowing where to start, or how interested she'd be in the first place. 'Is Mrs Morrison giving you hell, then?'

'Oh, I only work here one day a week. I got onto an animal husbandry course in Kirkcaldy. I thought I'd better stop messing around and start doing something with my life.'

'Wow. That's really great,' I say, hoping I don't sound patronizing. I don't recall Mona ever being interested in animals, unless you count the E-addled lads of Kingsferry, but it's good she's doing something.

'And I stopped drinking too,' she volunteers. 'It was totally doing my head in.'

'Well, good for you.' I smile, encouragingly, not knowing what else to say. Neither, it appears, does she. She shifts her weight from one foot to the other, her new figure accentuated by a very nice pencil skirt. It's not just her looks that have changed though – her whole manner is unrecognizable. Was her entire personality down to too much cider and Buckfast? How could we grow up in tandem for twenty years and be so familiar to each other, only to change completely after a couple of months apart? Then I get it – she doesn't need me to mop up her puke and give her lifts to Edinburgh any more. She's grown up.

Up on the wall, the big old sunburst clock beats out its eternal tick, timing our awkward silence to the second.

'Well, I'm just on a flying visit, and my dad wants to show me something, so I better go . . .' I roll my eyes to indicate how long-suffering I am, but don't quite pull it off, and my cheeks start to burn with embarrassment. 'So I'll see you at Christmas, probably.'

'Yeah, OK.' She smiles briefly and folds her arms, probably relieved that I'm going.

'Say hi to Mrs Morrison from me.'

She nods and waves, and for a second, as I shut the door, the jaundiced cellophane on the window makes it look as if she's fading from memory, a distant relative in a yellowing photograph.

Dad, in glorious Technicolor, shouts from further down the street, pointing to a row of pylons in the distance.

'Come on, Evie! I'm freezing my knackers off here! We must go up here and then onto Dun Links, and then it's a small trek up Kingston Hill.'

'That's miles away!' I break into a run and catch up with him, past the bus shelter where Mona and Teresa spent all their time. Not any more though. I wonder whether Teresa has undergone a similar transformation. Perhaps she's studying for a PhD in astrophysics.

'It is not miles away!' my dad says. 'It's a wee walk. You need some exercise – I bet you sit on your bottom all day long in the city, doing sweet FA. It will do you good, fatty!'

We trudge along in silence for what seems like ages, with Dad occasionally pointing out something that catches his eye, like an interestingly gnarled tree or a mutant pine cone. When we get halfway up Kingston Hill, my lungs are aching and I can hardly feel my nose.

'Nearly there! Come on – you are like an old woman. My mother could climb this hill quicker than you, God rest her soul.'

'Why are we going up here anyway?' I yell, but the wind takes my voice away. Once I've wheezed halfway up, he's still ahead of me, along with the dog, whose paws are effortlessly navigating the lumpy ground as if he's just wandering to the supermarket.

'It's good, isn't it? A great spot!' my dad says, already at the top, rubbing his hands together and warming them with his breath. Behind him is what looks like a concrete plinth, cordoned off with plastic orange mesh and flanked by a digger and a generator. It's only as I puff my way up the final stretch that I can see how big the site is.

'Taa-daa!' he says, stretching his arms out. 'The work has begun. *Windscape* will be not only a sculpture, but a real working turbine, which will provide renewable energy for Kirkness. This part will be clad in sheets of recycled aluminium, held together with rivets that will reflect light from far away . . .' He gestures to a random point in the distance and takes a deep breath of air into his lungs.

'It will be a beautiful silver beacon on the hill, not the eyesore the neighbours are all so worried about,' he insists. 'Beautiful and useful, working with the landscape and for the people. They will eat their words.'

I watch him proudly surveying his post, looking excitedly into the future, flecks of plaster blowing off his jacket.

'Good one, Dad,' I say, putting my frozen hand into the crook of his arm. We stand there, steeled against the wind, the blustery day stretching out before us, clear and cloudless and zinging with bright light. From up here there's a spectacular view of the coastline. The beach stretches out before us like a puckered golden ribbon with the white huddle of Culdrossie in the distance. A few miles away, Creggan Island sits immovable against the clean line of the sea.

'Anyway, we can't hang around here all day or we will die of hypothermia,' he says eventually, stamping his feet and warming himself up. 'We must hurry or Charlotte's cheese will go cold. Last one back to the house is a big girl's blouse.' Then he's off, like a fifteen-year-old, with Rothko skittering behind him on the rocks, a monument to energy.

Step Twelve – Tidy up Loose Ends

Now is the time to cast a quick glance over anything you might have missed, ensuring that any hanging threads have been snipped. An expert couturier knows that a little thing like an uneven hem or a ragged seam can ruin the entire effect, so make sure your dress is neatly finished off. Once these details are attended to, you will have the satisfaction of knowing you have created something beautiful, which, if cared for properly, may last a lifetime.

I can hear Alice's voice coming through the vent over my door. She's talking on the phone: 'I'm not sure whether it'd be a good idea, but it's up to you . . .'

The roller whites out the Utopia mural in big satisfying strokes, the squelchy pastel-coloured blobs disappearing in a snowdrift of Dulux emulsion. All those episodes of *Changing Rooms* have come in handy after all. Now the walls are cleaner and the carpet has been fumigated, I finally feel like I can call this place home. The window, where my sewing stuff is set up, has a good view onto the leafy street, and working in here has been stress-free – unlike Lorna, Alice seems to know when to leave me to it and when to distract me. She's usually at college from ten till five, and when she gets back she makes cups of tea and tells me about her day. Shamefully we've even started to watch *Neighbours*, sitting there silently like two old crones in a nursing home. Jess is on the phone a lot, with questions and commissions and requests for invoices. In fact, my stuff is selling well, and there's even talk of a waiting list. Amazingly, if it carries on like this I might have to hire an assistant. Duncan perhaps. Or Jezebel. I could get her to fetch the coffee and sandwiches, wobbling to the café at the top of the street with a bike chain wrapped round her head. Failing that, maybe Neil could strap on his seagull wings and fly there.

I carry on painting, aware I'll have to pack up and make myself presentable soon. Tonight, Alice has decided to throw one of her parties. It's the first one since I arrived, but I'm not exactly looking forward to it. Since the gallery opening, I've been avoiding Alice's port-a-crowd and concentrating on work, but the other day she bullied me into it, telling me I was working too hard and I needed a night off. I know her guest list will be a roll-call of the usual types. Johnny and his Bottle Rocket compatriots, Jess, Tomas Jankowski, Nadine probably, Mickey . . . hopefully not. His manuscript has been restored since Lorna went for it, and I've been meaning to return it. Lines from it stick in my head and some scenes are so vivid that I even occasionally dream about the place where it's set, even though I've never been there. But then his words in the gallery come back to me and I sling it back into the cupboard. *It's not what you know, is it?* I hear the harsh inflection, quite unlike his usual soft speech, every time I thread a needle or struggle with a seam, using it as a bloody-minded spur to continue.

'Tell Nadine . . .' I suddenly hear Alice say, her voice muffled through the vent, and she walks out of earshot. She must be talking to Tracy. The mention of her name causes me to flinch, and I splatter myself with a fine mist of brilliant white from the roller. I start to paint more furiously, covering up the custard drips.

'Evie, what are you wearing tonight?' Alice shouts when she's off the phone.

'I don't know,' I shout back.

'You should wear your red dress again. You look really great in it – everybody said so,' she says.

'Yeah, maybe,' I say casually. Who said so? Apart from Jess, I don't recall anyone at the gallery saying a word about it.

'By the way, I invited Mickey tonight and he said he might come along. I hope you don't mind.'

I pause, roller in mid air. Do I mind? Well, I shouldn't really.

'No . . . it's . . . it's fine . . .' I say, concisely, feeling unstable on the wobbly chair I'm using for a ladder. While I'm in the mood for obliterating the past I can give him the manuscript back and we never have to breathe another word to each other. I do some more painting, more erasing, but my hand is aching from gripping the handle of the roller.

'Evie? Can I borrow your black skirt?'

'Yeah, sure.'

From the hallway, I can hear a thump at the door and Tracy is let in, the sound of rustling carrier bags and her breathless exclamations echoing down the hall.

'Hey, girls!' she bellows. 'You wouldn't believe what treats I've got in store for ye!'

I hear footsteps and Tracy barges her way into the room, wearing a floor-length fake fur coat that looks as if it's made from yeti.

'Ooh, very nice. Although I have to say I'll miss that mural. It was the exact colour of a pool of vom I once saw outside Central Station. How you doin'?'

'OK,' I say, trying to convince myself that's true.

'Well, put down your roller and get excited!'

I put down my roller. Excitement, though, is not forthcoming.

'I hear Johnny's coming tonight – you'd better get the red carpet out,' she swoons. 'He's a daft wee chump, isn't he? I'm sick of the sight of him – he's on the cover of everythin' from *Heat* to the *New Fucking Scientist*. Hasn't he got any other facial expressions?'

It's true that Johnny's cheek-sucking pout is slowly becoming ubiquitous. The confidence that was comical when he was a nobody seems to suit him now he's got a platform for showing off. He was even true to his word and went out with a model, probably just because he wanted to prove he could. I wonder whether Johnny would be such a bad idea after all. Maybe he's the one who got away. He's not bad looking, he's in demand, he's probably going to be rich, and there are plenty of girls who would kill to be his girlfriend. I try to imagine hanging off his arm as he waltzes into some hotel lobby, or bunking up on the tour bus, or being enlisted to design their stage outfits – sewing bolts of lightning onto spandex trousers.

'And Mickey's coming too!' Alice trills from the hallway.

'Ooooooh. Mickey too, eh? You'll like that, won'tcha, Evie?'

I look down at her to see whether she's making fun of me, but she's glancing at the instructions on a packet of ready-to-roll puff pastry.

'Right, ah've got Volvo vents and sausage rolls and my pièce de résistance . . . devilled eggs!!' Tracy announces. 'Bet you cannae wait! Food poisoning, here we come!'

She stomps into the kitchen and I hear the opening of the oven, and Alice follows her, twittering over temperatures and cooking times. I climb down, unable to complete my decorating, and wipe my hands with a cloth. I really should start getting ready. Passing the point in the hallway where I first saw Mickey, entangled in his duvet, I lock the bathroom door and check myself in the mirror. There's a big lump of paint in my hair and I look like I've seen a ghost. Overhead, the marmot glowers at me.

I'm going to need to take drastic measures if I'm going to survive the evening. I start to run the bath, tipping in a generous glug of fancy bath oil. I'm a Kaminsky, and we can deal with anything. We can build monuments and start small dress-designing businesses and we can get over annoying men, too. If he's going to be a snob then I'm going to be so unbelievably superficial he won't know what hit him. I'm going to dress up to the nines, make frivolous remarks about Jimmy Choos and kiss loads of boys. Ha!

When I'm finally ready, Tracy is flapping around the kitchen, some music is playing, and the bitter aroma of scorched pastry is drifting through the hall.

'I've burnt the sausage rolls!' she's screaming.

Alice is standing by the door of her room in my black skirt and a green top, unperturbed, looking much better in it than I did, with her face made up and a pair of false eyelashes brushing her cheeks.

'You look nice,' I say.

'Ooh, so do you!' she shrieks. 'Hotty boombotty.' She blows me a kiss and sticks her arse out.

'Special occasion, is it?' Tracy smirks.

'Just something I threw together.' I sigh, giving a mock jaded twirl.

'You know what'd go with that, don't you? A devilled egg,' Tracy says, handing me an eyeball. 'Go on. They're a taste sensation!'

'No, thank you – I don't want bad breath. I'm going to be doing lots of snogging later on.' Even as I say it, it doesn't sound very convincing.

'Whoo hoo, missus!' she whoops. 'Well in that case, I think madam would probably prefer a drink, seeing as she's a total alkie slapper. Hey, Big Jamesy Warner's coming – you can show him your bra! Or maybe this time, you can show him your pie!'

I laugh, even though she's made my face go puce.

'Tracy, don't be disgusting,' Alice says matter-of-factly. 'Now, who can remember the name of that cocktail you mixed at the last party we had?'

'Keef's Teef,' Tracy and I say in unison, with varying degrees of enthusiasm.

Soon, the buzzer starts to go, and a steady trickle of friends begin arriving, some who seem to know me, even though I don't know them. My job is to take coats and greet people. The guy in yellow who I saw at the Temperance Hotel gives me a familiar hello, while some bald bloke who works at a record shop in town gives me his jacket with a wink. I wink back – so what? Two random girls see me and start giggling. Were all these people here the last time, watching me get full to the brim with Keef's Teef and jump up and down on a sofa? But it seems so long ago I can't be bothered to be embarrassed, I just accept it all, with what I hope is a completely superficial smile. I'm already half-cut. Soon, Alice slides up to me, her face alight with amusement.

'Get in here!' she says, whisking me into her bedroom. I haven't been in Alice's room properly since the encounter with Mickey, and when I put the pile of coats down on the bed and see the word 'LOVE' dangling on the wall, I feel unexpectedly seasick.

'This is so funny . . .' she gasps. 'You're famous. Everyone's like, oh yeah, I know Evie. Oh, and those girls want your autograph!' She collapses into giggles.

'Why?'

'You're the girl on the Bottle Rocket poster!' she squeals, silently having a spasmodic fit, aping the girls who used to hang around Johnny, shyly poking their drinks with their straws.

'Well, I am.' I grin, happy to have decided to let myself go. 'I'm fabulous.'

'Oh, I know. It's in all the papers. I read in *Woman's Own* that you have a yacht and you're going out with Ronnie Corbett.'

'All true,' I say solemnly.

She grins at me and puts her hands on her hips, her bitten nails still full of ingrained charcoal from a drawing project she had to do last week.

'Ah, Evie. How far you've come. You used to be such a frightened-looking thing, and now you're the belle of the ball. Tell me, what's your secret?' She thrusts an invisible microphone in front of my mouth.

'I owe it all to God and my agent,' I joke. Alice cackles, and not for the first time, I'm glad I'm here. I look around at the room that, although I've only really been in it once, seems almost achingly familiar. The colour wouldn't be my choice, the skirting boards could do with a good clean, and the lampshade looks like something from the moon landing, covered in a permanent layer of dust, but I don't mind. After two months of Lorna insisting I put my mug centrally onto the coaster, I think I can cope with a few dust particles.

'This is going to be a good party. I can feel it,' says Alice, moving to the window. 'Hey, check this out!'

I go over to the draughty bay to see a group of kids on bikes, wearing hoodies, who have cornered some guys on the street and are pestering them with shouts of 'Gees a song!' From up here, we get a bird's-eye view of Johnny, James Warner and the crazy drummer in the top hat trying to get out of a taxi. It's Bottle Rocket, wearing their new-found fame with reluctant pride. Surrounded by this lowly gathering of pre-teen fans, Johnny stands out, all in black, frozen under an orange streetlight, better dressed than before, but otherwise unchanged, looking as if he's posing for an invisible camera.

'He doesn't half look silly,' Alice sniggers.

'I quite fancy him,' I murmur.

'Do you?' she says, looking vaguely worried and drawing the curtains.

By midnight, Keef's Teef are starting to bite. Tracy has gone out to try and get some ice from the neighbours, while Alice is flitting around refilling drinks and giving people the full force of her charm. Occasionally she looks over and I can tell she's telling people about the dress. She's like the town crier – my very own PR woman. James Warner is blethering on about something in my ear, something about the food in Japan, a long and complicated prelude to getting another eyeful of my bra, no doubt. For something to do, I watch Johnny in the living room, beached on the chaise longue with a bunch of girls around him. The band's grand entrance was greeted with a barely perceptible flicker of excitement. Everyone was too cool to say anything, but I spotted a few quickly turned heads and urgent tête-à-têtes. Johnny moved through the party like a shark fin through water, dark and sharp and impossible not to look at.

Still, at least he's a welcome distraction. The jerky, goofy swagger he only recently practised outside the shoe shop is smoothed over and refined, and he's certainly not the boy he used to be. In a couple of months he's turned into a man of the world. I sip my drink, ice cubes clashing against my teeth and a flutter of butterflies suddenly descending in my stomach. Maybe I should have pursued Johnny all along, instead of wasting my time chasing scruffy, difficult layabouts. When I think about it objectively, Mickey is old news, probably lying in Nadine's accommodating arms right now, thinking about his opus. If only the book wasn't so good. If only he hadn't asked me to read it, making me think there was a connection between us when there so obviously wasn't.

'Everything over there is made out of fish,' James Warner is saying. Luckily, after drilling him with a come-hither look for the best part of five minutes, Johnny takes his psychic cue and catches my eye at last.

'It's Little Miss Prim herself!' Johnny says when he sees me, and the girls on the sofa all look at me with the same level, coolly disinterested expression. 'You're a real fashionistaaaa these days, aintcha?' he says, scrambling to his feet. He comes over, peeking at me through his hair and pretending to be shy. I notice a blue tattoo is blossoming over his waistband and for a second I want to find out how far down it goes. 'One cool cat.'

He hugs me. He smells of aeroplanes, the sterile smell of pressurized air and hot, tasteless coffee.

It seems strange that this version of Johnny would know me at all – his features are so engrained on my consciousness it's as if I'm meeting an actual celebrity. I want to giggle. His skin is still white, almost luminous, but his stray eyebrow hairs have been plucked and his face looks more symmetrical. Has he really changed or is it a trick of the light? Has he been in so many magazines that he's actually become airbrushed?

'Hey,' I say, trying to be casual. 'How are you?'

'Not bad,' he says. His voice is gravelly and tired sounding, as if he has a sore throat. 'How are you? And why are you slumming it here? Last I heard Alice doesn't care how her salt pots line up with her ketchup.'

The fake American accent is even more pronounced, and when he smiles he shows a chipped tooth, probably from some rock-and-roll incident with a beer bottle or a fist.

'Oh, ha ha.'

Looking over his shoulder, I'm vaguely aware that the group of girls are exchanging bitchy glances, some whispering. One openly gives me a look of disgust, which I ignore.

'You seem to be doing well for yourself,' I say, sounding more like a Kirkness shopkeeper than a temptress.

He rolls his eyes.

'I'm knackered. I just want to go to bed, y'know? It's all just . . .' He peers behind him and clocks the girls. When he turns round, they all change their expressions to ones of receptiveness and delight, as if someone has presented them with diamonds or a brand-new set of steak knives. 'It's not what I thought it was. Hey, Evie, let's get out of here, OK?' he says quickly, putting his arm round me and nudging me into Alice's bedroom without even thinking of poor James Warner, standing there bereft, all his careful groundwork ruined.

He shuts the door and faces me, leaving his hand hovering on my shoulder. I stand there, stunned, not knowing what might come next.

Me and Johnny. Is it really going to happen? I can't quite stretch to imagining it somehow, yet here we are, in the glittery green palace that seems to serve for the scenes of my crimes. But now I'm in here, I'm not sure I like the way this is going.

'Look, Johnny, I don't know—'

'I just want some peace and quiet,' he croaks, keeling over slowly like a fallen tree. 'I just got back from Japan.' He collapses in a heap on the bed, showing a line of skinny white belly crisscrossed with a web of black hairs. I look away, but I can see him in the mirror, looking disjointed and broken, as if he's been run over by a bus. 'They love us over there,' he whispers.

'Good,' I say dumbly. Is this part of his seduction routine? *Ooh, look at me, I've been to Japan . . . they love us, everything is made of fish.*

'It's a crazy world,' he murmurs. 'Y'know, the other day I got a phone call from Mick Jagger. Sir Mick. Ha! Last month, I was at my ma's in Kilmarnock and she was telling me to get a job. What the fuck's going on?'

'I don't know what's going on,' I say, sitting heavily on a chair opposite Alice's dressing table. 'You should enjoy it while it lasts.'

'Yeah.'

I glance over at him, half dozing, Tracy's yeti fur crowning his head. If he's trying to impress me, falling asleep isn't going to get him very far. I don't really know what to do with myself. The idea of going over to the bed fills me with a vague horror. I'm not sure about this at all. Do I want to be like those girls out there, waiting for their turn to get it on with a rock star? Am I really that shallow?

'Cos it ain't gonna last,' he continues. 'It's all soooooo shallow.' He yawns, stretching, as if he's picked up my thoughts. 'I'm playing a game. I'm not like you – I don't do anything. It's just a big funny, stupid game.'

'I'm sure you work hard,' I reply flatly.

'Och, I'm a chancer. You knew that the minute you laid eyes on me. I take what I can get.'

I lay my eyes on Johnny again, willing myself to feel something more than a dim sense of affection, a seriously platonic feeling. Once more, a ridiculous plan I've concocted is unravelling around my ears. What am I doing in here anyway? The more I look at him, lying languid and floppy on the bed, the more I feel twitchy and frustrated, as if he's a guy with a big head sitting in front of me in the cinema, obscuring the main feature.

After their initial hopeful flutter, my butterflies are dead.

Not that he's exactly raring to go, either. When I look over his eyes are closed and he's asleep, snoring softly, his stomach rising and falling. For a second I'm inexplicably put out and wonder whether there might be something wrong with my deodorant, but no, that's fine. That's great. We're friends. I don't want him, even though everyone else does. I'm the original Little Miss Prim, all right. And he's just Johnny from Kilmarnock, who can't believe his luck. I exhale and realize I'm limp with relief.

I take one of the coats and put it over him. He stirs and rolls over, but instead of pulling me towards him, incredibly, he puts his thumb in his mouth. There he is, international rock sensation, looking like he should be wearing a pair of *Star Wars* pyjamas and slumbering on the top deck of a bunk bed. Bless him. I can't help smiling. Nothing is what it appears, hey, Johnny?

Slowly I withdraw, making sure to be quiet, and leave him to sleep it off. The party is rumbling on elsewhere, with a few whoops and howls of laughter coming from the living room. I sneak out of the door, the bright light in the hallway making me blink.

'Evie?'

I turn round to see Alice, who is standing outside, arms folded, frowning. Her curls are sticking up at all angles, angry looking. They match her face.

'What's the matter?'

'Is Johnny in there with you?' she snaps, trying to peek through the door.

'Yes, but . . . he's asleep,' I say.

'You didn't . . . tell me you didn't.' Her face is almost anguished.

'No! I was just talking to him. He's asleep!'

'You're sure nothing happened?' She squints with suspicion.

'I'm sure, thanks very much. Why?'

'Do you remember Mickey? He's in your room.'

'What's he doing in my room?' I demand, annoyed, while fuzzily trying to work out whether I left anything embarrassing lying around.

'Go and talk to him.' Alice's voice is urgent and scolding, quite unlike her usual laidback self. I experience a jolt of shame, even though I haven't done anything wrong.

'Why?'

'Oh, come on,' she groans. 'Christ, you're both as bad as each other . . . you've been avoiding him, and he's been avoiding you, and all you've done since you moved in here is throw yourself into your work. Stop pissing about. I know you like him. He wants to speak to you. So sort it out, OK?' she finishes, frustrated, throwing her hands in the air and letting them fall heavily to her sides. Tracy looms up beside Alice.

'Aye, go on, the poor boy's dyin'! What, don't you fancy him or somethin'?' she asks. She sucks her drink through a straw, making a loud gurgling noise.

'What are you getting at me for?' I quiver, feeling wobbly and put upon. 'He's going out with Nadine.'

Tracy and Alice stand there for a second, their faces vacant.

'Nadine?' Tracy murmurs.

'Yeah.'

'No he isn't,' says Alice sharply.

Now it's my turn to be on the defensive.

'Don't you all talk to each other? Nadine and Mickey have been going out since the party. She told me at that club . . . whatever it was called. She told me.'

Alice gives Tracy a look. Tracy shoots it right back.

'EEE-EEE-EEE-EEE!' she squeaks, mimicking the music for the shower scene in *Psycho*.

'Oh, she's a piece of work,' Alice says, shaking her head. 'I can't believe that girl.'

'Still, you've got to admire her persistence,' Tracy cuts in. 'I think she should get some kind of medal. Do ye remember that time she tried the whole seduction routine and turned up at his house wearing just a coat and her pants? He was fucking terrified! I swear to God, he didn't speak for a week!'

They both laugh. My lips feel numb.

'What are you talking about?'

'Mickey's never been interested in Nadine. She follows him around all the time, but she doesnae get anywhere. I thought she'd have got the message by now, though,' Tracy explains.

'But she said they used to go out . . . I mean, it's not like she isn't pretty . . .' I protest, thinking about her slender neck and her powdery complexion, silky hair wound into a loose knot. There were *tears* in her eyes. 'She said they were back together.'

'They didnae go out!' huffs Tracy. 'She's a sleekit wee tart! What a liar!'

'I can't believe she said that. I knew she didn't like you the minute I introduced her. I'm gonna give her a piece of my mind when I see her.' Alice looks crest-fallen, her wonderland of like-minded people tainted by a devilled egg.

'Mickey doesn't go for girls like Nadine,' says Tracy with authority. 'She's far too uptight. She's always checking her hair and being vain and making sure her eyeliner is on at the right angle. I bet she cannae sleep if the top's off the toothpaste. He likes girls with a bit of oomph.'

'He likes you,' Alice pleads. 'Honestly.'

'Yeah right,' I splutter. 'He didn't like me the last time I saw him – did he tell you about that?' I ask, trying to get my mouth to move in a normal manner.

'Look,' says Alice, who, as usual, seems to know something I don't, 'if we're not right about this, I'll do the dishes for a year. Please just go and talk to him. OK?'

I take a deep breath and turn my head to see the door of my room, scarred with Sellotape and thumbprints of grubby Blu-tack. The angles of the hallway seem wrong all of a sudden, like somebody's put the skirting boards on upside down.

Alice and Tracy gently but forcefully move me towards it, until the blistered woodwork fills my field of vision. I feel sick.

'He's not going to bite,' Alice whispers.

'He might if she's lucky,' Tracy hisses.

I clear my throat, resisting the ridiculous urge to knock, and walk in. They might think it's all moonlight and roses and a cause for celebration, but they didn't hear him at the gallery.

The room smells of fresh paint, but like a bad penny that keeps on coming back, the Utopia mural has stubbornly emerged, custard drips still visible from under the first coat. Earlier on, I put the battered briefcase at the foot of the bed, so I could give it to Mickey and cut him off for good, walking away with my nose in the air. Now it sits next to him on the bed, as if connected by an invisible thread. He needs a shave and his hair is like a bloody haystack, but the sight of him in my room, not just a memory or a ghost wandering through the hall in a duvet, but here and breathing and alive, makes me dizzy for a second, as if I've been suddenly confronted with a mountain or a tall building.

'I was just looking at this.' He holds up *Paris Fashions the Easy Way*, my dressmaking bible, and meets my eye. 'It's like hieroglyphics. I can't understand a word of it.'

'Hmm,' I say.

'You'd have to be pretty smart to figure it out.'

I shrug modestly. 'Yeah, I s'pose.'

'And you were right about the character,' he says, gazing at the briefcase. 'He is a bit spineless, and he couldn't be that naïve, could he? He needs to pull himself together and work out what he wants.'

I look at him properly: his scruffy shoes, his wrist, thin and delicate, like a girl's.

'Yeah, he does.'

'Sorry about the thing in the gallery,' he mumbles, returning his gaze to his shoes. 'I didn't mean to imply . . .' He straightens up and sighs. 'But I couldn't pin you down and every time I saw you Johnny was there, singing songs about you and fawning over you . . .' He screws up his face, as if he's trying to remember his speech. 'I gave you the book because I didn't want to just be some random guy you met at a party. And there you were at the gallery, with him, and you didn't seem to give a shit.'

'I was never with Johnny,' I tell him, even though five minutes ago things weren't exactly so clear cut.

He blinks up at me.

'You should have just asked me,' I say quietly. 'Anyway, you were always with Nadine. And she told me to back off because you and her were . . . y'know.'

His eyes narrow.

'When did she say that?'

'In the club. That was why I left. I didn't feel ill.'

He looks pained and incredulous. 'She's crazy.'

'Well, yeah. Seems like a lot of people are round here. Everyone's a lunatic.'

He thinks for a minute and smiles that big, don't-be-a-stranger smile. I smile back, even though I'm supposed to be being tough. What a pair of losers.

'I like that dress. Is it one of yours?'

'Yes.'

'Thought so.'

He looks at it for a while, but not like Jess did. Something tells me he's not admiring the bias binding. I can feel myself starting to blush and try to override it. Calm down. Think about Malcolm Chance's hairy back or something. Dad's hairy arse. Hairy arses!

It doesn't work.

'Are you blushing?'

There doesn't seem much point in pretending otherwise.

'Yeah,' I say, shuffling from one foot to the other.

'C'mere, Evgeniya.'

When he says my full name it sounds pretty, rather than the way it usually does, like a Russian pig farmer clearing his throat. There's no pattern, or instruction, or Plan A for what happens next. I sit on the bed next to him, and he reaches out to touch the roughened edge of the frill on my dress, briefly looking down at his fingers, as if he's expecting magic dust to come off on them. And in a moment of contact as inevitable as Victor McDougall and his shelf of glass, he leans forward to kiss me. But there's no chaos, only the feeling of things rearranging themselves, tipping the right way up.

'Let's start again,' he says, and although my head is scrambled, for a second I'm dimly aware of Edith, gazing approvingly down from her elevated position on the wall. After being mauled by Lorna, it's nice to see that the rip down the middle hasn't disfigured her too much. She just looks like she's lived a little.

THE END

HAVE LOVE WILL TRAVEL

Lucy Sweet

Complete Misery Checklist:
1. Polyester tartan uniform
2. *Hello My Name is Jane* badge
3. 'Job' in Edinburgh Tourist office during the festival season
4. Ginger whinger colleague who's out to get you

Crap job, manky flat, and eight hours filled with questions like 'How long is the Royal Mile?' – that's what Jane Darling has to look forward to. Every day. It's a grim prospect.

Some people would think it was complete lunacy to travel halfway across the country just to reunite a man with his lost diary. But when you consider Jane's alternatives, and you look at his photograph . . . you'd pack your backs too,

'PUNCHY, DROLL AND FAB'
Cosmopolitan

'SPIRITED, AMUSING AND FUN'
OK Magazine

0552773018

BLACK SWAN

MAY CONTAIN NUTS

John O'Farrell

'O'FARRELL IS A CONSISTENTLY HUMOROUS WRITER WITH AN ACUTE EAR FOR THE ABSURDITIES OF MIDDLE CLASS PRETENSION. IT'S HARD TO FAULT HIS SATIRE ON COMPETITIVE PARENTING OR HIS CONCLUSIONS REGARDING SOCIAL INEQUALITIES'
Mail on Sunday

Alice never imagined that she would end up like this. Is she the only mother who feels so permanently panic-stricken at the terrors of the modern world – or is it normal to sit up in bed all night popping bubble wrap? She worries that too much gluten and dairy may be hindering her children's mental arithmetic. She frets that there are too many cars on the road to let them out of the 4x4. Finally she resolves to take control and tackle her biggest worry of all: her daughter is definitely not going to fail that crucial secondary school entrance exam. Because Alice has decided to take the test in her place . . .

With his trademark comic eye for detail, John O'Farrell has produced a funny and provocative book that will make you laugh, cry and vow never to become that sort of parent. And then you can pass it on to your seven-year-old, because she really ought to be reading grown-up novels by now . . .

'O'FARRELL IS ONE OF THE BEST CONTEMPORARY SATIRISTS IN THE BUSINESS AND HE HAS MIDDLE CLASS PUSHY MOTHERS DOWN TO A TEE IN THIS LATEST TOE-CURLING, HACKLE-RISING CHRONICLE OF HYPER-PARENTING . . . THE ONE-LINERS ARE SUBLIME AND THE COMEDIC SITUATIONS UTTERLY HILARIOUS. DON'T MISS THIS'
Daily Record

'O'FARRELL HAS SCORED A BULLSEYE WITH THIS SATIRICAL SALVO . . . TAPS INTO MIDDLE ENGLAND'S NEUROSES WITH TERRIFIC WIT'
The Herald

0552771627

BLACK SWAN

TABLOID LOVE

Bridget Harrison

'A REAL-LIFE BRIDGET JONES MEETS
SEX AND THE CITY'
Candace Bushnell

'FORGET THE BLURB – CAN I GIVE YOU
MY PHONE NUMBER?'
Toby Young

You're about to turn 30, you've got a great boyfriend, your own house and a steady job. Then you chuck it all in and run away to New York to become a tabloid journalist . . .

Bridget Harrison took off for Manhattan, and *The New York Post* – fulfilling a life-long ambition to become a news reporter. As well as covering everything from murder and muggings to celebrity gossip, Bridget was asked to write a column about looking for love, in the hardest city in the world to land a man.

The highs:
Finding a great apartment in the East Village
Dating a different man every week
Realising she loved her job

The lows:
Finding out exactly what her flatmates were like
Dating a different man every week
Realising she loved her boss?

'AS HILARIOUS AS IT IS TEAR JERKING. A REAL INSIDER'S COMEDY OF NEW YORK'
Plum Sykes, author of *The Debutante Divorcee*

'BRIDGET HARRISON IS SO MUCH SEXIER, SO MUCH FUNNIER AND SO MUCH MORE FUNDAMENTALLY HUMAN THAN BRIDGET JONES'
Giles Coren

0593057384
9780593057384

BANTAM PRESS

LOOK THE WORLD IN THE EYE

Alice Peterson

'I've lost my sister. If you've seen someone who doesn't blend into the crowd,' I sniffle, 'well that's her.'

Katie seems to have everything you could wish for – she's attractive, successful and has a rich, handsome boyfriend, Sam. But she has a secret: a younger sister, Bells, who doesn't fit into the perfect world she has created. When Katie reluctantly agrees to let Bells stay, bitter resentments resurface quickly, forcing Katie to confront her past. Bells pins tatty posters on Sam's pristine white walls, plays Stevie Wonder at full volume, strikes up conversations with strangers – including an attractive man in Sainsburys – and generally creates mayhem. Soon Katie's relationship with Sam is under severe strain. And problems escalate when Katie receives disturbing news about her mother. But, with help from Bells, Katie finally learns about real love, and that appearances can be very deceptive.

A deliciously warm-hearted, funny and moving first novel about families, secrets, falling in love and having the courage to look the world in the eye.

'I LOVED THIS BOOK. IT'S A WARM AND HONEST LOOK AT A FRACTURED FAMILY AND HOW IT MANAGES TO PUT ITSELF BACK TOGETHER AGAIN'
Bella Pollen

055277300X

BLACK SWAN

THE UNDOMESTIC GODDESS

Sophie Kinsella

'HOORAY! SOPHIE KINSELLA'S BACK'
Heat

The story of a girl who needs to slow down. To find herself. To fall in love. And to discover what an iron is for . . .

Samantha is a high-powered lawyer in London. She works all hours, has no home life, and cares only about getting a partnership. She thrives on the pressure and adrenalin. Until one day . . . she makes a mistake. A mistake so huge, it'll wreck her career.

She walks right out of her office, gets on the first train she sees, and finds herself in the middle of nowhere. Asking for directions at a big, beautiful house, she is mistaken for the interviewee housekeeper and finds herself being offered the job. They have no idea they've hired a Cambridge-educated lawyer with an IQ of 158 – Samantha has no idea how to work the oven.

Disaster ensues. It's chaos as Samantha battles with the washing machine . . . the ironing board . . . and attempts to cook a cordon bleu dinner. But gradually, she falls in love with her new life in a wholly unexpected way.

Will her employers ever discover the truth?
Will Samantha's old life ever catch up with her?
And if it does . . . will she want it back?

'AN ADDICTIVE READ'
Daily Mail

0552772747

BLACK SWAN